Mortis Velum

Chris Kane

This book is dedicated to my grandfather, a man whose kindness and respect were as boundless as the sky, and who continues to inspire me. His stories ignited my childhood imagination, sparked immense joy, and crafted a tapestry of unforgettable memories. He helped me understand that the echoing cacophony of others' opinions held no weight on my path. I will always and forever be grateful to him for being my idol and guiding me to become the person I am today. Every day, I miss you.

To my grandmother, from whom I inherited her sass, attitude, and sarcasm, which have become a part of my personality, whether or not I like it. Even though we no longer spend countless hours together in the cornfield and bean patch under the sweltering sun, the feeling of quiet peace from those times washes over me whenever I'm alone.

To the person who willfully remains one with the shadows and my biggest supporter. When I felt most alone, you were the one person who stood by my side without fail, never faltering in your support and expecting absolutely nothing in return for your dedication. You have been my encouragement to be better, the angel on my shoulder keeping me in check, and my backbone to hold me up when I'm not capable. The completion of this book is directly because of the encouragement that you provided.

-To my dog, who is my entire world, I dedicate this. As the most loving poodle in existence, you quickly became the inspiration that fueled Nova. Even when I have difficulty loving myself, you have been the boy who has always shown me love and has been a constant in my life. You are my reminder to be selfless, my hero to drag me from the flames, and my reason for remaining sane. We remain destined to find each other in every lifetime, our souls intertwined like threads woven through space and time, a connection felt across every realm. You are worthy of so much more than what I can offer.

A Personal Note from the Author

Greetings, dear reader,

I would like to begin by offering my sincere gratitude for the time and interest you have given to reading my book. It truly means more to me than words can convey. I am deeply honored that you stepped away from your busy life to take part in the imaginative journey I created alongside these characters.

When I first began writing this story, there was never any intention of publishing it. It started simply as a way to give shape to my creative thoughts—a personal refuge where I could escape the weight of everyday life by disappearing into a world of fantasy. I would write before drifting off to sleep at night, or sometimes in those quiet hours when the darkness itself seemed to stir my thoughts. What began as scattered ideas and scribbled notes slowly grew into something far more meaningful.

Bringing this story to publication has been an incredibly humbling experience, one I never expected but am profoundly grateful for. I hope that this is only the beginning, and that I may continue to expand and complete the world I have started—one story at a time.

If you would like, you can go check out my website at chriskaneauthor.com. Any extra information about myself, along with future book releases, will be updated there in due time.

I bid you farewell until the next story unfolds, Chris Kane.

Mortis Velum

Chapter 1: Sisterhood

"Octavia!" a voice cried, the sound carried on the breeze. The moment Ophelia came running towards me, I was jolted out of my spaced-out stupor, my gaze snapping upwards. I sat on a small bench in the public courtyard garden near the town hall, flanked by towering hedges. The moment I saw Ophelia's ethereal appearance, my thoughts completely dissipated. Ophelia was my older sister, though we only shared a mother. We were full sisters in all intents and purposes, bound by a connection that needed no explanation. She is likely the most beautiful woman in Faladorn, the reason for my survival, and the most compassionate person I've ever encountered. She truly had the looks to rival a goddess like Aphrodite herself. The eligible bachelors and bachelorettes, along with some people who were married, all paid attention and were aware of who Ophelia was. She had admirers galore, but she was blind to her own beauty. Her long, voluminous dark auburn hair danced in the wind, brushing against her face as it fell in lustrous layers just past her shoulders, shimmering as though touched by divine grace. She was born with the most stunning olive skin that I could only describe as being nearly a genuine gold in appearance when she was in the sun. Slightly pointed, almost elven-looking ears, but I don't think she even possessed elven blood. She's taller than most men, athletic, and perfectly proportioned for her height. Although she was the embodiment of femininity, she still commanded respect and displayed assertiveness upon entering a room. I noticed how our mother's feelings towards Ophelia changed, growing colder after she reached puberty. Ophelia quickly surpassed our rugged and rather plain servant mother in beauty and stature. As we grew up, the constant refrain from our mother was a bleak reminder: we were destined for nothing exceptional. "I'm so sorry, Ophelia. I didn't hear you." My words left my lips, and they seemed to hang in the air, weighted down by a depressing tone. "Never mind that, Tavia, get your ass up and moving! Quickly!" After jumping up, I quickly grabbed my sack of berries that was placed right beside me, and then I took off right behind her. I knew better than to argue with Ophelia, especially when she was in a bad mood. When we rounded the corner, a cascade of red hair swirled and danced, moving right into my path. I tripped over it and closed my eyes as I prepared to hit the cobblestones face-first. But I stumbled into a running fall as I then fell onto someone, arms catching me just before I would have hit the ground.

I felt a warm tongue on my cheek. Whatever it was, it completely caught me off guard. I opened my eyes, seeing the beast before me. "Nova?" I could have sworn he smiled at me. Well, he's no beast at all. He started wagging his tail and jumping several times excitedly. Nova, an apricot-red standard poodle, had a coat that shone like the morning sun. His height was accentuated by his slender build. His hair was always perfectly styled, not a strand out of place. I often wondered how a dog could be so effortlessly regal and goofy at the same time. People around here knew the royal poodle Nova, and most of us knew he belonged to Highborn Kenric Ravenspire; a dog of such a high-status breed was nearly unheard of in Faladorn. Most of us also knew of Sir Kenric because, Highborn being a rare title, but even more so seeing as how Kenric was one of the last descendants of his family's bloodline. Everyone knew his family fought valiantly alongside an army of mages, giving everything to save the Dryads of Efameral. The dryads were on the brink of annihilation and extinction, being hunted and burned as kindling by those too ignorant to know the repercussions of their actions. The entire Ravenspire family helped to mitigate and even reverse some of the inflicted damage. A feat few have forgotten. Their human family lineage earned the well-deserved title of Highborn by the Royal Council, a feat even more impressive given that their family had no mage powers whatsoever. I blinked as I realized what had happened. I could smell the amazing scent of.. citrus, licorice, vanilla, candied sugar, and tonka bean. What a surprisingly delicious smell. I was being pushed to my feet by the time it sank in who had caught me. "Oh, my goodness! Sir Highborn Kenric Ravenspire!" His stunningly handsome face caught me by surprise; he was genuinely a pretty man by any standard. My gaze caught his muscular frame and the tattoos he bore. Only after proving themselves worthy were the tattoos he bore given. The markings flowed down the sides of his neck to his arms and chest, and I couldn't help but wonder how much more of his skin was decorated. Ophelia was then at my side, grabbing me firmly by the arm, forcing me to stand straighter. "Please forgive my clumsy sister. Octavia is a bit of a mess sometimes, two left feet and all." He held up his hand and blinked with a 'Please' gesture. "No harm done so long as Octavia here is unharmed." I blinked rapidly a few times as I tried to mask being embarrassed. "Yes, Sir, I am fine, thank you." "Call me Kenric, please, for the love of all. You are making me feel as old as my father, with all these formalities." His voice was suave and smooth. I smiled at that. I had never known him to have such a warm personality. Well, I didn't know him, not really. Nova was pressing his head into my side, begging for pets and attention. I reached down, cupping the side of his face and floppy ear with my hand. What a sweet soul, Nova radiated pure happiness and goodwill. "Such a good boy," I crooned, "I don't even have any treats for you." He almost seemed to grin at me again. The damn grin was just so human, as were his eyes. Nova had eyes with so much intelligence, it felt as though they looked into my soul, making me feel uneasy. In a casual manner, Ophelia was pulling me along, or, as casually as she could manage. "If you would please excuse us and our terribly uncouth behavior, we really must be going." Ophelia consistently had a goal in mind, as she was always dedicated to a specific pursuit. Muttering to myself, I bent down to embrace Nova, recognizing that the pleasant aroma was originating from the poodle's fur, and said goodbye. I took off, trailing Ophelia once again. "STOP!" The abrupt yell rang through the air from Sir Kenric, causing the two of us to stop where we were. We turned to see Sir Kenric sprinting towards us in a fast-paced walk with a bag in hand. His hip - length straight hair flowing in the breeze, reminding me of the luscious mane on an enormous horse. He was carrying a sack in hand.

"My berries!" Sir Kenric frowned as he looked down at the bag. "I'm afraid some of your berries may have gotten damaged." I glanced at the bag, seeing the purplish-blue juice staining the side. I wasn't really bothered by it. "That's all right. There's more where that came from." Sir Kenric smiled a toothy grin and nodded before he handed me the bag. I took it politely before whirling around with Ophelia yanking my arm, and we were off.

When we got home, Ophelia was already stripping before the door shut. "Quick Octavia! Hurry, freshen up and get dressed. We need to get going to the Rights Ceremony; we're already going to be late as it is." I rolled my eyes. "But must we go, Ope? You know I don't like these sorts of things." My words came out in a whiny tone, and I cringed at the sound of my voice. "I know, but you undeniably have the gift. Do you know how many enchantresses and mages hope and pray to the gods that they get what you possess? Sell their very souls? They would give anything for just a chance to be invited to the Rights. Diviner Archmage Lady Alsendra herself invited us, mind you. If she recognizes your potential without even knowing you, why can't you?" I shrugged and let out a sigh of exasperation. I knew I should be grateful, I should want to be noticed, I should want all of this... but I just wanted to be invisible. I wanted to live a simple life of peace and solitude, surrounded by nature. With no expectations and no responsibilities. I knew it was selfish to want to keep my supposed gifts to myself, but why did I have to be the one to do more? Ophelia would've been far better suited than I. Prior to this, I was an unremarkable and unknown person. In truth, I did not possess any exceptional talent or ability. There was nothing extraordinary about me at all. I was just Octavia. A commoner, albeit now a commoner with an extra little connection to the earth and the surrounding energy around us. While I could sense certain things, I must admit that my abilities were not extraordinary. I couldn't manipulate time, control minds, or even use my abilities to defend myself as a spellblade in battle. So what good was I in reality? I only hope that Lady Alsendra had some insight to share with me. Ophelia snapped the last clip closed on the small chain that was woven through my medium-length brown hair as she helped put it up. I sat at our grandmother's small, old vanity with a mirror, staring at our reflection. A copper hairpin secured her hair at the back, with some long bangs and shorter layers left loose to frame her face. She is always so effortlessly pretty. She had on a white and lavender gown, accented with copper armbands and bangles. I was wearing a black two-piece dress. Silver chains connected the top and bottom, crossing around the abdomen in a flattering way. Chains made in the dress followed the contour of my cleavage around the top where the cut was on the verge of being indecently low. "Do you think this is... too much, Ophelia? Could this possibly be appropriate for the Rights? I never wear anything this revealing." Truth be told, I still wouldn't be wearing it had Ophelia not picked it out, insisting I would look stunning in it. Ophelia scoffed at me and rolled her eyes. "Always thinking so little of yourself, little sister. Octavia, you deserve to be truly seen. Go there today and leave a lasting impression, leave them talking, and leave them wanting to know more about this commoner girl at the Rights." She rested her hands on my shoulders. "I'm going to need you to believe in yourself as much as I believe in you. You have what it takes to outshine every other person there tonight. You can do everything those other snooty harpies there can do. You deserve it just as much as they do; believe that, Tavia." I gave her a forced nod and a half-smile, patting her hand on my shoulder as I stood up. "Well, I guess we'd better get going then."

We were almost at the ceremony as I felt the wind blow around me and leaves dance around my ankles. The leaves felt odd, almost electric. The wind carried an unnaturally cold element, something that made it alarming. The hair on my neck stood up as chills ran down my spine. "Ophelia wait. I have a feeling that something is trying to communicate with me. I just can't pinpoint what it is. Maybe we should go back home. I just have a feeling." "Seriously, Octavia — are you just saying this from nerves and not wanting to go, or are you seriously picking up on something?" "No, I believe this is really trying to tell me something. I just don't feel right Ope." Ophelia looked down at the leaves and then back at me, "Listen if you want to go back home and miss the Rights, your Rights, I will turn around with you right now and head back home with no further hassle. This will be your decision and yours alone. I will not tell you yes or no, because your future is at stake and not mine. I will not pressure you into any actions that you are not willing to do or cannot accept, as I will not be responsible for your mistakes. I'm not even sure if I make the right choices every day, so I won't try to tell you what's right for you. I just want you to know that I want only the best for you and for you to have every opportunity available to you. Including those opportunities that most people will never have. You deserve that, Octavia. After all the hell we've walked through together and how hard we have had to fight, how we had to fight and grovel to survive on our own with absolutely nobody and no help from anyone, I think we're owed a little good faith in life. It's about damn time the gods or whatever deities exist stopped trying to break and kill us every time we turn around. Maybe do something good for us for a change." Immediately after she finished speaking, a crackling sensation permeated the air, accompanied by a subtle static charge. "Did you feel that, Ophelia? You had to feel that, right?!" Her expression shifted, and she raised a single eyebrow in response. "Feel what?" A lengthy breath escaped my lungs as I exhaled slowly. "Forget it; let's just finish this already."

Chapter 2: The Rights- Part 1

We entered the foyer of the building where the Rights Ceremony was
to be held. The sound of our heels tapping on the brightly polished
white marble floor beneath us. A smoky scent met us at the door, a
blend of comforting herbs. I could pick up frankincense and myrrh
most noticeably, among others. Cream-colored walls with floor to
ceiling windows wrapped around the grand corridor as we left the
foyer. We made our way to the great room, where the Rights were to
be held. It was more of the same aesthetic. Tall marble columns with
intricate details carved around them. Large green plants, ferns I
believed, sat in oversized pots in front of each of the extra-large
windows along the back wall. Oversized burgundy-red draperies
adorned the windows, meticulously tied back and pleated to
perfection. I had to take a quick ponder on who had the eye for detail
— a perfectionist, perhaps. I glanced over at Ophelia, and her gaze met
mine. She gave me a nod of affirmation. We squeezed through the
bustling crowds, the murmur of conversations filling the air. It did not
go unnoticed how many heads turned in our direction as we made our
way through. Some grimaced with a face of disgust at why a lowly
commoner like myself would be at the Rights. But many of the stares
were for Ophelia; she was easily the prettiest woman there. We finally
found our seats, which had been reserved for us by Lady Alsendra,
and I didn't hesitate to plop down. My feet already ached from the tall
heels I wore, wishing in this moment I had more comfortable shoes for
the walk.

    I then spotted Lady Alsendra making her rounds before

the ceremony, stopping by each special guest to make introductions, only pausing for a brief conversation before moving on to the next. Ophelia and I sat talking about the different decorations. Discussing the surrounding architecture and pondering the amount of wealth it would take to create and maintain such a lavish structure. We then found ourselves lost in conversation, recalling a memory of a time when we were walking home as young girls and got harassed by a perverted old man. The incident that led us to being here today. The thought of the gross old man we encountered that day still gave me chills. The old pervert stopped us, spewing lewd and vulgar comments about us being such 'pretty little girls'. He would move closer to us every time we tried to move away, smiling at us in a way that was stomach-turning. He eventually tried reaching his arm out to rub against mine. I let out a shriek in response. Before I had time to grasp what was happening, I saw Ophelia fly through the air to land on the man's back. She bit down on his ear as she landed. The man stumbled back, turning in circles to throw her off. Ophelia had been carrying a walking stick in her right hand. She always carried that stick to thwart any potential animal attacks when we walked alone. In a flash, Ophelia had the stick pressed against the old man's throat, her arms locked around it at her elbows, pulling with all her might. The man, wide-eyed and flailing, eventually fell to his knees. Ophelia let go and hopped off, darting around the man in my direction. The man left gasping for air, quickly recovered, jumping up and grabbing Ophelia by her braid. A sudden yank forced her to the ground, and she ended up lying flat on her back. He got to his feet. I stood there in horror, not knowing what to do. I screamed, "Ophelia!" I felt vibrations in the wind around me and a nudge pressing against my back. Then I heard a whisper in my ear saying, "Here Octavia, look here." I looked down and to my left toward that voice, as if intuition were guiding my sight, seeing a large stone near me. I grabbed it quickly. By this time, the man was standing over Ophelia as she screamed. I ran as fast as I could manage while carrying the heavy stone, feeling the help of the wind carrying me at my back. I leaped up higher than I had any right to go for my size, bringing the stone down over the man's head. I dropped the stone and felt the wind die down, my hair settling back around my shoulders. I turned to look at Ophelia. She was still on the ground, holding herself up with one arm, face full of shock and her mouth agape. I said, "What is it, Ophelia? Are you okay?" She looked at me in confusion. "I'm fine, but Octavia... what was that? What just happened?" I shrugged, not even sure what I had done that was different. I turned back to look at the man, noticing that he was still breathing. "Well, he's still alive." "What a pity." Ophelia spat at him. "Hurry, let's go before he wakes up." We picked up the items we had dropped before Ophelia ran back to the man one last time, kicking him in the side. "You big jerk!" Then we took off. That is how it happened — on the specific day on which we discovered my special abilities.

As we were concluding our reminiscing thoughts, I saw in my periphery Lady Alsendra walking up. I quickly hopped up from my chair, Ophelia following suit. Lady Alsendra had a pursed-lip grin on her face as her eyes met mine. She looked so good for her age. She must be at least seventy, I estimated, if not older, but she did not have a single wrinkle to be seen. Nearly flawless porcelain skin. She was about my height with perfect posture. Not short, but not as tall as Ophelia, I noted. She walked tall and proud. A powerful air followed her as she moved. She was exceptionally curvy with long, thick white hair that was grandiose, nearly radiant. It was done up in braids on each side of her head, wrapping around the sides with a few pieces left out to cascade in a deliberately messy-elegant look. The braids on either side converged at the crown of her head, merging into one long braid that tumbled down her back. The rest of the hair was left down, to flow around her shoulders in ornate loose curls. Several small golden rings were woven into the sides of the braids. She wore a bright silver cold-shoulder dress. Dainty pieces of fabric forming the appearance of sleeves that stopped at her elbows, draping off of her forearms. The dress fell just to her knees, cut at an angle with the front of the dress being short while the back cascaded down behind her legs. A sash incorporated into the dress design cinched her waist, accentuating her figure. The sash hung off her left side, slightly touching the floor when she was standing still. Tall heels, with thin silver straps against her skin, containing a delicate silver butterfly that shimmered just above her toes, completed the look. She walked so effortlessly in the high heels; I wondered to myself if she could even own a pair of flats. I longed to have her graceful movements as I watched her flow through the space at that very moment. She stopped just in front of us; Ophelia and I giving a quick curtsy. Alsendra nodded in recognition of the gesture. I exhaled, preparing for my next choice of words. She spoke before I could say anything. "Forgive me if I forgo the polite courtesies and cut right to the chase, Octavia. Care to tell me why it is you don't think you should accept my gracious invitation to the Rights Ceremony? Do you assume to believe that I do not make the correct decisions when I choose who should be here? Do you not believe yourself worthy?" I stood there, unsure what to say, trying to think if I should say anything at all. "Answer, girl!" Her voice wasn't any louder than it had been before, but carried enough power to almost take my breath away. I gasped, feeling my breath leave me in response. "N-n-no, Lady Alsendra." I squeaked out before collecting myself. "I know that as Diviner Archmage; you know things beyond my reach." "This is true!" She spoke quickly. "I see and know many futures, many paths, many outcomes, and several pasts. So tell me now, why do you think you do not deserve to be here, Octavia? Do you think you know better than I?" "Well, I'm just not anything special. I'm a commoner. Poor. Not particularly pretty. Not talented. Not extraordinary in any capacity. Yet I still get invited to the Rights without me having a clue…" She held up her hand. "Enough!" The power behind her voice stopped my words instantly. "My gods, girl, you really do not know, do you?" I didn't dare speak as she seemed to study me. She pursed her lips into a straight line. "Yes, now that detail I failed to see prior to this conversation, it would seem. Most peculiar. Divination is a fickle master. At any rate, it seems I have much to teach you. You are capable of many great things, Octavia. As it stands now, you clearly don't have any grasp of your own abilities. We will tend to that soon. You will perform the Rights tonight, isn't that correct?" She asked, but already knew the answer. I nodded. "Complete the Rights Ceremony and we will speak again soon." She gracefully turned, her sash flowing in a quick twirl as she walked off. It appeared Ophelia was holding back a multitude of thoughts, appearing to have a lot to say. "Yes, Ophelia? You might as well spit it out." She huffed before speaking, "Well, Lady Alsendra is a badger of a lady, isn't she?" "Shhh, Ophelia, you know how well respected she is." "I do, and that doesn't mean I have to like her for it." Ophelia crossed her arms and adjusted her weight to one leg. "Let's just get through the Rights Ceremony, Ope. We can figure out everything else afterwards." She let out a dramatic sigh as she sat back down, her face holding a scowl, drawing the attention of several nearby guests. I kicked her foot. "Behave!"

Lady Alsendra's voice echoed through the room, drawing all eyes to her as they turned to find the source of the noise. "All participants in the Rights Ceremony, make way to the front. Grab a dagger and candle to the right of the altar and take a stand behind me." She clapped loudly once. "Proceed!" We all hopped up and, with her words echoing in our ears, went to carry out her instructions. I looked over the other guests, observing their attire and the way they carried themselves. They appeared wealthier than I could have imagined. Well-trained, poised, and educated in socialite etiquette. I was the third person to reach the tables to the right of the altar. Candles on one side, daggers on the other. All the daggers appeared identical. Steel blades with decorative gold handles — nothing particularly special stood out. There were candles in an assortment of colors. Black, gray, white, blue, purple, green, yellow, orange, red, pink, silver, gold, and brown. A few of the girls proceeded to grab a candle, then headed over to stand behind Lady Alsendra. Oh gods, I didn't know what color to grab. I could feel my heart pounding with anxiety. I leaned in closer to the girl behind me, whispering. "Do you know what color we're supposed to get, or is it random?" She looked me up and down, letting out a "hmph" before grabbing a candle and moving on without a word. A short, petite girl bobbed up next to me a moment later with a smile, giving me a little startle as she did. Flaxen-haired in a simple updo and with a fair complexion, she couldn't have been any over five feet tall with heels. She leaned in to speak in an upbeat voice, "So what you want to do is focus. Maybe close your eyes if that helps. Grab the color that stands out to you. The one that is right for you will make itself known." She then stepped forward, looking the candles over for a moment. Smiling, she picked up the pink candle and, giddy with excitement, said, "There you are," then skipped off, glancing back over her shoulder. "I'm Gabrielle, by the way." I gave her a genuine smile. "And I'm Octavia." She beamed back at me. "Good luck!" She hopped off to stand behind Lady Alsendra. It was then that I noticed Lady Alsendra looking at me through narrowed eyes. It gave me a jolt and brought my attention back to finding the right candle. But I couldn't feel anything. They were all the same, just different colors. I remembered what Gabrielle had said. "Close your eyes if that helps." I closed my eyes to focus, picturing the candles and all their colors on the table before me. Nothing. I concentrated harder, picturing each one and where it was on the table. Imagining how different colors might have distinct scents. Then I felt that electric feeling again, the same one I felt when Ophelia and I were speaking before we got here. A breeze brushed the back of my neck. I focused harder, willing a color to make itself known to me. A gust of wind blew around me with a sharp howl, blowing my dress and making the chains on it clink. I lost concentration immediately upon hearing a few gasps from the audience. As my eyes fluttered open, I surveyed my surroundings, taking care to confirm that my dress was still properly situated, and that nothing had come loose. Everything seems to be all right. The only thing different was a dark purple candle tipped over on the table, facing my direction. Is this the candle that made itself known to me? I pondered, picking up the candle. This is a pretty color, at least, I shrugged to myself and headed over to stand behind Lady Alsendra. I once again noticed Lady Alsendra looking at me, this time with a look of amusement. I noticed Gabrielle beaming at me again as she was waving her hand back and forth to grab my attention. When I noticed, she pointed to the floor beside her and mouthed "here", motioning for me to take a stand beside her. I gladly did as she suggested; her warm gesture gave me hope. Especially since it saved me from having to be with one of those other snooty harpies, as Ophelia called them. "Now then." Lady Alsendra boomed through the room. She then extended her arms out wide to each side, bringing her hands together quickly to clap in a thunderous rumble that echoed around us. The lighting dimmed throughout the great room. Sounds of awe and surprise, characterized by "oohs" and "aahs", permeated the air and were heard by all. She smiled. "Let us begin!"

Chapter 3: The Rights- Part 2

Lady Alsendra moved to the altar with one swift movement. The altar was essentially just a table with a raised ledge along the back. A large white cloth draped over the top, hanging to the floor on all sides. Candles lined either side, with the tallest candles towards the back and the shorter ones towards the front. The candles were white, plain, and uninteresting. Wax dripped down the sides of a few to collect on the black candle holders, giving the overall appearance of a tree made from wax. A large silver bowl sat in the center of the altar with water, an assortment of leaves and flowers floating about. A basket of flowers and petals sat to the right of the bowl. Bark and stones sat to the left. Behind the bowl rested a brazier on short, spindly legs. A low fire danced on top of the coals. In front of the bowl, in a straight line, looked to be a type of fine dirt. It was hard to make out with the dim lighting and my current position, but it looked as though clumps of moss were mixed with the dirt. Various types of crystals were dotted around the top of the altar. Balls of some type of plant material lay along the inner perimeter of the dirt line. An ornamental piece of twine was tied around them for cosmetic appeal. Above the altar was a banner holding three symbols: witch's knot, pentagram, and triquetra. From the balcony overhead, the large doors were open, allowing the breeze to enter and cause the banner to ripple gently. This place was truly designed from top to bottom to incorporate all the elements. This was a representation of unity, where all five elements could come together to coexist. All five were needed to give life. To take life. To sustain. I closed my eyes and inhaled slowly and deeply. A moment of peace and clarity offered by the tranquil space.

The girl in the front-left corner stepped up to the altar first. Lady Alsendra had instructed the girls to start from left to right, beginning with those at the front. The girl had skin as black as midnight. Hair the color of dark ink. Her eyes were just as dark as her hair, unable to differentiate between pupil and iris. The contrast was truly striking against her red dress. The light from the flaming brazier glinted off her dark features, making her skin appear reflective, as if it were wet. The thought occurred to me: could she be a selkie? Never had I met a selkie in person. I wasn't even sure if they still lived, but she fit the description based on what I knew of them. I glanced over at Ophelia, curious if she was paying attention and wondering the same thing about the girl. I brought my attention back to the girl, now standing in front of the altar. She said a small blessing from what I could tell, placing the silver candle she held on the altar as the words left her lips. The girl then grabbed one of the plant material balls wrapped in ornamental twine, followed by gently picking up a bamboo punk, placing it above the flames of the brazier and bringing it back to light the candle. The silver candle glinted and sparkled as the flame sizzled up briefly before simmering back down to a low flame. Gabrielle leaned over, whispering. "Silver, you see?" I shrugged. Gabrielle put her hand on her hip. "Silver? You know? Lunar energy. The moons, intuition, dream work, and clairvoyance. That's an interesting choice, don't you think?" One girl in the row behind us made a "shhh" sound in response to our quiet conversation. To be honest, I didn't have a clue what any of the colors meant or what they represented. Nevertheless, I nodded in recognition and turned my attention back to the girl at the altar. She held the strange-looking plant ball in her left hand and the dagger in the right. She mumbled some things; we were too far away to hear what was spoken. Afterward, she carefully slipped the dagger beneath the twine, setting the twine aside with care before gingerly placing the dagger down. She cupped the plant ball using both hands, proceeding to hold it in front of her face, closing her eyes. Without pausing, she fell into a rhythmic chant, its words echoing around her. Because of my lack of knowledge, I could not tell the difference. Her words grew quicker and louder. I could feel the low reverberations from her deep voice. With a gentle splash, the bowl of water dispersed, and a minuscule droplet landed with precision, extinguishing the flame flickering atop her candle. A trail of smoke whipped up from the wick. Having opened her eyes, she brought her cupped hands down to place the plant ball in the bowl of water. I expected something spectacular, but what was that? Another crackle erupted from the candle, yet only a wisp of smoke escaped, without a flame. As we stood there, waiting in anticipation, I noticed Lady Alsendra take two steps to her right. The precise moment I perceived it was then. A beam of moonlight made its way down from the overhead window, moving as if it were sentient. I could swear I saw it dance in a back-and-forth sway, a rhythmic sway through the cool night air. It reached just above the altar. Then I noticed the girl's black eyes and the way they sparkled in the dim light. They glowed faintly, a subtle luminescence that seemed to whisper the moon's secrets. The girl raised a hand to meet the moonlight. It quickly darted straight down to the bowl upon her touch. The water glowed with a soft, beautiful, cool blue light. I watched in awe. The light seemed to swirl a couple of times and then disappeared into the plant ball. Everyone stood watching with full concentration; you could have heard a pin drop. The plant ball appeared to have the slightest tremor, barely noticeable. Then, the ball unfurled before our eyes, turning greener and more vibrant in an instant. It fully unfurled to reveal a shining silver lotus. The moonlight left the lotus to spread out onto the leaves and strand out into the water, appearing as if the moonlight were the roots. The lotus spun slowly. Water whirled around it. With a small final splash, the silver lotus popped up out of the water just above the bowl. The girl, whom I now strongly believed was indeed a selkie, reached her hand out as the lotus popped up, landing gracefully in her palm. She paused there, not moving. Then Lady Alsendra broke the silence. "How splendid! Well done!" Low applause broke out across the audience. I heard the girl behind me sneer in disgust. The girl with the silver lotus smiled, her teeth deeply contrasting with her dark skin. Lady Alsendra motioned for her to move to a bench in a row to the side of where she stood. The girl nodded graciously, then moved past, her perfume leaving a faint scent.

There was one girl left before Gabrielle, and then it would be my turn. The girl up next was of average height. Her light tan was a perfect match with her dark brown hair. She was a large girl sporting an A-line dress. Small shoulder pads gave the top a little more shape, while the petticoat she paired with the dress provided extra volume around the flared bottom. She wore shorter, closed-toe heels. She approached the altar with a brown candle in hand, following the steps the first girl had previously displayed. It sounded like she said a different, yet quite similar blessing or chant. I couldn't completely tell from where I stood, but the rhythm sounded different. She lit the candle with the bamboo punk and used the dagger to cut the twine as the other girl had. I leaned over to Gabrielle, lowering my voice to whisper in a hushed tone. "So what about the brown candle?" She let out a little chuckle. "Brown promotes a connection to the earth and the natural world. Grounding and balance. I've heard brown is also used to help gain a connection to ancestors and heritage. You know? Old things like the hamadryads. Although I've never actually confirmed that for myself." She crinkled her nose in thought. I turned my attention back to the girl at the altar as she cupped the plant ball a little differently than the girl before had done. After she finished speaking, silence hung heavy in the air, broken only by the sound of her own breathing. Except this girl placed her plant material ball in the basket of bark and stone. Everyone watched intently, but nothing seemed to happen. Her brown candle remained lit with a low, steady flame. Then I couldn't tell if my eyes were deceiving me or if the skin on the girl's lower arms seemed to turn rough and brown. I quickly realized that her arms now resembled tree bark. As that thought left my mind, she reached forward, giving the ball of plant material a hard thump. A small noise rang out. Almost like a high-pitched whine or cry. Not a soul moved as a heavy silence hung in the air. Then the plant ball lurched. Wiggled this way, then that. The candlelight illuminated the dust motes dancing in the air as the ball rustled nearby. It unfurled, taking its time as we anxiously watched. It didn't unfurl in the same way as the previous girl's had. There was no light. The leaves didn't turn greener or more vibrant as it moved. This was something I found to be equally captivating. Another noise rang out. This time it sounded like a grunt. The dirt line directly in front of the basket with the bark and stone moved ever so slightly towards the plant ball. The girl gently placed her left hand over the dirt line and then her right hand directly on the plant ball. Both sounds stopped, with no movement to be detected. I could hear no sound. A moment passed. Then, with a *poof*, a little puff of dust whipped into the air around the plant ball. A couple of exhales from the audience could be heard. Then a small, what appeared to be a stick, stuck out of the ball as it continued to unfurl. I realized this was not a stick, but a leg! This stick leg bent and moved in a way a small stick on a small bush would bend. Except this was thicker and shaped in a way that uncannily resembled a human leg. It kicked, and another grunt and what sounded like a tiny groan emerged from the unfurling ball. Without further delay, the plant ball burst completely open with a thud. When I looked forward, I could not identify what was present in the distance. It appeared as if it were humanoid, but also a tree. What was this fascinating, heterogeneous being? It must have stood about a foot tall. It appeared to have a long beard made of green moss. Green, faintly glowing eyes. Twigs that looked like antlers protruded from the top of the creature, while it had more of the green moss for hair. On its back rested what looked like a woven mix of vines, leaves, and twigs fashioned into the shape of a bird's nest. The little creature's hands extended into what looked like small tree knots with four "fingers". The fingers were long twigs. It looked as though they were claws, and I suspected they could be used as such if needed. After glancing around, the creature directed its attention at the girl who created it, and then in a small voice yelled angry words. It stomped twice, then threw a small rock that hit her on the forehead. The girl reached up, pressing her hand against where the rock had hit. The little creature, content with its actions, chirped with glee. A girl behind me snickered, her voice like a mocking echo. The girl back at the altar lowered a shoulder bag to just in front of where the little creature stood, opened it up, pointing while repeating, "in, in". The little creature still looked mad, but begrudgingly walked over to stand in the small bag. As she picked up the bag, I could still see the little tree man's head peering up above the fabric, glaring around as she put it over her shoulder. Lady Alsendra once again broke the silence. "Marvelous! Well done, my dear!" A soft applause from the audience. Lady Alsendra continued; "You have displayed quite a feat, but I do hope you plan to make haste and deliver this creature to the deep forest immediately. Leshies belong in the untouched sacred forests, not here at our ceremony. Provoking them could have unfavorable consequences for anyone involved." Oh, so that is a Leshy. It has to be a baby, or perhaps whatever the term is for a very young one. How in all the realms did she bring a Leshy here? Did she summon it or create it? I made a mental note to find out more about that later. From a young age, I have heard tales that speak of the terrifying Leshy. I've been told stories of some standing as tall as the trees themselves, striking fear and intimidation into anyone unfortunate enough to gaze upon them. They played pranks on hunters and anyone foolish enough to wander that deep into the forest. They have kidnapped people, and especially children, but typically released them after playing their pranks. Fate determined whether a Leshy would be helpful or dangerous, as these creatures were known for their unpredictable nature. They were symbolic of the border between civilization and the wilderness. I knew enough from the folklore and warnings about Leshies to know that leaving them an offering of bread or tobacco was in your best interest if you intended to be in their good graces.

Next was Gabrielle's turn. Her gaze met mine for a fleeting moment before she made her way towards the altar. That was the first time I had seen her face with anything less than happiness and enthusiasm. She looked worried. Concerned. Oh, gods, that made my own nerves even worse. I gave her a quick "good luck" before she was out of earshot. I wonder if she had anxiety about what she would be performing. I was confident that she already knew what needed to be done. Gabrielle seemed well-informed and far more educated than I was on these things. She assumed her position at the altar. Following the same steps as the other girls with minor differences here and there, giving it her own unique twist. Following that up by placing the bright pink candle on the altar and lighting it with the bamboo punk. I wished in that moment I had asked her what the pink meant or represented. Why did the pink catch her attention? She picked up the ball of plant material, cut the twine, and once again began speaking things I couldn't make out. I thought I heard the water bowl vibrate with a faint ringing sound for a moment. The same way a wine glass would ring when you rubbed a wet finger around the rim. She stopped; nothing happened. I was paying extra close attention because, damn it, I was truly rooting for her. Gabrielle was the first and only girl here to show me kindness. She treated me with respect and dignity. Spoke to me as a fellow peer, never looking at me with disgust like the other courtly parasites here have done. She deserved to do well, whatever it was she was going to do. I was still curious about what this tiny girl with the bubbly personality would conjure up. In her left hand, she held the ball of plant material and carefully lowered it into the water. She cautiously grabbed a couple of different crystals from the altar. One looked white, while the other appeared aquamarine blue. I knew I had seen crystals like those before, but I couldn't recall exactly what they were. Gabrielle dropped them into the bowl of water, holding her hand over the bowl, palm down. She closed her eyes, and her face took on a look of intense focus. I noticed a pink feather floating down from above. Aside from me, it seemed everyone either didn't see it or disregarded it. I couldn't be sure. The water bowl let out a couple of bubbles, followed by a few more, coming from the crystals at the bottom. This continued until the water's surface was disturbed by rising bubbles, as if on the verge of a low boil. A mist started rolling out of the bowl, staying low to the top of the altar. Then, the ball of plant material started to either sink or dissolve. No, it was absolutely dissolving. The plant material was rapidly dissipating upwards into the mist as it dissolved, not into the water. There was an ever so faint glow of pink in the mist now. It looked as if fine glitter had been sprinkled across the misty scene, catching the light. By this time, the mist was rolling off onto the floor around the altar, flowing out as if it had a purpose. The pink feather drifted gently to the floor, landing silently near Gabrielle. Slowly, the mist drifted, eventually enveloping the feather in its damp embrace. As the feather reappeared above the mist, I couldn't understand what was happening; my brow furrowed in concentration. Oh good gods! My eyes widened.

What came up was a mass of feathers. I realized that this was, in fact, a living being. Again, nobody paid attention, or perhaps they simply overlooked what was unfolding. Gabrielle's gaze mirrored mine; it was clear she saw it too. I looked over and saw Lady Alsendra watching me through narrowed eyes again. Was she unable to witness the current situation? Did she know and not care? In that moment, it was impossible for me to make sense of it. I gazed at the beautiful creature the one feather had now become. It was the size of a small gazelle. Slender, deer-like legs with a body shaped like a fox. The head of the creature held a delicate face that was doe-like, with a long, elongated snout. Its expressions were emotionally readable with empathetic eyes and small, alert ears. The eyes were large and luminous, with heart-shaped pupils. The ears, slightly tufted like those of a lynx or fennec fox, adding a whimsical look. A smooth blend of short, silky fur and soft, downy feathers made up its coat. I noticed the soft, downy feathers, especially around the shoulders, chest, and tail. The texture shimmered in the moonlight. Both the fur and feathers were shades of blush pink, rose gold, and pearl white. With a faint iridescence over the creature, like the surface of a soap bubble. It had a fox-like, flowing tail. Wings the length of its body lay flat on its back and sides, a mix of soft, downy feathers and thicker, larger feathers towards the tips. The creature appeared light and agile. Moving gracefully and silently, as if it were gliding with its walk, added to the overall ethereal presence. It moved towards Gabrielle. Yet, it went completely unnoticed by everyone. The creature made a circle around Gabrielle's legs, rubbing against her slightly. She looked down as she watched it without moving or making a sound. It turned a much darker, vibrant pink around her. The iridescence of its coat danced around in the moonlight as it moved. The creature walked away from her and stopped, making eye contact with me. It flared its nostrils a few times, shaking its wings out with fervor, then gracefully moved towards me. I noticed the color of its fur and feathers fading as it got further away from Gabrielle, before then darkening again as it neared me. I noticed a radiant, heart-shaped gem in its chest as it was just in front of me, sparkling in the dim light. It was pulsing with a low light, more so as it moved closer. I looked around in confusion. Most eyes were on Gabrielle, but none were on me aside from Lady Alsendra. I don't believe Lady Alsendra could see the creature based on her expression, but she must have known I was involved in this somehow. The creature made a circle around my legs as it had Gabrielle's. I could feel its aura. It was strong, emotionally enlightening, making my nerves almost disappear as I let it in. The creature made its way around me full circle, stopping once it completed its circle to arrive before me once again. I stared into those heart-shaped pupils as it gazed up at me. It flicked its tail a few times, shaking its coat before closing its eyes. *POP* The sound rang in my ears, causing me to flinch as if someone had popped a balloon directly in front of me. I gasped, earning me a few stares. In the blink of an eye, the creature was nowhere to be seen. The mist from before left the air and slowly rolled out in all directions. Now, the mist, everyone seemed to see and notice. I saw something pink under the mist as it was clearing. I bent over to pick it up, shocked at what I now held. It was a beautiful, large, heart-shaped, powder-pink blossom wrapped in dark pink feathers, as if it were in a tightly bound nest. Lady Alsendra glared. I could feel her eyes on me, even without seeing them, just like everyone else in the audience. Gabrielle's eyes were wide with a bewildered expression, clearly confused by the situation. Lady Alsendra once again broke the silence. It seems she has a habit of doing that. "Absolutely splendid!" She boomed. "You achieved something we have not seen before — most impressive!" Gabrielle walked over, and I placed the heart-shaped blossom in her hands. Lady Alsendra motioned for her to take a seat with the other girls. Now it was my turn.

Chapter 4: The Rights- Part 3

I made my way to the altar, following the example of the girl before
me. Standing here, a sense of somber came over me. My nerves were
calmer than they had been prior to the encounter with the magical
creature Gabrielle had created. I spared a glance at Ophelia. She gave
me a big smile and a wave, letting me know she was there and paying
attention. I glanced over at Gabrielle; she beamed at me again while
giving me a thumbs-up. A quick glance at Lady Alsendra told me by
the subtle look of disdain on her face that she was growing tired of me
not moving it along. What was I supposed to do? I wasn't born for
this. I wasn't raised in a wealthy family that could afford costly
lessons for things such as this. I didn't have abilities that compared to
what those other girls did in any capacity. I didn't even know I had
any gifts until the day Ophelia and I had to deal with that nasty old
man. Most of these girls were born and bred specifically with this in
mind, hoping for the chance to make it where I now stand. As soon as
they could walk and speak, their education began. While Ophelia and I
were forced to learn how to survive on our own while we were
starving and trying to live. Our mother was around when she felt like
it and wasn't out spending her time with whatever man was her
current muse of the week. Or when she needed to use us or needed us
to do something of benefit to her. She really was a narcissist through
and through. So, we learned early on to rely on each other without a
parent. It taught us things these girls would never know, made us
forge a bond stronger than most soul mates, and for that I was truly
grateful. At least one positive thing can come from that cesspool of

terrible circumstances. I snapped my focus back. Lifting the bamboo punk up to the brazier, bringing it down on the wick to light the purple candle, snuffing out the punk before carefully laying it back to the side of the altar. I grabbed the dagger and a ball of that plant material wrapped in twine. It was lighter than I had imagined. Hard to tell exactly what it was, but the outside layer looked to be dried banana leaves or possibly tobacco leaves. Then again, I didn't smell the distinct scent of tobacco. I cut the twine, setting the dagger aside. Cupping the plant ball with both hands, I froze. I knew from watching the other girls that this is where I say something, but what in the nine hells was I supposed to say? A blessing? A chant? A prayer to some God of old or an entity? I pondered for a moment before deciding I would just make a plea to whatever is willing to listen on the wind to come to my aid and assist me in any way possible. I didn't want to fail this. I didn't want this to go horribly wrong after Lady Alsendra herself saw enough in me to give me a chance to be in this very spot. It would be utterly humiliating, and I would be made a mockery of if I failed this now; I was sure of that. I must have taken a moment too long, as I heard one girl waiting for her turn at the altar. "Oh, come on, get this mundane plebeian out of here already." Her voice wasn't so loud as to draw attention, but was loud enough to be heard throughout a large part of this room, I suspected. I hadn't moved or so much as blinked after the girl spoke until I saw Ophelia stand up with a rustle. With the eyes in the audience moving to her as I lifted my gaze. Well, rot me sideways, here she goes.

Ophelia was yelling and pointing before anyone knew what was happening. "And why don't I come up there and drag your scrawny ass, you bloated goblin!" "SILENCE!" Lady Alsendra boomed with a crackle through the air that trailed. The girl to whom Ophelia's words had been pointed dropped her smug smirk in an instant, hanging her mouth open before catching herself. She turned a bright shade a pink, nearly red. I could feel her seething anger directed at Ophelia. I tried to imagine being called out like that by the tallest and prettiest woman in the room, who was more than capable of giving you a good bashing you'd never forget. All because you wanted to be snarky. Ophelia sat back down without another word, arms crossed and giving a venomous stare with her head tilted slightly forward at the girl she had addressed. I knew Ophelia well enough to know she would make it her mission to stare that girl down and make her as uncomfortable as she could manage for the rest of our time here. Part of that made me giggle inside, easing my nerves. Ophelia was exceedingly kind and generous. She would give the clothes off her back to anyone truly in need, but she was also an adept judge of character. In any fight or circumstance she deemed unjust, she would stand her ground, defending both herself and me, and refusing to yield. She was a fighter like that. Most who knew her only knew her as kind and polite until they vexed her in a way they shouldn't have. Lady Alsendra boomed once again. "Please continue. I trust we will not have any further interruption less anyone cares to test my patience this day?" There were underlying challenges in her words. She almost wished someone to interrupt. I wondered what Lady Alsendra could really do when provoked in anger. I hadn't known her to be powerful in other ways aside from her fierce divination gifts. She was the Diviner Archmage, so we all knew she was clearly the best and most powerful at what she did. She is a highly respected and radically gifted clairvoyant in a multitude of ways. Could she have other abilities that were strong enough to be used to any extent outside of that? I'd like to ask her that one day, if given the opportunity.

I once again brought my attention back to the task at hand. With the little ball of plant matter in my hand, I held it up close to my face, nearly reaching my mouth. I remembered what Gabrielle had said about the candle and how effective that had been. Focus. Close your eyes if that helps, I repeated to myself. I focused, but nothing came; nothing happened. I did not think of anything to say. I decided I should focus on the flaming purple candle before me. With the low dancing flame, the little crackles it gave off, I pictured the wax melting around the wick, imagining the flame changing colors as it would when the burning temperature changes. I imagined how air is needed to fuel a fire and how wind can fuel the smallest ember into a giant roaring fire. I felt a breeze before a nudge at my back. Then I heard that voice, yet not quite a voice; it spoke low and slow. "Octaaviaaa. Hear my words. Repeat what I say, child." I nodded slightly to myself as if it could see me respond and whispered, "I am ready." The voice began speaking again, slowly. I repeated word for word. "Umbrosi spiritus, flammarum potentes, Antiquissimi, vos nomino in umbra. Per radix profunda et lapidem sacrum, Per cruorem et animam viventem, Adeste, et ducite me per tribulationem et mortem." (Translation: Spirits of shadow, spirits of flame, ancient ones, I call your name. By root and stone, by blood and breath, guide me now through trial and death.) A howling wind roared around me, the sound like a thousand angry voices, as it tossed my hair and dress. The chains on my dress swayed back and forth with soft clinks. I felt a nudge at my back, but I didn't dare move, opening my eyes a moment later. The sight before me gave me a start. The flame on the purple candle must have been a foot tall and roaring, whipping around in the wind as tall grass would in a meadow. The cloth draped over the altar whipped in a repeated back-and-forth pattern as the wind swung it up and then released it. Swinging up and releasing. Repeat. The ball of plant material in my hands became scorching hot in an instant. Too hot to keep holding. I jolted. Tried to bounce it in my hands to prevent the burning, but I dropped it. It fell into the bowl of water with a soft 'plop'. "Oh no," my stomach twisted with the feeling of blunder. Did I ruin everything? Was the ball supposed to get hot? I watched intently as the ball smoldered, little puffs of smoke wafting up in what was now just a breeze. With a small gust of wind, I heard that voice saying, "here child," from where the candle rested on the altar. I felt compelled to reach out without knowing exactly why. I stopped inches away from the flame. The voice again "here". I inched my hand closer. Suddenly, before I had time to react, the flame jumped to my hand. It swirled around my arm, running up faster than I could realize what was happening. I felt the fire on my back. I heard a loud reaction from the audience. I tried to let out a scream of shock and horror, but only a squeak came out.

My attempt to scream seemed to fuel the flame, making it jump out higher and brighter, almost blue-purple where it touched my skin. Then the flame swirled down my left arm as quickly as it had my right. My left hand had hovered over the bowl of water where the ball of plant material floated. The flame shot off my left hand with what seemed like lightning speed, hitting the ball. Water splashed out of the bowl on all sides. The flames on my body and arms disappeared as quickly as they had started. Then I realized I wasn't harmed. No burns and my hair felt intact. I looked back at the ball of plant material; it was roasted and red with embers. Then a twitch from it. The water rippled. I heard a high, whiny sort of noise off to my side, followed by a bit of a commotion; it was coming from where the girls who had already completed their Rights were sitting. I looked over to see the brown candle girl was now fighting with her shoulder bag. Fighting with the Leshy, I realized. I turned my attention back to the burned ball in the water bowl as it gave a sudden lurch and a hum. It went still. No noise aside from more commotion coming from the girl and the Leshy. Without warning, the ball of plant material erupted up in a spiral of flames. With a gust of wind and the flame shot out to both my left and right. People ducked. It did not escape my attention that Lady Alsendra had already moved beforehand. I stepped back as I felt the heat from the flames, almost losing my balance. I squinted as something within caught my eye. Was that a face in the flame? The flames pulled back, taking shape. I let out a jagged breath at what took form. It looked like a flaming devil. Or a demon. It had a body and a face, but you also couldn't quite make it out as it was covered in rolling flames. It was standing in the water bowl where the ball had previously floated. Water boiling from around this thing's "legs". It was looking at me as I studied it. It must have stood around two feet tall, if not slightly more. It was at eye level while standing on the altar. I could smell a smoldering scent. Flames came off its head in a way that appeared to make horns that resembled those of a ram. It smiled at me. Was it amused? I didn't feel threatened or in danger. I noticed something in my periphery. I looked down to my right at what was moving. It was that Leshy! It was now scrambling up the side of the altar, using its twig claws to stab into the cloth and pull up. It was faster than I had thought possible for the little tree man. Although not unbelievably quick, it was making haste. It reached the top of the altar, screaming and shouting angrily in that small voice. I couldn't exactly understand what it said, but I could pick up on the tone that it was very unhappy. The fire demon flared up as it looked down at the Leshy. I could no longer make out the face as it burned brighter. The Leshy picked up a stone from the basket on the altar, throwing it at the flame. The stone landed behind the altar while the flame remained unfazed. The Leshy leaped forward, ramming into the side of the silver water bowl with all his might, tipping it over. The flaming demon moved back as water splashed off the altar, steam rolling up into the air. Then the flame crept backwards, slowly dying out as it rolled off the side of the altar. Perhaps it simmered out. The Leshy made little whoops and held up its arm, cheering. I heard gasps from around the room; the Leshy and I both snapped up. I looked to see what the gasps were about. Was it about the Leshy? Then I felt a hard nudge at my back again; as a silent command for me to hear what was being said.

What was this about? I thought maybe I should open myself a little to the nudge, just a little to see if I could figure out what it was telling me. The impact of the nudge against my back was so forceful that it stole my breath away and caused me to suddenly stumble forward. There was no voice, only raw power rippling through my body, using me as a vessel. I felt myself channeling it unintentionally, because what was happening was instinctive and primal. A fury of wind came in every window and door of the room, surrounding me. It buzzed around me before soaring around the altar, a wild current weaving the short distance. As the cloth covering the altar came loose, it fluttered away, eventually coming to rest close to those in attendance. Most things left on the altar top got thrown around or knocked over; a few of the lighter or rounder items rolled and bounced off onto the marble floor. The candles around the altar were no longer lit. No sooner had I caught my breath, a wild flame shot out from the left side behind the altar as the surrounding wind fueled it with a yearning lust. From the right, another flame unexpectedly shot out. It now spanned the entire width of the room. My eyes shot upward, and disbelief washed over me. It was... wings, or shaped like wings. Dark blue and purple flame in the center, then orange, with yellow framing the entire "wings". Just as I took in the sight of the wings, I felt another gale-force fury of wind. Having been secured, my hair came undone and was now moving about in a chaotic fashion because of the wind. Occasionally getting in my face. Somehow the little chains Ophelia had clipped in held fast, but they were now hanging down or flying about when my hair caught them. However, I was not prepared for what the last fury of wind brought forth. An enormous demon took form and stood behind the altar. It was then I realized those big wings were in fact part of this creature, as they extended from its body. This colossal elemental being was surely born from the flames of hell and chaos. There was still no solid form to be found, no flesh. Its entire form was a writhing, ever-shifting mass of fire and smoke, shaped vaguely like a humanoid predator forged in nightmare. The flames composing its body flickered and roared. Its presence dimmed the surrounding room, not with shadow, but with overwhelming brilliance. At the center of its chest and along its "spine" or where a spine would be, the fire burned a deep ultraviolet-blue. Its core radiated raw, seething power, rippling outward into a luminous purple, then a fiery orange, and finally edged with a brilliant, molten gold — a holy color twisted into hellish majesty. Its wings were now a breathtaking and terrible sight. The flame-woven appendages now spread out like the sails of a dragon long damned to the underworld. Each wing layered in living fire. Glowing blue-violet at the base, encircled by vibrant orange, and then outlined with licking arcs of golden yellow flame. Curved horns made entirely of compressed flame glowed from within, trailing smoke and embers with every movement. Its eyes were the only distinct feature I could make out on its face. Two narrow slits in blinding white fire, crackling with ancient rage and intelligence. Another gale-force gust of wind came. I braced myself, nearly collapsing to my knees. When the devil moved, the air warped, and the floor scorched. The colossal devil looking at me speaks, with a voice like an inferno erupting from a chasm, every word accompanied by a thunderclap and a rush of searing wind. It belches out: "Master... cloaked in my fire, thou art beyond harm. Beneath thine shadow of my wings, thou art untouchable. Let the world burn ere a hand is laid upon thee." Am I the master it speaks of? Lady Alsendra yelled something in her booming voice, but I couldn't make out a thing. At that moment, I realized that most of those present had already exited the room; only a select few stayed behind. I glanced over to see Ophelia ducking behind a bench with her head peeking over it. Oh, thank the gods she's fine. Then I saw something fly from my periphery. It was the Leshy, now on the floor, standing beside the silver water bowl that had fallen off the altar, who threw a wine goblet at the creature. Residual wine spilling out and sizzling off the heat of the devil. It let out a bellowing hiss. This damn little weed was going to get us all killed. The infernal flame devil leaned over, spreading out a trail of fire that resembled an arm towards the Leshy. The Leshy squeaked out some words, then dove under the silver bowl on the ground just seconds before the flame reached it. The flame of the creature burned everything around it. With a nudge at my back, I instinctively let it push into me; the fire soared up. I gasped, oh no, it was going to kill the Leshy. "STOP!" With a sudden hiss, the flame jerked back. I ran forward to kick the bowl, feeling the heat of the surrounding fire. The Leshy stumbled out, its mossy head smoldering as it slapped at it. The flame was coming back for the Leshy. I stepped out in front of the flame, kicking the Leshy back. The flame stopped just inches from my face. The heat went to my core, but it didn't burn my skin. With a nudge at my back, I stepped forward; the flame rushed at me, engulfing my body in an instant. I expected to incinerate to dust and ash, but nothing happened as the flames whirled around me. I now realized I was directly under the infernal devil. Those eyes looking at me from above. "Master... while thy flame burns hot, no harm shall dare touch thee. Let the world burn, for I am your wrath made manifest."

Then I noticed Lady Alsendra, red-faced and yelling as she waved her arms, ordering someone around with a tone that brooked no argument. I couldn't hear a thing in these flames, just the roaring of the wind and the crackling of embers. The selkie from earlier was there. After I noticed three more, it prompted the question in my mind of whether they were part of her family. They had to be; they were too eerily similar not to be related. One man, two women, all three equally stunning in the moonlight as the girl performing the Rights had been. The brilliance of the flames reflected off their skin like the blackest depths of a lake. They all had varying shades of sea-spray-black hair. The male selkie made a movement, running for an extensive set of double doors to the side of the room that led outside to a courtyard. At the center stood a large fountain with a mossy base, encircled by a brick pathway, surrounded by various rose bushes and plants rustling in the breeze, and a few benches sat invitingly nearby. I saw beams of moonlight dance around the first selkie in the courtyard. The moonlight leaping artfully, dancing to the next selkie, who was just inside the double doors, then to the next. The last selkie was standing next to the girl from the Rights. Both must have been close in age from the looks of it. The last two selkies shared in the dancing moonlight as the brilliant light bounced back and forth between them. The selkie man in the courtyard, now standing in the fountain, vibrated as he changed shape. His dark, alluring appearance contorted as his clothes ripped, the moonlight continuing to beam around him, spreading out into the water of the fountain. The fountain now glowing a stunning cyan blue glow, strands of moonlight branching off from the few lilies in the fountain, once again appearing as their roots. What was a dark and tall selkie man, now sat a large black seal with dark eyes glowing with moonlight. The second selkie at the door shook again. She contorted into a mass, her clothes ripping, and took the form of a seal. She looked more ordinary, smaller. Not as dark in seal form, but keeping the graceful and attractive sensuality she had before. The last two selkies — the girl from the Rights and the one next to her didn't change. Instead, they held hands as their eyes glowed with little moons, moonlight bouncing back and forth between them. The selkie in the fountain let out a bark, jumping up and making a small splash. The glowing moonlight reached out around it. The water defying gravity rose in shimmering ribbons, each droplet dancing upward like stars towards an unseen moon. Pulling together in the moonlight beam, the cascade of water rushed towards the second selkie. She let out something between a bark and a groan, bouncing in place as the water reached her. The water, traveling through the moonlight beams in great quantity, dropped in a cascade, touching the back of the selkie and bouncing back up to gush through the moonlight. The surrounding moonlight trickled out into the water like earthworms through mud. The water wove up and down in the moonlight to the two selkie girls standing before me, hands clasped tightly together. With both their eyes glowing with the softest moonlight glow, they each held up a hand. The girl on my right was holding up her left hand, and the girl on my left, holding up her right hand, while they kept the opposite together between them. The water was swirling around the two of them, making a bubble shape, reminiscent of a whirlpool in a deep lake. Moonlight protruding outward from their hands, it rushed for the colossal infernal devil above me.. Surrounding both it and myself. At least I thought it did. The brilliant gold flames of the giant flaming beast made it nearly impossible to see if any moonlight made it nearby. The water bobbed and weaved, like a snake dancing to a snake charmer's flute, heading for me and the giant infernal. The infernal devil vibrated with energy. "Master... giveth thy desire. No harm shall befall thee." I looked up, peering into the white eyes. The malice, the desire to consume, the power to burn the sins of any mortal who peered in, eagerly waited for me to give approval. I said nothing, closing my eyes to listen to the whirl and rush of the surrounding power. The nudging at my back channeled through me like static electricity in a lightning storm. I opened my eyes; the selkies had already sent enough water at us to encapsulate the colossal in a giant water bubble. Or maybe it was four walls; I couldn't be sure from inside the flames. The water whirled around with a hum, the flames of the giant infernal whipping about. The selkies were creating a vacuum, pulling out the surrounding air. I once again closed my eyes, this time to focus and concentrate. I pictured that little purple candle in my mind, the color, its warmth, the way the flame might flicker in a subtle draft. How the color purple might smell. Then I pictured the flame getting smaller and smaller until it smoldered and then finally snuffed out. I opened my eyes just as I was collapsing on the floor, gasping for air. The selkies, realizing what was happening, snapped their hands out in one quick, unison movement. The water around me burst outwards into millions of droplets, falling to the floor.

Chapter 5: Ensuing Aftermath

A moment later, the two selkies had changed back to their human
selves. The naked selkie man stood at the door, still alluring and
striking in his appearance, holding a hand over his groin while
leaning against the edge of the door frame. I had the feeling that the
gesture was more for everyone else's benefit and out of respect than it
was for his own benefit. He didn't catch me as the modest type. He
was of a slim and tall build, with rippling muscle definition over his
entire body. The way his deeply dark skin caught the light revealed
the hard ridges of his body. He had muscular legs with defined thighs
and large calves. Well, okay, so I could admit I found him super
attractive. The idea of waking up with a seal flashed into my mind,
and I wondered if it was possible to ride one. Would he need a saddle?
Could you ride a seal while swimming in the ocean like a mermaid
queen? Would he take orders? I dismissed the thought. The girl selkie,
now also changed to human, stood beside him. Equally alluring as she
was stunning. She was also naked, but with what looked like a ripped
shirt or tunic wrapped around her hips. Even in the way she stood —
the posture and position — siren-like and hypnotic. Her breasts were
on full display, but she seemed more than fine with that fact. She was
only a few inches shorter than the selkie man. Her hair was the
blackest sort of sea-foam green. Not ink black, but looked black from a
distance when the light wasn't bouncing off the shine. She was
relatively defined. She had little fat on her stomach, curvy hips, long
legs, and large thighs. Her arms were muscular and toned while
remaining feminine. Truly a stunning body. Her power and femininity

were perfectly balanced. The rumors about female selkies being extraordinarily beautiful humans were true, I concluded. Okay, I may have found both of them to be remarkably attractive. Far more attractive than I thought they would be within reason. Were they all this beautiful? I snapped myself back to the present as Ophelia was running to me. The tap of her tall heels echoed through the great room like the taps of a hammer. "Thank the gods you are fine, Octavia! You nearly gave me a heart attack! I thought you were toast. I thought we were all done for, truly! Did you know you could do that?" Lady Alsendra, looking a little worse for wear, was making her way over to where I was now standing, brushing myself off. She looked pensive and brooding. I suspected she was not happy in the slightest, but I didn't feel resentment from her either. She cleared her throat before speaking. This time there was no boom in her voice. "Well then. That was certainly a three-ring circus of incompetence. Of piss-poor taste, my dear. An ostentatious and vulgar display of foolishness, ignorance, and lack of preparedness. The latter is through no fault of your own. You are something I didn't see coming. That is indeed a rarity these days. It would appear we have many things to discuss. I feel that we've all taken away some very useful but disturbing lessons tonight. Thus, the efforts were not entirely fruitless. I suppose the Rights Ceremony is suspended for the time being, seeing as how my participants and honored guests scattered like ants and ran for the hills. Disappointments, really." She turned with a tsk-tsk under her breath, the long sash twirling to follow her. I felt a little disheartened to myself as the bottom of her sash was now blackened and wet, when she had appeared so flawless and graceful before I brought that infernal devil to life. I stretched my shoulders and neck, leaning my head back, rubbing the sides of my neck with my hands. I saw on the ceiling large scorch marks of ash and soot spanning the width of the room, in the pattern of large wings. I caught a rapid movement by the door at the back of the great room, an arm waving back and forth.

Gabrielle! I waved for her to come over; she started our way with a hastened walk. I peered around at the damage done, the mess, the things people left behind as they ran out. A deep sense of disappointment washed over me. I saw Lady Alsendra jump up, moving quicker than I had seen her move to date, weaving around some of the bench seating where the girls had previously sat after completing their Rights. "Stop that right now!" A streak of wind and fur, all grace and wild momentum, whipped around the corner of one of the wooden benches in the blink of an eye. Head down and tail high in the air. It was Nova! That beautiful poodle, still prim and proper, darted around the corner of a bench. "Halt right there, you pesky beast!" Lady Alsendra's thunderous voice filled the air. Before I had time to blink, I realized exactly what Nova was after and why he was so worked up. That stupid Leshy. The little tree man was ducking under the benches, this way and then that, waiting for Nova to run around just to duck back under a bench. Nova was too big to fit under them, bless him. He was so focused on catching the Leshy, he didn't make a sound, sheer determination replacing the need for any vocals, only the clanking of his name tag against the metal buckle of the collar to be heard. I swear I could hear the little tree man cackling in a small voice. Sir Highborn Kenric dashed through the double doors at the front of the room. He didn't hesitate for even a moment as he moved swiftly, arriving at the benches and halting close to Lady Alsendra. He watched as Nova darted around the bench once more. Sir Kenric swiftly raised his leg up level with Nova's chest. With a sudden jolt, Nova stopped after crashing full force into his leg. The muscles in his legs coiled like a spring held in check. Nova let out of whine of discontentment. The Leshy popped up from under a bench like a groundhog from the ground, a fact Nova noticed with full attention. Nova once again sprang into action with impressive speed, aiming to dart right around Sir Kenric. Sir Kenric calmly reached his hand down to grab Nova's snout with great care and ease before spreading his hand out flat in front of the large poodle's face. He pointed a finger back. "Now sit!" My heart fluttered for an instant. I had never heard Sir Kenric speak with such commanding authority before. Nova plopped down without hesitation, body straight and proud, holding his head high with what looked like a grin, mouth open and tongue hanging slightly to the side, panting. He looked so happy with himself, equally regal as he was goofy. I couldn't resist chuckling softly. I noticed Gabrielle held a hand up to her mouth in polite etiquette while she tried not to laugh aloud. Lady Alsendra straightened, bubbling resentment below the surface of her expression. A puckered tsk sound left her lips before speaking; "Well, I have had just about enough excitement and mishaps for tonight, followed by a fortnight more."

Another puckered tsk under her breath. "Unless someone offers constructive input to improve my current mood, I will make my leave posthaste." She started for the front of the room, bending down to grab the Leshy with one hand wrapping around its entire body, arms and all. "And as for you, Leshy, I've had just about enough of your shenanigans and pranks. Your actions have created a multitude of issues. You will behave, less you wish to become the kindling to heat my tea." The Leshy glared at her, not moving or making a sound as she walked off. Sir Kenric patted Nova on the head, flattening the curly puff of hair atop his head with each pat. "Proud of yourself, aren't you?" Sir Kenric chuckled. "Let's get going home, boy." It was obvious he adored that dog; their bond was plain, as they were always together, like two peas in a pod. It was easy to observe their respect and love for each other. I decided Sir Kenric was likely a good man. The respect Nova had for him would only be given to someone with a pure heart of gold. Highly intelligent animals such as Nova reflected that kind of adoration in their personality and disposition. Sir Kenric strode by, heading for the front of the room, the large and regal poodle at his side walking tall, radiating with dignity and the air of royalty. Sir Kenric, looking around at us, nodded and said with a velvety smooth voice, "Have a good night, ladies." He glanced over at the male selkie, "and gentleman," he followed up. The selkie man's chest rose and fell with a soft, breathy chuckle, and his lips curved into a smile. I could've sworn he blushed a bit, but his midnight-black skin made it impossible to tell.

"I quite like those two." Gabrielle beamed. "So do I," I smiled back at her. It was nice to be talking to her again after all the events that had transpired tonight. She had a good aura, calming and heartening to be around. She was happy, but not in an annoying or overbearing way. She was authentically herself. I decided I needed to speak with her again before we parted ways for the night. "Gabrielle, may I ask you a few questions? I feel you will have most of the answers." "Oh well, I'm not so sure about that, you perhaps place more faith in my limited knowledge than you should, but you're welcome to ask." "Can you tell me about your pink candle and the significance of it?" "Oh! Is that all? If I recall my teachings correctly, pink candles represent the purest forms of love, compassion, friendship, and relationships. Pink helps balance and heal the heart."

That makes sense, I concluded with a nod. "What about the creature? What was it? Could anyone else see it, or just us? It was so pretty!" Gabrielle looked off to the side for a moment to concentrate and think, looking back to me after a moment. A more serious tone to her words now. "I believe it to have been a Coravelle now that I think about it." "A what?" "A Coravelle..." she trailed off as she appeared deep in thought. "The Coravelle is often used to teach emotional intelligence, empathy, and the courage it takes to love again after being hurt. Or even serve as a familiar for those who have spearheaded great emotional growth. They do not appear to just everyone, though. When they appear, they are drawn to true friendships, reconciliation, and the forging of deep bonds, often being those who have overcome conflict, loss, or pain together. If one lingers, it may be to remain near a group or individual who embodies empathy, loyalty, and kindness. Coravelles also emit a soft aura that calms the deepest anger, eases sorrow, and repairs emotional rifts and despair. The power is limited, however, only working where both parties wish to be healed. After a Coravelle disappears, it often leaves behind a gift. A pink feather that never fades, to soothe heartbreak. A blossom shaped like a heart, known to bloom even during the harshest winter. Or a whisper in a dream, offering encouragement to take emotional risks." She bobbed her head to herself, seemingly happy with her deduction. "So you can see why I believe this was the creature that appeared to us. To add further interest to the Coravelle, legends say the very first Coravelle was born from the tears of two estranged lovers who reconciled under a blossoming tree during the full moon. As their hearts opened again in trust, the energy formed a glowing spirit with feathers of soft pink and a pulsing, luminous heart. I do not know why it showed itself to us, or what I did exactly to summon it." I thought that over, wondering if it was a sign for Gabrielle and me. A testament to the start of a strong friendship bond, perhaps. I saw Ophelia listening to our conversation, one arm across her chest while her other arm was propped up with her finger pressed just under her chin. She was deep in thought as well. "Okay, what about the purple candle I chose? Did it have anything to do with this mess?" Her chest rose and fell as she let out a deep sigh. "Well, I don't think you are directly responsible for creating that devil or for choosing the candle color. Remember how we choose what speaks to us? It is decided by fate before we make a choice. Purple candles are always associated with power, spiritual enlightenment, and raw ambition. Associated with intuition, self-assessment, and spiritual growth, often being used for rituals related to self-improvement and spiritual development. Perhaps in your case, it gave you a little too much power and growth, although I'm not exactly sure what that was. I'm not even sure if what you did here tonight and what you brought forth has been done before. You'll need to enquire about those details with Lady Alsendra, she would know far more than I would about that, but I have a feeling that even she won't have all the answers for what that was." "Thank you so much for all this information. It helps me make sense of some things. I think in time I will have a great deal more clarity when I understand what is actually happening." Gabrielle nodded in agreement. "Glad to help when I can, but I'm still learning myself. I don't want you to take anything I say as hard truth, or presume I know what I'm talking about. I just like to read and pay attention to my classes sometimes." She shrugged. "That's understandable, but you still know far more than I do. Oh, and what about that Leshy, the troublesome tree man? Did that girl create him?" Gabrielle playfully rolled her eyes. "No, silly, Leshy can not be created. Or destroyed. They just are. You can invoke the spirits if you know how, as that girl did tonight." "It was so small that I thought it was a baby," I furrowed my brow in confusion. "I've always heard tales of some Leshy being as tall as trees." Gabrielle nodded in agreement. "While it's true most are big, they will be found in a plethora of sizes. While I'm not sure, I think some of it may coincide with the Leshy's responsibilities. The forests or places each one watches over, maybe even their personalities or strengths play a part in their size. As you saw with the little one tonight, the small ones are still just as problematic as the large ones." Ophelia stepped in. "I think we should get going, Octavia. We have long overstayed our welcome, and I think we need to unpack what happened here and get some rest. I, for one, am exhausted after this ordeal; you might need a horse to drag me out of bed tomorrow." I wholeheartedly agreed with that; fatigue set in with a vengeance as I thought about how tired I was. There were only a couple of faces left to be seen as we waved everyone off, saying our goodbyes. Exiting the great room, the rhythmic tap of our heels on the marble led us down the corridor and into the expansive foyer. On the way home, neither of us spoke much. I think we were both truly tired, deep in thought, and trying to wrap our heads around what had happened. We followed the sidewalk in the cool late-night air, the glow of the streetlamps casting shadows around us. When we were finally home, both cleaned up and ready for sleep, we briefly discussed the event of the evening before heading straight to our beds. I closed my eyes as my head hit the pillow. Before the darkness took hold, I recall I still needed to find out a few more things, and then, without a fight, I embraced it.

Chapter 6: Reconciliation?

An abrupt knock at the door woke us from our sleep. There was an unfamiliar deep voice at the door. "Hello! Anyone home? I am here to speak with Miss Octavia," Ophelia groaned unhappily, yanking her comforter and sheets back, throwing her feet to the floor. She walked over to the doorway into the nook that held my bed, raising her hand in the air while looking at me with an "Are you going to get up and get that or not?" gesture. I moaned and stretched with the deepest ache of relief. My whole body was sore and tired. Sleeping let the reality of the day before nestle in. I slowly got up, sitting on the edge of the bed, eyes dry and not working properly yet. Another unnecessarily hard knock banging at the door. Okay, he was getting on my nerves. "If you hold on, I'll be there after I'm decent, or you can piss right off." The words I spat out were sharper than I'd intended, like shards of glass. In an instant, I decided I didn't care about the situation anymore. Anyone who showed up to wake me did so at their own peril. Morning was something that we always held in contempt. If we woke early, it was typically in silence, neither of us speaking a word. Most of the time I made us coffee or tea, while Ophelia sat around making grumbling noises of displeasure over having to be up early. She would go without having anything to eat or drink in the morning before she would go through the trouble of making it. I, on the other hand, refused to leave the house or function as a normal human until I had something soothing and warm in my stomach before I got going. It was one of the very few small, simple pleasures I got to enjoy in life, and an enjoyment I was not willing to pass up to spite myself. I was almost in a bad mood by the time I was standing. The extra pillow on my bed fell to the floor as I stood up, knocking it off in my half-asleep stupor, where I then almost fell as it got caught up beneath my feet. I angrily kicked the pillow as I regained my footing. It flew across the room, hitting the wall before finally falling to rest on the floor. I gave it the middle finger, just to make sure it knew how much it displeased me in this very moment. I had worn a small crop top cameo to bed with just my panties on the night before. My midriff and nipples were far too visible through the thin fabric as I looked down; I couldn't answer the door like this. As quickly as I could manage, I grabbed an old, oversized blouse and a pair of loose, yet comfortable shorts out of the old, busted dresser Ophelia and I shared. I pulled both on over what I was wearing as I headed for the door, taking both my hands up to rake my hair out from the collar of the heavily worn tunic. I yanked the door open. The daylight of early morning pierced my eyes as I squinted hard, at first only able to make out the silhouette of the tall man standing there. I realized he was a little older and very well-dressed. He was probably as tall as Ophelia, though far larger framed than she. Wide shoulders, enormous arms, and a hulking, defined chest. His abdomen was slightly slimmer, but still wide, as his whole physique narrowed into smaller, spindly-looking legs. I paused for a moment, and an upside-down triangle formed in my mind. His legs seemed of normal size when compared to others, but they seemed too small for his build. Maybe his chest and shoulders were just that broad. The man turned to look at me without speaking a word. "What do you want?" As my patience dwindled, my voice was on the verge of turning into a snarl. He took off his expensive-looking brim hat, holding it to his chest before giving a small, courtly bow. "Miss Octavia, I presume? I am very sorry for disturbing you at such an early hour." He glanced at my baggy old clothes before looking back into my eyes. When I didn't speak after a moment, he continued. "I am Eryndor Roswyn. I am here on behalf of Lady Alsendra, as right hand and chamberlain to the Lady herself. She has asked you to meet her at once, as she has a subject of a rather more urgent nature to discuss." I rolled my eyes. Of course she does. "Fine." I groaned. "Tell her I will go see her later today." Eryndor stood a little taller before speaking. "I'm not sure you understand, Miss Octavia. This was not a request. You have been summoned, and I am here to deliver." "Summoned?!"

Ophelia croaked from behind me. "Who are you or that old woman to summon one of us? We're neither dogs nor slaves. You can't snap and order us around at your beck and call." I looked over at Ophelia, eyeing her to let her know she had said enough. The large man seemed to let out a genuine, soft smile. "Please, I am ordering neither of you to do anything, but Octavia has been summoned and therefore I will deliver as my duties require. You completed the Rights, mind you, Miss Octavia, therefore you are obligated to answer a summons from any prominent member of the High Council. Lady Alsendra holds eminent authority on the council; otherwise, I would not be here. I would like you to come of your own free will and volition, but we can get there however you would like to go, Miss Octavia." Again, a soft smile settled on his face. He said the words so calmly and unthreateningly that I knew he meant every word and would see it through. He was well-spoken and refined, but there was a certain backing to his words that told me we didn't stand a chance against him if we tried to fight or run. There was no malice or ill will behind his words, I noted, only dedication to completing the objectives tasked to him by Lady Alsendra. I sighed. "Alright, but you will give me time to get myself presentable and ready to go." He shrugged. "Very well, there is no problem as long as you remain in my sight." "Oh no, I'm not." I retorted with a snort. "I'm not having anyone watch me strip naked." "He's going to watch you do what?!" Ophelia almost screeched from behind me. "Let me get my knife." She spoke the words as she leaped up, the old floor vibrating with each stomp as she went for her dagger. Eryndor, holding his hand up politely with that soft smile, "Please, there is no need for anything like that, my lady, truly. I can remain right here in this spot until Octavia is ready, no need to see anyone... indisposed." "That works." I said with a shrug and shut the door in his face.

Ophelia got ready as I quickly washed up and dressed, making myself presentable enough. It went unsaid, but I knew Ophelia would go with me without my asking or saying anything. We were always stronger together, smarter. That we were both a little nosy didn't elude me. If one of us were to be "summoned," as Eryndor said, we would both be there to find out the news because it most likely meant trouble for one of us. Where there was trouble for one of us, there was trouble for the other. I looked over my shoulder at

Ophelia as I finished pulling on my boots. "Are you ready?" She nodded. I grabbed an apple from the counter before making my way to the door. I was starving, so at least it would be something to nibble on as we made our way with Eryndor. I swung the door open. I saw Eryndor leaning against the large oak tree in front of our house as we walked out. He gave us another soft smile with a nod. Now that I was properly awake, I realized he was indeed a distinguished gentleman. He was maybe 15 years older than me, I suspected. Older, but not terribly old either. He was physically healthy and in great shape. A few gray hairs sprouting up around his dark, warm, chestnut-colored hair. He had a mustache that was thick and a goatee that was pointed. The mustache was long, curving up at each end in the most elegant way. It looked as though he must meticulously trim it daily. The subtle appearance of fine lines arching down from the corners of his eyes became just visible when he smiled. Ophelia shut the door behind us as Eryndor stepped forward to meet us. "I believe Lady Alsendra was expecting you to come alone." Eryndor glanced back at Ophelia. "If you would like me to join you, the understanding is that she will be there. I mean, you can try to stop her, but then I suspect you will have to go explain to Lady Alsendra why you got tussled by two little girls." He grinned again. "Little girls? Is that right, Miss Octavia? I don't know if I would use that description myself, but if that is how you would like to see it." He tilted his head to the side in a half-shrug, conveying casual indifference. "Very well, shall we?" He held up his arm to my side, expecting me to grab it as a proper lady would do. I responded with a "hmph." I am most certainly not the girl to be led by any man. "I appreciate the sentiment, though." And I did. Eryndor was respectful and courteous. That wasn't something you came across a lot. I mean, sure, you ran into men pretending to be gentlemen every day, but Eryndor was genuine, debonair, and refined to the core. As we approached the street, Eryndor waved his hand nonchalantly. It was at that moment that I noticed a large, all-black coach approaching us. A true sight to behold as the two all-black large Friesian horses at the front arrived trotting in unison, each leg raising and tapping down in an almost unbelievably effortless high-stepping trot synchrony. Long, flowing-wavy mane and tail nearly to the ground, swishing to each side, swaying in the breeze with their every movement. Long, silky hair encased their hooves, feathering around the lower legs. These horses were someone's pride, exceptionally cared for and immaculately clean. It was clear someone was dedicated to the care and training of these majestic beings. The coach was another thing entirely. Gloss black, darkened windows, even the large wheels themselves looked to be covered in a glossy black lacquer of some sort, giving an overall sleek and menacing appearance. I could just make out ornate curtains and valances surrounding the interior windows. Then there was the coachman driving the ensemble, who was not a man at all but, in fact, a woman. Adorned in black from head to toe, with hands wrapped in lacy black gloves, she clasped the reins of the steeds steadily. A large, flowy black dress covered her entire body, even the full length of her arms down to the bottom of the coach where her feet rested. Her dark hair was neatly braided into a twisted bun, with a black veil affixed covering her entire face. I could not make out any features of the woman, not even skin color, as she almost appeared to blend in as one with the coach. She was nearly frightening; I wondered for a moment if she was even human at all. The horses came to a halt directly in front of us. They both turned their heads in unison to look at us and let out a snuffle as the steam from their nostrils wafted up in the cool air. The lady at the reins never made a move to be seen. The horse closest to me sniffed my hair, then reached down before I had time to take in the scene and bit the apple I was holding in half. "Well, guess you needed it worse than me." I walked around the front to the other horse, offering the other half of the apple. The second horse was a little more suspicious, hesitating to bite the apple before deciding to take it. He chewed a bit and then spat out the rest, curling his lips out with a whinny. "I guess he wasn't a big fan." I shrugged. Eryndor spoke up. "Shall we then, my ladies?" He was at the side of the coach, holding the door open. I noticed a little folding step coming down from the coach. Ophelia had stepped into the coach by the time I made my way back around. "You know, you must be something special, Miss Octavia, for Vantor and Draven would normally flatten anyone that close. They are trained not to trust anyone." "Vantor and Draven? What lovely names!" I noticed as I spoke their names, each horse twitched its ears around, glancing in my direction. "Smart too." I stepped up into the coach, allowing Eryndor to assist, holding onto his shoulder only for a moment to keep my balance. I was a bit taken aback by the interior.

The lush, over-padded seats were a vibrant dark red, as was the carpeting on the floor. While the walls, ceiling, curtains, and extra odds and ends were black. I sat beside Ophelia, Eryndor ducking beneath the door behind me to sit opposite us. He gave the top of the coach a knock with three quick taps in succession before the coach lurched forward in haste. Vantor and Draven let out neighs of excitement as they set a steady pace, the same almost otherworldly unison trotting. I still had my eyes fixed on the magnificent trot of the horses as I let my words trail out. "Eryndor... Vantor and Draven, they must be the most breathtaking and majestic horses I've ever seen." I meant it, too. Eryndor grinned softly. "Yes, they tend to leave quite a lasting impression on people. These two are among Lady Alsendra's many prides. She would lay waste to lands before she let any harm come to either, especially since I have my own orders to protect them at all costs. Oh, and you may call me Eryn if you'd like, Miss Octavia. Lady Alsendra and the Council refer to me as so, and I have a feeling we will see much of each other over the coming days." "What exactly am I being summoned for, Eryn? Am I in trouble about the Rights last night?" He gave me another soft smile. "No, nothing like that. While I believe you will have some repercussions to deal with, I think the High Council isn't sure what to do with you. As I hear it, you have quite the talent, nearly burning every person at the Rights to a crisp. That is indeed a sight I wish I could've seen myself. I might've had fun with that one." Eryn shrugged slightly before straightening back in his seat. The coach fell silent as we listened to the enchanting unison clip-clop of the gigantic horses' hooves on the cobblestone.

We rode to the outskirts of town down a narrow, winding road with trees on either side of us. Before long, the narrow road opened into a clearing with a vast stone building standing stately at the center. It is not a castle in the traditional sense, but a display of both wealth and social standing. If I were to give it a name, I would lean toward calling it a mansion, possibly a grand manor. A curved cobblestone path led through a large stone arch; iron gates swung open to the inside as we rode through. We rode up the path to a curved circular pathway, going up in front of the doors of the manor, and then back around to merge back into the path we arrived on. As we approached the large wooden doors to the entrance of the stone building, Vantor and Draven slowed to a crawl before gracefully coming to a halt. I noticed I never saw the veiled woman move a muscle. She never spoke or moved a finger to adjust the reins. I wondered how she communicated with the two horses. She clearly did so skillfully, seeing as how the ride was one of the smoothest and most enjoyable rides I'd ever taken, while somehow also being faster than the normal coach. Upon stopping, Eryn reached over to open the door before then bending over to drop the small step to the outside. He stepped out swiftly, giving a glance around before reaching his hand up, offering assistance as we got out. I accepted his offer. Because my bad morning mood had mostly passed, I could now reason that it would be better to graciously accept help from the gentleman Eryn was than to fall here on the cobblestones. Doing that before meeting Lady Alsendra would not win me any favoritism with her, to be sure. Ophelia exited the coach behind me. I glanced up at the coachwoman in black, pondering whether I should speak to her. It seemed poor manners not to thank her for such a delightful ride. As if picking up on my thought, Eryn promptly shut the coach door, giving a few knocks in a two-knock, pause, then three-knock pattern. Vantor and Draven were off at once. I watched for a moment as the coach rounded the corner of the manor, going out of sight as quickly as it had first appeared. Something about that was so strange. The large wooden doors of the manor were tall, easily reaching a height three times as tall as Ophelia, the top of each door taller at the center, curving down on each side slightly before straightening to a corner. I noticed a square wooden plaque framed in bronze trim to the right of the large doors, "Deerstone Court." Under the manor name was a smaller engraving: "Sanctum of Lady Alsendra, High Council." Eryn made way in front of us, opening the doors and then standing back to wait for us to enter before him. I stepped inside with Ophelia directly behind me. The interior was a combination of upscale yet cozy and comforting. Large exposed wooden beams ran the width of the room overhead, while stone and mortar columns spiraled up to meet the supports in crucial areas. Varied stone colors in varying materials composed the unique checkered floor of square tiles. A large candelabra chandelier hung above the center of the large room. A wooden and stone staircase at the back of the room led straight up to the next floor. The walls were lined with miscellaneous armor pieces, bundles of dried herbs tied with different colored twine, and a few partly sewn quilts hanging in one corner stretched over quilting frames. Eryn motioned for us to move down a side hall, spanning across the front of the left wing. Tall, narrow windows lined the outside wall along the stretched hall. More of the large wooden beams sat above the hall, facing side to side down the length. We got close to the end when Eryn moved towards a heavy-looking wooden door to the right. He once again opened the door and stepped back, waiting for us to walk through. When we entered the room, Lady Alsendra sat in a large, throne-like carved wooden chair behind a large, beautiful dark wood desk. She gave Eryn a straight-lipped smile. Eryn bowed courtly before moving to the side. On her left and right were two smaller chairs. To the left of her sat a woman of average build. Dark brown skin, reminding me precisely of the color of an acorn. Her head was bald and shiny, accentuating the large metal earrings she wore. She wore leather pants with corset stitching down the sides of the thighs, a low-cut loose cloth top draped off her shoulders with a bustier showing just above the breasts. The woman to her right was older than the woman on the left, but younger than Lady Alsendra. Her skin was darker than Lady Alsendra's, but remained on the lighter side, reminding me of the color of honey. She wore a dark green top and skirt matching set, with what looked like brass bangles and jewelry around her arms, wrists, and fingers. She had very light, almost moonlight-white hair. That's different, I thought. She didn't look old enough to have white hair from age. I gave the women a slight curtsy, Ophelia following my lead. Lady Alsendra, now wearing fitted black pants and a one-shoulder gray blouse, gave us a nod of acknowledgement before standing. "Give us room, dear." She motioned with her hand at Ophelia, dismissing her from standing by my side. I heard Ophelia scoff, but she at least knew better than to have an outburst here, of all places. She walked to the back of the room to stand next to Eryn. Lady Alsendra turned her gaze back to me with a pursed-lip expression. "Now what to do with you, Octavia."

Chapter 7: Rectification

"You know what to do with her!" cooed the bald woman behind Lady Alsendra. The woman with white hair stared at me before speaking in a singsong voice. "Indeed, you know what must be done!" Lady Alsendra held up her hand to hush them without otherwise acknowledging what either had said. The room remained silent for an almost uncomfortable length of time before Lady Alsendra broke the silence. The demeanor of Lady Alsendra struck me as being notably dissimilar to her usual behavior I had previously seen. Her voice carried less of that impactful power, sounding tired. "As you can see, it would seem there are some rather strong opinions on what we should do with you, Octavia. Then there's the matter of your training." Lady Alsendra had a telling look on her face, one perplexed and a little concerned — taking long pauses to think before speaking again. "The outcomes are so uncertain, like viscous fluid weaving through a sieve. On the one hand, you could be one of my greatest mistakes and regrets; on the other, you possess the potential for great and amazing achievements unseen by us in over a century. Most of those here saw exactly what you are capable of last night, Octavia. Word of what you have done has spread and continues to spread as we speak. That leaves us with the matter of how we, as influential council members, must maintain assurances and put minds at ease. It is our duty and responsibility. People rely on us to maintain some sort of control over any enchantresses or wielders of arcane with potential would-be devastating abilities. If we do not act, your very life will be in danger from those who believe someone with gifts of your level should be stopped before being given a chance to grow. Had the selkies not been there to intervene and assist, do you think you would've been able to control yourself and that devil made manifest?" That was rhetorical, I noted. Another long pause. "I could simply strip you of your gifts, you know that, right? Nullify your natural born talents. That is the general consensus among the council and others, and I have the full authority to do so at my discretion." "Do it," the two women behind Lady Alsendra cooed in unison. She once again didn't acknowledge what they said and continued speaking after a pause. "However, that is a serious and damning decision with its own consequences that I will not take lightly, nor would I wish that for anyone such as us. Last night would have gone differently had you been properly trained and your gifts honed. I have seen possibilities others have not, both good and bad, therefore leaving me with significant reason for hesitation. I fear the decision made now could become a far more troublesome burden than we can handle." Another long pause that felt like an eternity, where I only heard my heart pounding, then she exhaled deeply before making a move.

Lady Alsendra approached the distant wall of the room in which we were located, proceeding toward a credenza that was both tall and narrow. She still wore tall heels, walking so gracefully that I didn't notice at first. She reached down and gently pulled open a small drawer, grabbing something with her hand before she carefully closed the drawer. She made her way to stand in front of me once again, holding out her empty hand. I concluded in the moment that she wanted me to lay my hand in hers, which I did after realizing. Lady Alsendra brought her other hand over mine, a small silver chain dangling between her fingers. She then dropped a necklace into my palm while humming some kind of chant under her breath. She spoke up, startling me for a moment. "Take this; keep it on for the foreseeable future. This charm gives someone with my specialty in divination skills the ability to see the wearer. I will sense if you are using any abilities above your capabilities to control, sense if you are in danger, or should any harm come to you. While it may not seem ideal to you, with this I can counter the council for the time being as they will see how you remain under my observation." I looked down at the necklace in my hand. A small glass vial hung from the dainty silver chain. Inside the vial swirled a liquid that appeared to shimmer with a pastel blue to red, briefly swirling a purple between the two. A small, dark object rolled around inside the liquid. Could it be some kind of crystal or stone? I realized Lady Alsendra was waiting for me to put it on. I unhooked the small clasp, bringing the chain up around my neck. Just as I was trying to hook the clasp back together, Eryn stepped up behind me. "Please allow me, Miss Octavia." I was thankful for the help. The chain was just short enough to be a pain to get on; the vial hung just between my clavicles, below my throat. I thought I caught Lady Alsendra giving a small sigh of relief as she blinked her eyes closed for a moment before opening them again. "That's better." She spoke the words softer than I had heard her speak prior.

Lady Alsendra spoke up again, this time her voice regaining some of the power and boom she had the night before at the Rights. "Now, with that out of the way, I have made my decision." Every eye in the room was on her as we waited anxiously to hear her next words spoken. You will make leave for Liraquor at once. There you are to meet up with Althira Thorne. The two women behind Lady Alsendra let out inaudible gasps in unison. "You wouldn't." One mumbled. "Preposterous." Coming from the other side. Lady Alsendra held her hand up once again to silence them. "Althira and I honed our skills together many years ago. Where I can see many things, Althira can control and influence many others. She has as much knowledge as I do, and I wholeheartedly trust her capabilities to take care of you while under her guidance. I will contact her immediately to make preparations awaiting your arrival. You will leave here and make haste there, do you understand? You will avoid main roads and paths. Stay on the ones less traveled; fall into the shadows if you must, but do not draw suspicion to yourselves. You will travel with plain horses and little luggage to remain inconspicuous and free to move quickly if needed. Too much attention has already been brought your way after the stunt you performed last night. I meant what I said Octavia, there will be many who will see you dead if possible. I am unsure of the outcome, but I know there are several possibilities. Most not being in your favor. Therefore, I'm giving you strict instructions for your best chance of success. You are the unknown as of now, something people fear after hearing of the powers you potentially possess; others see you as something potentially precious, and that unequivocally makes you a target, my dear." She paused again before continuing. "Eryn, you will accompany Octavia to Liraquor as her escort and remain with her once there, unless Althira gives you different instructions. I trust you to ensure no harm or malice befalls her. You have heard the orders I gave Octavia; I expect them to be followed meticulously." "Yes, my lady, it will be with my greatest pleasure." Eryn gave her a soft smile, and for the first time I've seen to date, Lady Alsendra seemed to give Eryn a little more than a straight-lipped smile. It was a warm, albeit small, smile. It was clear she did indeed trust him to fulfill her orders. "I do not currently trust any arcane I know well enough to travel with you; despite the knowledge that having an arcane along would make the trip easier for you. However, you may bring along any one person, but know this person must be completely trustworthy, or you may have to take their life yourself, Eryn. Is there anyone you would like to request?" Eryn thought it over for only a moment before answering. "Highborn Kenric Ravenspire, my Lady. He and his noble family are well-respected. I have seen him fight with great skill; he would be more than proficient in battle should that arise. Therefore, I trust him with my life." Lady Alsendra seemed to approve of that. "Very well, I will send word for him to meet you right away." I thought the conversation was over just when she spoke up again. "Oh, and Ophelia, you will remain here. The smaller the group, the less attention it will bring." Ophelia spat out, "What?!" Lady Alsendra boomed with more power to her voice than I had yet seen. Everyone in the room flinched. "You will remain apart. I will not have you foolishly putting both of your lives at risk. Do I make myself clear?" Ophelia staggered back slightly before regaining her composure. She nodded back without speaking a word. Lady Alsendra returned to where she had been. "I want you two girls to understand something as I make this abundantly clear one last time; this is a very serious situation. I am doing this hoping that this entire venture will have a fruitful outcome. You might not be aware of this, but Eryn here is one of the kindest and most capable men I've ever known, despite his modesty." "Nah, you give me too much credit, my lady." A large, genuine smile crept across Eryn's face. Lady Alsendra continued. "He is more than capable of cutting down a small army if need be, but let's hope it doesn't come to that. I believe you will have little problem getting to Liraquor unfazed if you follow my directions closely. It is a three-day ride if you make haste, stopping only when necessary and to let the horses rest. You will spend the rest of today preparing and getting yourselves ready for the trip, leaving first thing in the morning. Remember, you will bring only the essentials you can carry in a small sack. I will send Eryn and the coach for you at first light." She turned, giving Eryn a nod of dismissal. Eryn opened the heavy-looking wooden door, extending his arm out, gesturing for us to move through before him.

We made our way back out, retracing the same steps we had taken on the way in. As we exited the oversized double doors at the front of the manor, the coach with Vantor and Draven was again pulling up to come to a halt before us. The coach was so peculiar, always where it needed to be at the right moment. Eryn once again opened the door and assisted us in. Another series of knocks on the ceiling of the coach and we were off. On the ride back, we mostly sat in silence. Engaged in some casual conversation about the journey. Ophelia and I were discussing whether she should come to Liraquor shortly after I arrived. I didn't see why she couldn't. Lady Alsendra said nothing about that. A safer trip, with extra items, could be made a few days later. Before long, we no longer had anything to discuss at that moment. Then I got to thinking about Eryn. Evidently, he was especially capable, possibly even a mage, and according to the praise from Lady Alsendra, he must be a very gifted one at that. "Can I ask you a few questions, Eryn?" "Go right ahead, Miss Octavia." He said with a soft smile. "Why did Lady Alsendra say you were so capable?" "Well, you see, I am a spellblade. Many often assume I'm more capable than I am. I'm not that special." There had to be more to it than that; Lady Alsendra regarded him too highly to be a simple spellblade. "I see. I know a spellblade is a hybrid warrior-mage and that they are good at battle, but can you specifically do more than that?" He chuckled lightly before answering. "You could say that if you studied me, but I think the Lady just holds me in higher regard than I should be held after saving her life once or twice. To answer your question directly, however, yes, I can do a little more than most. Spellblades wield their magic as battle weapons. That comes in a variety of ways. Most predominantly elemental abilities. Some spellblades manifest speed with their arcane. Some manifest weapons. Some manifest armor. Some can add great strength to their blows or even toughness to their skin. It depends on each individual to learn their own strengths based on what they naturally gravitate to. I can do a little of everything, along with sometimes having a few nasty tricks up my sleeve when I get bored with the fight. While I'm highly focused on one task, I can swiftly switch to others when necessary. That is why Lady Alsendra thinks I'm a little more talented than most, but I wouldn't say that myself. I'm just a brute that's good at a little brawl from time to time." That explained a lot, yet nothing at all, because how was this refined and mannerly gentleman a wild and adept killer in battle? I almost couldn't imagine him doing anything of the sort. I was still lost in my thoughts about Eryn and what he must look like in battle when the coach slowed, gently coming to a halt. That trip was fast; this coach was much quicker than normal, indeed. We got out and said our goodbyes before heading in. We decided we should get everything ready and prepared for my departure the next morning. I packed the essentials. Hairbrush, toothbrush, a few hair accessories, two changes of clothes, and three pairs of underwear. I wasn't about to go a day without changing underwear. Then what if I peed on myself or something? Oh, gods no, I certainly had to have an extra pair or two with me. Better bring five. After that was done, we ate a small meal. Some toast with chicken gravy we had left from roasting a chicken a few nights ago. The gravy stayed good for a few days when in a jar in our small root cellar. We would reheat it, sometimes adding in some different meats or vegetables we had on hand. I was always so thankful for the warm meal. When we had finished eating, we sat around discussing the trip I'd be embarking on in the morning. Ophelia got up to get something before coming to sit back down beside me at the small round table. She handed me her old dagger. She had owned the dagger since her early teenage years. A plain and aged silver blade with a rather plain black hilt. Off the end dangled two decorative chains, one chain bearing a small dragon charm. Something Ophelia added in her belief it was good luck to have the eye of a watchful dragon with you. I couldn't remember a time when we were on our own that she didn't have that dagger. "Why are you giving this to me, Ophelia?" "I want you to have something to protect yourself. I have my new dagger, as you know, so I won't be needing this one. So if anyone tries to attack you, I want you to stick this right in their throat." "Okay, I'll take it if it makes you feel better, but we both know I'd probably panic and forget to use it." "Well, you'd better remember it, Octavia! If you get hurt and don't die, I'll finish the job when I get to you for being stupid!" I let out a laugh followed by a yawn. "We should get some sleep. I'm still tired from the night before, and tomorrow is a big day." With that, we both got ourselves ready for bed and went to sleep.

Chapter 8: Preparations

I was up before Ophelia the following morning; the nerves of what was yet to come kept me from getting a good night's rest. I decided I would trim my hair a little before I got ready. It wouldn't look the best, but I did not know when I'd have the chance to do it again. Shortly after I finished brushing up the loose hair with the old straw broom we've had for years, I heard Ophelia get up. "Why are you up so early?" She asked in a voice that was still thick with sleep. "I guess I'm just nervous, Ope. Lady Alsendra dropped a lot of information on us yesterday, and now I feel like my whole life is being turned upside down right before my eyes. Then, to add to the mix of all these wonderful activities, she believes people actually want me dead! Can you believe anyone being so concerned about me that they want me dead? They know nothing about me, but evidently want me dead based on some stirred-up rumors over what happened at the Rights." "Except they aren't rumors," Ophelia interjected. "Well, regardless, you know what I mean." "Yeah, but do you really think it's that serious, or is Lady Alsendra being dramatic and overzealous? It seems like it may be a bit blown out of proportion; perhaps she's merely being cautious." "I'm not so sure, Ope. I thought the same last night until I slept on it and had time to think this morning. We know Lady Alsendra knows most things before they happen — well, possible things — so why would she be so stern and insistent on this unless she has seen something? I think she knows a great deal more than she's sharing with us. Part of me also wonders if she isn't intentionally withholding information not to draw extra attention, whether that be from the High Council or prying ears." Just then, a knock came at the door. We both jumped. Neither of us said anything, giving each other a look of suspicion. Before we had time to scare ourselves further with paranoia, a familiar voice sounded from the other side. "Miss Octavia, I hope I'm not disturbing your rest again. I am here to pick you up." It's Eryn! Oh, thank the gods. Knowing he was here put my worry about someone bursting down the door to kill me to rest. I hopped up, making way to open the door. "You can come in for a moment if you'd like, Eryn. I'm about ready; I just want to finish speaking with Ophelia." Eryn gave me another one of his soft grins. "As you wish, my lady, so long as we don't take too long. I don't think Lady Alsendra will be in any kind of mood for us to keep her waiting." I grabbed the small handbag I had prepared with the few clothes and items I'd be taking, slinging the little rope tied to it over my shoulder as I walked over to where Ophelia stood. "Well, I know this isn't really a goodbye and we'll be seeing each other again soon in Liraquor, but I wish you were coming along. I'd feel better about the entire trip." "I know Octavia," Ophelia spoke softly. "Do you have my dagger?" I checked my pockets, squeezed the bag around to feel inside, and realized I didn't have it. "See, you're already making me mad." Ophelia shot me a scowl before walking over to my bed, picking up the dagger, and handing it to me once again. "Thanks, I'll keep it on me, I promise." "Mm-hmm." Ophelia rolled her eyes, her arms crossed. "Let's hope Eryn can do what Lady Alsendra believes he can, because he'll have me to deal with if anything happens to you." She said the words loudly enough for Eryn to hear clearly from where he stood. He chuckled a little. "I am hoping for a rather uneventful trip to Liraquor, but rest assured, I will make sure no harm befalls your sister to the best of my ability, Miss Ophelia." "You had better!" She retorted with extra attitude.

We stepped out of the house, Ophelia walking with us. We were halfway to the cobblestone road before I saw Vantor and Draven pulling up, with such an uncanny knack of always arriving at the perfect time. How peculiar. "Too bad we can't take the coach to Liraquor." I groaned. "We'd make better time and be more comfortable doing it." Eryn sighed softly. "Indeed, we would. You saw firsthand yesterday how much of a spectacle these two can be when they show up. Taking the coach would make us an easily trackable target, not to mention we'd have to stick to the main roads. I also don't think Lady Alsendra would be fond of these two traveling that far without her. If anything happened to them, she might have me burned at the stake!" Eryn let out a breathy laugh, but he sounded serious about that too. "Maybe if we had a mage or enchantress with us who could disguise the coach, but Lady Alsendra believes nobody is to be trusted right now." Eryn pulled himself into the coach behind me, pulling up the little step and closing the door behind him. He gave a quick series of knocks again, and we were off. I glanced back to see Ophelia still standing there, watching as we departed, arms crossed. I gave her a little wave from inside the coach, unsure how well she could see me through the darkened glass, but she saw just fine as she picked up her hand with a little wave before dropping it back down. Just a few minutes later, we came to a graceful halt again. I glanced around outside, looking through the coach's side windows before I spotted Sir Highborn Kenric; he gave me a nod as we locked gazes for a moment. Upon the coach coming to a complete halt, Eryn bent over, opening the door to poke his head out before speaking to Sir Kenric. "Come aboard, good sir!" Eryn hopped out on the ground to stand at attention, waiting for Sir Kenric to get in. Sir Kenric reached inside the coach, dropping a sack of his essentials. "Hello again, Octavia, was it?" "Yes, that's right. And you are Sir Highborn Kenric." I said jokingly, but it almost came out sarcastically. "Please, I already told you to call me Kenric. I can't bear to imagine how tiring it would be for you to only refer to me as 'Sir Kenric Highborn' for the entirety of our time together". He said the name mockingly. I rolled my eyes and looked out the coach window. Something caught my eye on Eryn. It was a sword sheath with bits of metal on it, just visible behind his overcoat as the early morning sun glinted off it. I quickly realized there were in fact two sword sheaths, one on each side of his torso. I thought they must be small, as they were concealed so effortlessly. I wondered if he had them on his person the day before, but I'm positive I would've seen a glimpse of them at some point, but maybe not since it wasn't until now that I noticed them today. Kenric placed a large sword inside the coach, lying it on the floor while pressed against the bottom of the seat opposite me. It looked expensive and ornate. The handle had a hand-engraved design around the full hilt. The pommel at the end was also a silver metal, reminding me of a faceted ruby, with an end looking sharp to a point. "Now, there's just one last thing, and we can get moving." Kenric chimed as he turned back to a closed gate along a stone wall fence. Opening the gate as he reached it, he made a noise before I saw the bobbing of a fluffy tail running in his direction. Nova, something about the dog always made me smile. Nova ran out the gate, Kenric closing it behind him. "Let's go up!" Kenric ordered, Nova making a run right to the coach, hopping in with full grace and momentum... at first. He over jumped, hitting the back wall of the coach as he slid a few inches on the floor. "See, and that's what you get for not taking your time," Kenric playfully scolded. "Is he coming with us?" I asked. Kenric snapped his head in my direction with a frown. "Why wouldn't he?" I shrugged while raising my eyebrows, not sure what to say. I didn't have a problem with Nova coming with us; in fact, I'd be glad to have him there. I was more concerned about his safety. I wondered how Nova would fare running along with the horses for several days. A heartbeat later, Nova hopped up on the seat beside me, sitting up in a way that was regal yet eerily human. He threw his head back and to the side to look at me, that silly grin on his face, before he started panting with his tongue hanging out, worked up from his run to the coach. I found him to be hilarious, with a knack for making me laugh. I reached up to pet him on the side. "Oh my, was that a mistake?" I squeaked out. As soon as I tried to put my hand down, Nova nudged my hand with his nose in protest, then licked my arm. "Ew!" I couldn't help but laugh despite the grossness. Kenric snapped his fingers, pointing back. Nova stopped at once, sitting back as Eryn pulled himself up into the coach, quickly closing the door behind him as he sat beside Kenric. After a succession of knocks, we were off at once.

We arrived at Seerstone Court in what seemed only a brief moment later. Erin hopped out of the coach first, as per his usual accord, to assist those getting out. Kenric handed his things out to Eryn, Eryn setting them down on the stone walkway for the time being. Before Kenric exited the coach, Eryn reached up, offering his hand to me with a bow. "Miss Octavia." He grinned that soft grin at me again. It was impossible for me not to develop an affection for Eryn. He felt safe to be around; he was warm, caring, and courteous. I accepted his offer of help, stepping down out of the coach. Nova hopped down behind me, Kenric following. Nova ran around, nose to the ground, sniffing and tail high in the air. He quickly stopped to pee on a dark green grassy spot. Kenric, picking up a few of his items on the ground, was whispering loudly to Nova, "Why did you pick the nicest grass to go on? Get over here. You'd better not cause us embarrassment." Eryn had grabbed my handbag for me without asking. Lady Alsendra met us just inside the large double doors. "Right this way, after me; we have little time to waste." She paused a moment to look down at Nova, who by this time was sitting on the floor beside her with his nose pressed to her leg, looking up at her thereafter. "You better not make a mess in my manor, less you'd like to go live in the woods with the wolves and bears." She let out a "hmph" before turning, the long braid woven into her hair now making a twirl behind her. "Now come along." She boomed. We all followed behind her as she led us through a series of rooms and corridors, out of what I suspected was the back of the manor. I now realized that the manor was designed in what was a large U-shape. Across the back of the manor, closing off the U-shape was a long line of stables. Roof over the entirety, swinging wooden gates on both sides of the stables appeared to be open on most. Horses were scattered throughout the area. Some were in the center of the manor's U-shaped yard, some were out in the meadow behind the manor, and some were under the stables eating or drinking. "Yes, they are free to come and go as they wish. I do not imprison any animal without need." I looked at her, confused as to why she answered before I asked. She waved her hand in a dismissive gesture. "That is what you were going to ask, wasn't it? You know what my gift of sight is like, in addition to you being easy to read today, as it were." Lady Alsendra bellowed out three individually distinct whistles. A horse in the stable whinnied loudly before turning to gallop towards us. Two loud, echoing whinnies behind the manor followed as two beautiful horses began running at full pace in our direction. I noticed I didn't see Vantor and Draven, nor the black coach. Maybe they were out giving someone a ride, I wondered. Only a moment later, all three of the horses she called stood before us. Lady Alsendra walked between all three, giving them each a biscuit while patting their heads. "They get biscuits?!" I asked in shock. I was thinking the horses ate better than Ophelia and I. Lady Alsendra let out a tsk before speaking. "Perhaps it would be prudent to consider all possibilities before blurting out nonsensical judgments. These are stale biscuits, leftovers thrown out from the bakery. I have them collected to give to the horses. The beasts love them and don't care about freshness. You're welcome to consume them for yourself, though, my dear." She made the offer with challenging sarcasm. "At any rate, these three will take you to Liraquor. This misty gray horse with the watchful gaze is Sylareth. The marbled horse with black mane is Mareion. This ash and gold mix is Virelen. A little dense, this one, but she's swift-footed and sweet. They will serve you well and treat you as well as you treat them. Stop to let them rest; there is no sense in running a good horse to death when it can be prevented." We all nodded in agreement. "Eryn, come help get them saddled quickly." She turned and walked towards the stables.

Chapter 9: To Liraquor!

Our remaining belongings were loaded onto the backs of the horses. It had been a while since I had ridden a horse, but Ophelia and I grew up around horses. It was years ago that we learned how to ride them in the correct way. I'm not sure what it is, but once you learn a horse and how to ride, you never really forget. Kenric was already up on the horse he chose, Virelen. They were getting to know each other, as Kenric had put it. Nova was occupied sniffing various scents as he ran about. As I prepared to mount my horse, Eryn stood beside me, his hand already reaching out to steady me. I ended up with Sylareth; she did have a watchful gaze, as Lady Alsendra pointed out. She seemed a tad calmer than the other two, with a sense of otherworldly intelligence behind her eyes. I could use all the help I can get; a smart horse would benefit me when I'm not communicating with her properly. I put my left foot in the stirrup, swinging my right over the horse in one big movement as I jumped and pulled myself over. Eryn stood ready to catch me should I need it. I completed the task requiring no help from him. "At least I haven't forgotten how to do that." I said proudly. "Yes, indeed, Miss Octavia! Well done, I do say!" I grew fonder of Eryn by the minute. I felt my heart sink a little as a thought came to me: he was acting as a father to me. Or maybe I just perceived it that way, considering neither me nor Ophelia ever had a father. I had a moment of regret for what could've been, wishing we had been so lucky as to have someone like Eryn as our father. I felt tears pushing to the surface of my eyes and forced them back. Lady Alsendra shot a glare at me from the ground. "Are you alright, Octavia?" That was irritating, to say the least. Now she knew when I was emotional. Was that the stupid necklace I wore, or did she already have that ability? "I'm fine, just ready to get this long trip over with." She nodded without questioning me further. Eryn hopped up on Mareion, the only male horse of the three. Mareion was slightly more muscular than the other two girls. I wondered if Eryn wanted him for that reason. A more powerful horse might be useful to a spellblade. All three of us lined up in front of Lady Alsendra. When she spoke, her voice boomed a little louder than it had before we were all on horses. "Remember, Octavia, I will be with you the entire time via the necklace. Should you find yourself in a dire life or death situation, I want you to clasp the necklace and focus on me. Send intent loud and clear, and I will hear your plead without falter." I bowed my head in a small manner of recognition. "Thank you." "Off you go then. I have sent word to Althira to await your arrival. I expect to hear word of your arrival as well." She clapped her hands together lightly. "With nary a moment wasted, let the winds of fate carry you forward. May the spirits guide you, the gods favor you, and the arcane envelope you. Off you go!" With that, we were off to Liraquor.

A wide coach would never have fit on the path we rode down, which was barely wider than our horses. Eryn and Kenric discussed our riding formation for a while. Both agreed that while a staggered triangle was ideal for defense, the narrow roads and paths prevented its effective implementation. So, we ended up in a half staggered one front, two-back formation. Eryn insisted on leading front and center, both to scout and to take out any potential threats that could arise. Kenric rode on my left, only slightly ahead of me. From time to time, Nova would be at the back, smelling different objects, and afterward, he would come up to us, spending some time walking alongside Kenric. The landscape was mostly uninteresting. Flat lands and woods on both sides, trees hindering our view for over forty yards away. Eryn said the road we traveled would go through a highlands area near Thalmyr's Cradle. He seemed to think the view would be worth seeing. He cautioned us against running into criminals in the area. There was a decent-sized group of elves in that area known as the Ravynari, equally scummy as they were treacherous. According to Eryn, they lost all elven honor years ago and were to be avoided at all costs. We heard many stories of their kind growing up. During the Orriveth civil war, the Orriveth elves exiled the Ravynari, who became a group of outcasts and rebels. The Orriveth prevailed in running out the Ravynari, where the Orriveth then cut all ties to the Ravynari because of the Ravynari's unusually cruel and twisted ways. The Orriveth are a noble bunch of elven. A proud people, many possessing abilities to wield the arcane, they were said to be exceptionally gifted. The Ravynari are the opposite of the Orriveth in almost every regard. I've heard tales of the Ravynari commonly partaking in cannibalism, incest, and some of the most horrid acts of cruelty one can think of. A story of the Ravynari skinning a child alive while the mother was forced to watch came to mind. I shivered. We had been on the road for several hours by now. My inner thighs were hurting from sitting in the saddle, and I was getting angrily hungry. I told Kenric and Eryn as much. They assured me we would stop before long. They wanted to wait until we had a bit of a clearing, a safe place to heat some food and stretch our legs. When we finally reached such an area, I almost couldn't get off the horse fast enough. Sylareth was a nice horse, and she had been easy to ride, but I wasn't used to riding. I felt it in the worst way. Eryn quickly got to work making a small fire, Kenric made his way to a nearby stream to refill our water jugs, and I sat on a large log, stretching my back and legs in every way I could think of that might help. Nova was running around, bringing me sticks to throw for him to go get. I swear the large poodle never ran out of energy. I was petting Nova's neck behind his ear when he suddenly sprang up, growling. He was fixated on something in the woods. I hadn't seen movement, but I noticed Eryn was now directly by my side. I jumped; how did he get there so fast? We sat there in silence for a moment; Nova escalated his growling to a few mean barks. A few moments later, Kenric came dashing out of the woods with our water jugs in hand. "What is it, boy?" he asked Nova. "I heard you; tell me what it is." Nova zigged forward and back again, stopping to point towards the woods with his tail high in the air, alerting to something there. I heard rustling in the bushes and caught my breath. Kenric had already grabbed his sword, standing at the ready. Eryn looked as dapper as ever, almost even relaxed, yet on high alert with his attention fixed towards the danger in the woods. I had the feeling Eryn didn't need his blades in hand if we were to be attacked. Nova stopped dead in his tracks, not making a sound, just staring into the bushes. None of us moved, barely breathing; only the sound of the wind on the leaves could be heard. Suddenly, the horse closest to the bushes reared up on its hind legs, neighing loudly in terror. I jumped, letting out a shriek. Nova's barking intensified, becoming a chaotic chorus. Something cut out of the bushes, a dark mass of movement, headed right for us.

Nova got startled, yelped a small cry of fear before running around to stand behind my legs. Quicker than I could almost make out what happened, Eryn stood in front of me holding two blades at his side. The blades instantly caught my attention, making my eyes bulge at the sight. Syreth blades. I dragged in a jagged inhale as the realization hit me. I had seen nothing remotely close to the real thing, but I knew enough from the myths surrounding the blades to know what these were at first glance. Syreth blades, called such deriving from an old elven dialect meaning "whisper of silver", the name referring to their near-silent motion through the air and the soft chime-like resonance they make when drawn together. The blades were forged in a crescent curve, forged from a luminous and translucent metal known as virelith glass, an arcane alloy that resembles moonlit crystal but is stronger than even the strongest tempered steel. Only the most skilled Orrivethan blacksmiths could forge the material. Each crescent-curved blade contained glowing runes down the spine, in an old elven language only few could still read. The blades extended out to over two feet long. Syreth blades were once only given to Moonblades, a secretive order of arcane dualist spellblades who acted as royal agents and veiled protectors within the elven Royal Court. Little was known about the inner workings of the Moonblades, but one thing was certain: nobody was foolish enough to cross one. I have heard of people spending years hunting for just one of the priceless blades, to no avail. I always believed they were works of fiction or no longer existed, yet here they were before me. For a split second, I heard a brief hum of arcane energy from the blades. I am beginning to understand Lady Alsendra's faith in Eryn; it seems they omitted crucial details about his skills and capabilities. Who and what exactly was this man? Eryn held up the blades. The runes along the blade's spine ignited in a soft silver-blue light. There was a brief flash. The low-running mass tumbled to the ground, rolling in the dirt, a plume of dust exploding out from around the chaotic tumble. The light from the blades must have had some kind of disorienting effect on it. Through the swirling dust, I squinted, attempting to make out what was in front of me. Eryn already had the blades put away before I had time to see. A little creature stood up, hands in the air. Oh, gods, it was just a goblin. Eryn spoke to the creature slowly. "Can you understand our language, friend?" The goblin nodded. "Understand... talk... no good." "That is alright." Eryn replied. "Go on and get out of here. I trust you will not come back and bother us or try to steal from us, correct?" The little goblin shook his head, then started bowing to the ground as if he were praying to a god. Eryn spoke again. "Come on now and get out of here. That is unnecessary." The goblin looked confused. "But you.. you are the-" Eryn cut the goblin off mid-speech with a louder, more power-backed voice. "Leave!" The goblin jumped back a little before turning to run away at full speed in the direction from which he had come. It was a completely unique feeling to see Eryn at the helm of the power emanating from him. The same debonair and suave gentleman not only had the voice of authority but was the wielder of Syreth blades, if only for a moment. Ophelia would have loved to see this side of him. I felt saddened for a moment that she wasn't here to experience any of this. "Just a Moors Goblin," Eryn said in a dismissive tone. "They like to scare people and steal any valuables you may carry, but are otherwise harmless in my experience. However, it is curious what the creature was doing out here in the thicket of the woods, away from the moors. That's unusual considering they almost always prefer the clear grasslands and meadows." Kenric was carefully putting the large sword in his hand back into its sheath. As I observed him, I realized Kenric was never required to act; Eryn had preempted the entire situation. I wondered why Eryn wanted Kenric to come along if he was so capable. Maybe I'd bring up the subject later to ask. Eryn finished heating our meal. Small pieces of carrots, chopped turnips, and shredded cabbage with some kind of shredded cheese sprinkled over the top. I wondered whether he had really packed cheese in the sack he had brought along.

The meal was fine, nothing glamorous, but I was starving, so anything was good right now. Kenric gave Nova part of his portion, adding some pieces of what looked like dried meat to the top. He was squatting on the ground next to Nova while the regal dog delicately picked at his food. Kenric rested his upper body on his knees a bit, smiling while running his finger through the curly hair on Nova's chest. We all sat around for a short while, relaxing. Nobody said anything as we tried to recover some energy. The horses had already drunk a fair amount of water and were now grazing around the small clearing, nibbling on grass. Eryn was the first to stand up, packing away our belongings before moving to kick dirt over the fire and then spreading out the black coals. "It's time we got going, I'm afraid." He gazed down the narrow path ahead. "I believe we have a good four or five hours of riding left before sundown. That should get us to the knolls that lie on the outskirts of Thalmyr's Cradle, before reaching Ravynari territory. I believe it will be a safe place to make camp for the night." Without speaking another word, we mounted up. As we were exiting the small clearing, Kenric stopped, looking back behind him. Eryn and I stopped immediately upon noticing. Nova sat in the same spot he had been in, now looking up at Kenric, not moving. Nova let out a long whimper of dissatisfaction. Kenric laughed softly, turning around to dismount. "You're full and now not good for anything. Isn't that right, boy?" He bent over, scooping Nova up with both arms under his body, briefly throwing the large poodle over his shoulder before mounting back on the horse. Nova had to weigh over eighty pounds, I estimated, but Kenric made it look effortless. He reached into his saddlebag, pulling out something that resembled a folded shirt. With the item now draped across one of his shoulders, Kenric took a section from it and wrapped it around Nova, as the poodle was on the saddle, placed in front of him and directly behind the saddle horn. "Oh, great heavens of old, you spoil that dog too much, Kenric!" Eryn looked genuinely bemused. With that, we were off again. Now with Nova sitting tall and proud between Kenric's arms, leaning back against his chest, Nova having that silly, almost human grin on his face and tongue slightly out the side. I laughed to myself, leading Sylareth back into the half staggered one front, two-back formation we established earlier in the day.

Chapter 10: Thalmyr's Cradle

We rode at a steady pace for a couple of hours, something between a trot and a lope. Eryn said we needed to pick up the pace without going so fast as to tire out the horses. I noticed Kenric was more attentive to the road ahead now that Nova rode in front of him, against his chest. We slowed occasionally when the road forced us, whether it was too narrow or the path became rockier. We didn't want any of our horses to injure themselves. I had recently noticed the woods thinning, the dense thicket slowly giving way to a grove of scattered trees, sunlight now filtering through. We slowed once again to cross a small stream. I mentioned to Eryn that we could see further around us now. He shook his head. "This is Sylvan's Clearing. Stay on alert. There are certain things here that would not welcome us." Partway across the stream, I glanced downstream, seeing how clear and blue the water was, how the small stream curved its way through the clearing. Small trees and bushes, their leaves rustling in the gentle breeze, dotted the sides, partially obscuring our view. I thought I saw something, or someone, further downstream on one side. It looked as if someone had possibly stood up from crouching beside the stream, but it was too far for me to be certain. I turned to Eryn, who was now closer to me at my front left, Kenric to my back right. "I thought I saw something down there," pointing in that direction. "I'm not sure, though." Kenric gazed downstream for a moment. "If something was there, it doesn't appear to be now, possibly a deer drinking. If it were something else, let us just hope they have no interest in us as we keep moving." We crossed the stream, speeding up at once, feeling a little more eager to move than we had before crossing it. We rode on for what I suspected was another hour or two at most, with nothing eventful to speak of, seeing only a few animals and a lot of trees. We made small talk here and there when we slowed down. Eryn slowed ahead to let us get closer. "I believe we will reach Thalmyr's Cradle within two hours, seeing as how we've made good speed, possibly even quicker. If we are lucky, we'll have enough spare daylight to check out the area before setting up camp for the night." He sped up to get ahead again. A short while later, as I was lost in a daze with the hours of riding, Eryn held up his hand, telling us to slow down or stop. Kenric and I slowed immediately, keeping a bit of distance between us and Eryn. I wasn't sure what made him suspicious at first until I saw someone on a horse in the distance heading in our direction. Eryn slowed quickly to let us get close. "They have already seen us; too late to hide without making ourselves suspicious. Do nothing to draw attention. Do not speak. Eyes ahead and stay moving."

As we got closer, we maintained our slow, ambling gait. Kenric tightened the fabric around himself and Nova, then moved to unfasten the clasp on his sword's sheath without drawing attention, pulling it out slightly to keep his hand on it. Eryn did nothing of the sort. He maintained his normal stature, staying poised and proper. The person was now within range to make out a few details. A tall elven woman sat atop a horse of no distinguishable breed, possibly a mixture of several breeds from the looks of it. The woman had beige skin, wearing a long brown cloak with a hood pulled partway over her head, her pointed ears sticking out slightly as the hood tucked behind them. She had brown hair, not so different from the color of pine tree bark. The elven's face appeared gaunt, with sunken, dark eyes. She had a small blade affixed to her thigh, just visible as the cloak draped around her. Eryn tipped his hat to her as he passed, otherwise not speaking. The woman glanced at him as we approached. Kenric kept his focus ahead. Nova let out a few low huffs at the woman, to which Kenric hushed right away. I looked at the woman as we rode by, her horse going slightly slower than ours. We had almost passed her when the woman made a movement, straightening up a bit, then turning her head entirely to glare at me. I looked into her dark eyes; for a moment I could have sworn I saw a red flash of color within them. She smiled slightly, showing teeth with unusually large canines, lines filed across all front teeth. I shuddered. She turned back ahead, continuing to ride in the direction she had been headed, as we did the same. After she was well out of range to hear anything from us, I sped up a little to get closer to Eryn. "Do you think she was from the Orriveth elves?" He shook his head before answering, his voice low. "I'm afraid she didn't have any of their attire or metal. That was a Ravynari." "What?!" I tried not to scream the word out loudly. Eryn nodded. "She didn't seem too concerned with us; let's hope it remains that way. I don't think we grabbed her attention. We should pick up the pace, Miss Octavia; we need to get to Thalmyr's Cradle sooner rather than later." I noticed Kenric left his sword sheath unfastened; I wasn't sure if that made me feel better or if it fueled my paranoia.

We saw a change in the land as we came out of Sylvan's Clearing, the knolls Eryn spoke of earlier now coming into view. The knolls were low rolling hills, getting higher and steeper as they made way to the highlands, wrapping around into a massive half-circle leading up. If we had taken the path up, it would have led us into Ravynari territory. So, according to Eryn, we would stick to the low trails that weaved in and out of the hills through Thalmyr's Cradle to remain unseen and inconspicuous. The three of us stopped as we exited the clearing. Eryn was right about the view; it really was breathtaking in almost every regard. The path exited Sylvan's Clearing on a hill before descending slightly across the knolls. From the small cliff overhang we stood upon, I could see clear across the knolls, right down into parts of Thalmyr's Cradle. The highlands are visible at the top of the large hills to the left. The late evening sun cascaded down through the clouds, rays of sunlight beaming through the hills so magically that I wondered if some God was responsible for the beautiful artwork. Perhaps a mage was using their abilities to create an illusion, because surely something that gorgeous couldn't exist naturally. Maybe it did indeed exist, and I was just so accustomed to the flat wooded lands around Faladorn, our hometown we were raised in, that I never knew something like this existed. Eryn was waving lightly to get my attention; I snapped back from my gazing trance. He pointed to something beyond the path to the Highlands, not too far from where we stood. Maybe a thirty-minute ride away. It was smoke from a small fire, from the looks of it. "Let's move to the right on the outskirts of the knolls. That will be a safer bet for the night, away from the potential eye of whomever that might be." "You think it's Ravynari, don't you?" I asked Eryn. Unable to read any certain expression on his face or body language as he answered. "May the fates never have us learn that knowledge. I would rather both parties remained a mystery to each other." Eryn carefully guided Mareion's reins down the semi-steep, winding trail, the sounds of their hooves muffled by the soft earth as they descended into the knolls; I followed behind on Sylareth with Kenric and Virelen trailing close behind me. We stuck to the outskirts of the knolls, leaving the worn paths shortly after making the descent from Sylvan's Clearing. We stuck to the edge of the treeline and the bottom of the hills, making a way through the green grass. Occasionally having to move around a few smaller boulders or to avoid tall grass. We rode for a while longer, darkness getting closer to us by the minute. We finally reached an area between two hills with a hill at the back, which would obscure our view from the path leading up to the highlands. Eryn was smart in picking this place. The only side that left us easily visible was towards Sylvan's Clearing. Eryn seemed to think that was the lesser of the two concerns, Kenric agreeing. We had little to set up, with a few drop cloths on the ground, using our small bags as pillows. The weather was cool, but not yet cold. So, we would be fine through the night with no blankets. Eryn said he would not start a fire until well after the sun was gone, as he didn't want the smoke to gain us any attention. He kept the fire small, just big enough to heat our food while providing the smallest amount of light. We ate the same food we had earlier in the day, but I would not complain. Any food was better than no food currently, and we would soon be able, fingers crossed, to get a decent meal from Althira Thorne once we reached Liraquor. The rest of the evening passed uneventfully. We sat around eating; Kenric fed Nova, and I assisted Eryn in making sure the horses drank water before they were tied up to graze and rest for the night. There was a trickling stream not far away. It wasn't much of a stream to swim in or get wet if we were to cross it, but it was enough to get some much-needed water. After we were all done, we adjusted our bedding situations to get comfortable. Nova lay down beside Kenric, and Eryn got up one final time before kicking dirt over the little fire. With one last glance around in the black of night, listening to the low snorts of the horses between each other, I was out.

Chapter 11: Half Onward

We woke just as daylight broke the horizon, the brilliance of the earliest sun rays of the day willing us to get moving. I saw Eryn was up before anyone, Kenric in the process of getting up. I rolled over with my arms crossed. It wouldn't hurt if I dozed off for just a few more minutes. My thighs and legs felt as though they had been trampled by a herd of cattle; my back muscles were burning on each side when I tried to move, and the upper part of my arms at the shoulders ached something fierce. I suspected most of my aches were from riding as hard as we had the day before, but I thought it likely at least a small portion of this was from sleeping on the hard ground. I begrudgingly got up when I woke from my doze again a few minutes later. Eryn, somehow already looking fresh and tidy, saw I was up. "Good morning, Miss Octavia!" I shot him a snarl. I almost asked him what was good about it, but decided he didn't deserve that much attitude; he was always so kind to me. He held his hands up innocently with a soft smile. "Well, I didn't disturb you from your rest, as you see. I recall that didn't go over too well." That almost made me smile. I looked around, noticing Kenric and Nova weren't here. "Eryn, where are Kenric and Nova?" "Sir Kenric went to freshen up before we get going for the day, I suspect. I would suggest that you do the same. As you saw yesterday, we could very well be on the road half the day before we stop again." I groaned, "Don't remind me." I grabbed my little sack of supplies with what I assumed was too much attitude and headed to the small stream the horses had drunk from the night before. It wasn't too far away, but there was a small incline to the left, making the small stream unseen until you got partway there from where we had camped for the night. I heard rustling up ahead, then a few splashes, and then leaves rustling again. It didn't sound like trouble, so I disregarded it. As I overcame a bit of an incline, I saw Nova zip by. Kenric was at the small stream saying, "You stop that at once and get over here!" Then I realized Nova was chasing a rabbit, going under this bush and that. I wondered whether he could actually catch the poor rabbit. I've seen how fast the poodle can move. Deciding I couldn't be bothered to intervene at the moment, with my body hurting the way it did, I started walking toward the stream again as I looked up. Oh! I only just noticed Kenric. He was standing in the stream, the water barely covering his ankles; his waist-length hair was wet from where he had been washing it. Clad only in wet thigh-length drawers, he was shirtless. My hand flew to my mouth.

I quickly recovered before he noticed. He was rolling his hair up to hold with a short metal stick he had brought for that exact purpose, the way he had kept it up most of the trip until sleeping. The man was undeniably beautiful, and that was the truth. His arms were up in the air during the process, every muscle around his ribs, chest, and torso strained against the skin. The tattoos, of which I had only previously seen pieces on his neck and arms, wrapped around his chest to the sides of his abdomen, curving down on the sides towards his hips before tapering off. Accentuating every muscle and bony area with great artistry. The tattoo lines in the center of his chest ran from his neck down to curve out under his breast area before continuing down the center of his abdomen, following each abdominal muscle outwards and again curving off towards his hips slightly before coming to a point. The lines went down to his drawers. I glanced lower, wondering how far they went, seeing the outline of... Oh! I caught my breath, gods forgive me for being so perverse. I honestly didn't mean to stare like that. I pulled myself together, feeling heat rush to my cheeks. Nova zipped by again. Kenric, seemingly unbothered by any of it, and thankfully not paying attention to what I was doing, was in the process of splashing water on himself to clean off. First on his face, then under his arms, and so on. Every action taken with natural grace and elegance. I moved over to the stream, taking out my toothbrush to use first. I brushed my teeth while perched on a small boulder, using a brush that I dipped into a small, repurposed pomade pot filled with chalk and baking soda. Nova came over to plop down between me and Kenric, panting heavily. Looks like he gave up his rabbit chase for now. I decided I should do what Kenric had done and wash my hair quickly. I could feel the dirt and grime from riding covering my body; washing my hair would make me feel more like myself again. After I finished that and then washed my body as modestly as I could manage while half my clothes remained on, I started gathering my clothes and things to take back. I'd let my hair finish drying before I decided whether I wanted to put it up or braid it for the ride. I glanced over at Kenric. He was bent over while partly squatted petting Nova behind the ears. Once again, I looked at his tattoos, admiring the intricate artwork. They traveled down the back of his neck from the center, down the spine and feathering out onto the back of his ribs. The lines were carefully placed, emphasizing the muscles of his physique. I felt my eyes widen. Get it together, Octavia. I shook my head and walked onward before I saw anything else I shouldn't, as I already saw too much.

When I got back to our makeshift camp, I asked Eryn if he wasn't making us food. He looked at me regretfully, shaking his head. I don't think we should risk starting a fire here during the daylight; we would be too visible from the highlands. "It's a risk I don't think we can afford. I offer my sincerest apologies, Miss Octavia." With a reassuring smile, I told him everything would be all right. He offered me different things if I wanted something raw. I thought about taking a carrot for a moment, but shrugged and told him to just cook for us next time we stopped. As we were getting ready to mount back up, I noticed briars around two trees right at the treeline. I couldn't believe it. Dewberries! "You're going to give me a moment. I've got berries to pick!" I said it with more of a jingle than I meant to. Grabbing a square-cut cloth from my sack. Though intended as a handkerchief, the soft linen would be perfect for gathering the plump dewberries. I almost skipped to where they were, near giddy I could have such a treat. I carefully picked the berries between each briar vine, as quickly as I could manage without cutting my arms and hands up, eating a berry here and there between filling the makeshift berry bag. After just a few moments, the bag was full of plump, juicy berries. My hands were now stained purple and red with the juices; I found myself less than bothered by that fact. I ran back to Sylareth, carefully throwing my berries into the small side saddle pocket. Kenric was snickering at me from behind. "May I help you?" I asked with petty annoyance in my voice. "Well, I do recall you taking a tumble over poor Nova here, dropping a sack of berries very similar to that one there." "Oh yes, poor Nova." I rolled my eyes. "What is wrong with carrying a bag of berries? They are delicious and are only around for a small part of the year." "There is nothing wrong with it. I've just never seen someone like berries as much as you." He was still snickering to himself. "Well, don't eat any then. These are mine and for me alone! You'll be sorry when I have these delicious berries to snack on and you have nothing!" I turned Sylareth with my nose in the air away from Kenric and started trotting off, Eryn running by on Mareion to get in front of us again before slowing down as we once again found our pace. I heard Kenric still snickering, talking to Nova behind me. I rolled my eyes again. He and that silly dog — I was glad they came along if I were being honest. I had grown very fond of Eryn in our short time together, but Kenric and Nova gave us some fun entertainment to pass the time that we wouldn't have had otherwise, and for that I was truly grateful. We rode through the green grass around the knolls for a while longer before making our way back to a more traveled path. Eryn, slowing down to speak again, "I believe we may have another hour of riding before we are out of Thalmyr's cradle. I think the going should be good from here on, at least for a while. Just keep an ear up and your eyes out for anything potentially alarming or suspicious." Me and Kenric nodded in unison before we all went back to something between a trot and a canter, slowing down occasionally to make sure the horses weren't getting overworked.

        I got to thinking about different things while we rode, as my mind wandered from the monotonous riding after a while. I reached into the little saddlebag occasionally, grabbing a few berries to pop into my mouth. One was so sour, my entire face puckered involuntarily. I tried to chew quickly, swallowing before anyone noticed. I'd be damned if I let them think the berries I brought with me weren't anything other than delicious, every last one. Seems like I was successful. I glanced over at Kenric, thinking about his tattoos again. "Kenric, do you mind if I ask how you got those tattoos? Aren't they the ones earned, the kind given by the Woodwoses?" He appeared to be lost in thought for a few moments before answering. "Yes, they are earned. — I spent three years with the Woodwoses after my mom passed away. A few of them were living together deep within the woods near Velasari Glades. They were struggling with people attempting to run them out of their homes. The woodwoses fought hard, protecting their forest homes to no avail. The more they fought, the more people would run deep into the forest in droves, all in a hateful act to kill the peaceful Woodwoses or force them from their homes. I stumbled upon the Woodwoses during a hard time for myself. They tried to attack me in an attempt to make me flee. I dropped to my knees in front of them, telling them to do as they wished. I had no fight left to give. They realized my despair and utter desolation, how I posed no threat to them or their home." Kenric smiled then. "Those beautiful, hairy protectors of the woodlands brought me food and water, and then even provided me with shelter. I realized their dire situation, how hard they were fighting just to survive and save the forests they loved. So I offered them all I had at the time: my blade in battle. Just as my family previously did with the Dryads of Efameral, I fought for the Woodwose people. I leveled the field a little against the would-be death and destruction brought by civilization to the Woodwose's front door. After I helped them either kill or scare off any further intruders, they welcomed me to stay with open arms. I graciously accepted. While living with them, one of their elders gave me these. These markings are a great honor to me, as I will always be welcomed by the Woodwoses now with open arms. They seem to think the markings come with some gift of power, but I don't believe that to be the case as much as the wearer of these markings carrying with them great pride and respect. I will never forget what those wonderful wild men of the woods did for me, what they taught me, and what they granted me during my time there. They made sure none of their people forgot with these tattoos and gave me a reminder of the time they gave me kindness when I didn't have any to give myself." I sat there in silence, taking it all in full, shocked by Kenric's story. I'm not sure what I expected exactly, but not this. The story painted Kenric in a completely different light. I thought he was always well to do and wealthy, with very few troubles. I did not know the troubles he had faced or the feats he had achieved, but I wondered if the rest of his family had been the same as him. If that indeed is the case, I can see why they earned the title of Highborn.

Not too long passed before I became a bit bored again, my mind wandering to Eryn and the Syreth blades. I thought maybe I shouldn't ask at first, but I don't think Eryn would mind if I did. I sped Sylareth up to get a little closer to Eryn. "Eryn, can you tell me about the Syreth blades? Such as why you have the blades of myth as one?" He didn't answer for a long moment; I took that as his politely declining to discuss the subject. "I'm afraid that is a rather long and complex story, Miss Octavia. I can give you the quick and easy version now, then fill you in with the full story at a more appropriate time. How does that work?" "That would be wonderful! I can't wait to hear everything about them." He gave me a soft grin, his eyes crinkling at the corners. "Let's start by saying that in order to tell you how I became the wielder of the blades, I would have to tell you the full backstory and the surrounding circumstances. That's still part of a bigger story for another day. However, I can tell you the blades are bound to me by blood. They can never be taken from me. Someone could certainly try, and might even succeed, in physically removing the blades from my grasp." He paused for a while, his face taking on a pensive expression. "But the blades will always return to me when called. Being bound to me in blood, I can call the blades from anywhere. The elven call it the el'un-shimmer. When called by the one they're bound with, the blades will vanish in a shimmer, reappearing in the wielder's hands moments later as if pulled from thin air. It's not something that can be done often or repeatedly, seeing as how they use some of my arcane power with such abilities. That is quite tiring." He tapped his left side, where the left blade rested under his topcoat. "This one is Syreth'alun, Whisper of the Moon." He tapped the right side. "This one is Syreth'vahl, Echo of the Veil." I nodded in acknowledgment. "They are the twins that make up the weapon they become. They can also do quite a few other things, such as using the lumination of their runes to reveal hidden magic and even disorient foes sensitive to magical auras. As you saw a glimpse of with that Moors goblin. You may know how they can cut through the air and strike their targets in complete silence, making the wielder completely stealthy in battle or combat. Attackers would have to physically see me or an ability I used before they could hear me. That's a commonly known rumor about the blades." He was right; I had heard about how the very name of the blades referred to their silence. He continued.

"Then there are the very rare abilities. Some are so rare that they are often an exclusive ability to the wielders of the blades. One such ability given to me by these blades is Isil-tyelle." He paused briefly again. "It means moon step in our language. The Syreth blades grant me the ability, when used in tandem, to create a momentary illusion. This will cast a brief shadow-image of myself and my movements, thus confusing attackers and creating a flickering double for one strike. It's a gift I have rarely ever used and hope to avoid if possible. I'm afraid it makes me untouchable and twice as lethal, while also being extremely tenuous and draining to perform for myself. We can delve into the intricate details and the full story at a later time; let's leave it for another day." "Thank you, Eryn. I truly have known nothing about what they do other than myths, and of course I've never met someone with Syreth blades, as I'm sure you can imagine." He grinned softly. "Indeed, Miss Octavia, I can imagine."

Chapter 12: Combative Penitence

We had been riding for what seemed like hours longer than it had
been. Eryn assured me we were only two to three hours in, the pain in
my body protesting any rationality. Eryn spoke up in a reassuring,
matter-of-fact tone. "Just another hour or two and we will stop to rest
and eat. Just hang in there, Miss Octavia. We need to make ourselves
clear of Thalmyr's Cradle, getting out of direct line of sight from the
highlands. It will be safer after that." I nodded, but groaned. I knew he
was right, but I would not act thrilled about it. Just then, I heard
thunder in the distance. I looked up; dark skies were rolling above the
highlands. "We might have storms coming our way." I said to nobody
in particular. Kenric and Eryn both glanced over, lightning crackling
out of the dark clouds as they did, and both turned back to the path
ahead. It had been dark and gloomy for about the last hour, but the
storm coming in looked like it could be rough for us. I wondered if we
should keep an eye out for a safe place to shelter before it made way to
us. I supposed Eryn and Kenric would keep an eye out for that exact
thing, so I put the worry aside for now. We rode on for a while longer
before Eryn slowed to speak. "The storm may very well be upon us
before much longer. Let's pick up the pace. Ride hard for the time
being. We will let the horses rest after we're out of Thalmyr's Cradle. I
don't feel good about riding out a rough storm here." We did just that,
riding swiftly and fleeting. I felt a raindrop hit my face occasionally, as
I suspected the storm would catch up to us at any time. We could see
the edge of Thalmyr's Cradle in the short distance now, only a few
hills between us and the wooded area ahead. The path we rode was

flat, curving its way through the low hills as we approached the outskirts of the knolls once again. Lightning crackled not far from us. "I fear we may not have much time before we are forced to hunker down until the storm passes." Eryn sounded a little annoyed with that. As we rounded the next hill, Eryn came to a hard halt. Me and Sylareth almost ran into him and Mareion. Sylareth dodged to the right at the last second to avoid colliding before she came to a stop. I was so thankful for this incredibly smart horse. Kenric and Virelen had a better time stopping, as he slowly halted at my side. Then I saw the reason for the abrupt stop. Ahead of us sat two elven on mixed-color horses, hooded cloaks draping over both as only their ears protruded from the sides of the hoods. They both sat at an angle, facing each other slightly, to ensure the entire path was blocked. The elven girl on the right smiled as she looked at me, large canines and lines filed across her teeth. A lump caught in my throat; this was the same elven girl we had passed the day before. "Octavia, turn and head in the direction we came. Now!" I'd never heard Eryn speak to me so harshly; his abrasiveness was almost hurtful. Before I had time to comply, what looked like five or six more elven walked out into our view. Some had cloaks and hoods; a few of the taller ones were men, from what I could make out, wearing what looked like chemises with the sleeves torn off. Kenric to my left sighed loudly. "May the gods be with us," Eryn to my right said lowly and too calmly, "May celestial mercy wash clean our earthly stumbles." Eryn snapped in my direction and growled, "Octavia, move it, NOW!" I flinched and yanked the reins of Sylareth to turn us around. Kenric yanked the cloth that held Nova in the saddle. Pulling the poodle tight against his chest, he reached down for his sword before I had made the turn to run on Sylareth. Lightning cracked, lighting up the sky overhead. Just as Sylareth sprang forward to run at full speed, a loud noise from behind followed, followed by a couple of shouts. I heard Eryn yell at the top of his lungs. "GET DOWN!" Then, with a sickening thud, something hit me hard in the back.

Sylareth tumbled as I flew forward, hitting my shoulder and neck on the dirt now sprinkled with raindrops. I blinked; the pain was too unbearable to move or make a sound. Out of my periphery, I saw Kenric fly off Virelen, being hurled through the air backwards before slamming into the ground. He held Nova tightly, and as they slid, the sudden roll caused Nova to yelp before he came to a stop with Nova still securely held in his arms. I couldn't make out what was happening behind where I lay. I forced myself with all my might to roll over, just enough to see where Eryn was. I watched in horror as Eryn hit the ground, blood running down his face with his eyes closed. Mareion reared up, standing in front of Eryn, then letting out a guttural, squealing whinny. Something had hit or hurt the horse. Mareion took a faltering step backward, his efforts to find his footing resulting in him stepping on Eryn's leg. I gasped for air as I tried to scream, but no sound came. Mareion plummeted forward, stopping himself with his front legs at the last moment. Then he hauled himself up and bolted. Eryn lay in the same position, unmoving. I sat still in the same rag doll position I had landed. I was in too much pain and shock to move. The elven lady from the day before rode up on her horse, jumping down as she approached. It was now raining hard enough to wet everything, the musty smell of wet moss and dirt filling my nose. Trailing behind her was another elf, no, a Ravynari. She walked by Eryn, stopping for a moment to kick him hard in the side. He didn't react. I felt tears flowing uncontrollably down my face. She now made her way to me, a snarling smile fixed across her face. I felt disgusted and chilled. Before she reached me, one of the elven men had run to me while she was kicking Eryn, this sickly and evil-looking Ravynari man now standing over me with a leg on each side of my body. He bent down, sniffing me with an enthrallment that turned my stomach. He started flapping his tongue and thrusting his pelvis at me, hissing the words; "I'm going to have fun with her. I'm going to take my time, nice and slow, so that she feels and remembers every moment in detail. Bet she tastes good." Drool was running down his chin to drip off in a long string. I grimaced as I shivered to my core in revolt. The Ravynari girl spoke in response, just as she was reaching me. "Yes, we will get many uses out of this one." That vile snarl still on her face. A faint rustling reached me from behind, but I remained still, my eyes fixed on Eryn and the crimson stain blooming on the earth beneath him, slowly diluted by the relentless rain. I felt a faint hum at my throat, realizing it was the necklace Lady Alsendra had sent with me. I didn't want to chance reaching up to it, with the Ravynari standing above me. I closed my eyes and focused with as much intensity as I could manage, picturing my energy going into the little glass vial of swirling liquid. I felt it vibrate against my throat. Gods, I could only hope Lady Alsendra heard, and maybe, just maybe, she could save us. I stopped concentrating to realize I was now sobbing, almost unable to find my breath, as the rain hit my face. Lightning briefly lit everything around in a brilliant flash. The elven girl almost spat this time as she spoke. "Is the weak little spellcaster about to cry for us? That makes this all the sweeter." The last of her words left her lips with a hiss. I rasped out as venomously as I could speak; "You are the abhorrent failure of the elven race! Ravynari scum!" The bottom of her boot followed up behind my words, making its impact across my face. I couldn't tell if blood ran down my cheeks or if it was the trailing tears and rain trickling over my skin. "Festering pus bag!" I yelled the words as I spat at her feet, seeing blood leave my mouth. She brought her leg back up; I closed my eyes, preparing for another strike. I felt my ear twitch at that moment. The noise behind me — a wet, rhythmic splashing, like running through puddles — was rapidly closing in on us. Something was coming at a full run, then I saw something leap right over me for the Ravynari. I cried out as I realized what it was. It was Nova, the sweet and goofy poodle. The elven woman swung her leg with all her effort, bringing her foot down to connect with the side of Nova's chest. Nova got cut out of the air mid-jump. He let out a screeching yelp as he was flung backward. I watched as he hit the ground, rolling. I was crying so hard that my vision was now blurry and hard to see. Consequently, I felt a rage ignite inside me. A torrential wrath consumed by a burning tide of volcanic fury. How dare this heartless wretch inflict such pain on these people. They were merely attempting to assist me and had been nothing short of exceptionally kind. Nova was one of the most loving animals I had ever seen, and this disgusting blight on the elven race had hurt him badly. I saw Nova trying his best to get back up. The Ravynari girl, pulling the blade up from her thigh, started walking towards him. I gasped again as my eyes widened. No, the foolish poodle was going to get himself killed. The rage inside me felt so hot, feeling like it might melt my body from within. I seethed with a wrath older than the earth, flowing through me, all molten fury surging through my veins. I felt a mandatory nudge to the back. The wind blew up around me, carrying large raindrops to hit my skin even harder. "Child, I am here; take my hand." That voice again. I opened myself whole and fully. No,

I willed it into me like water siphoning into a sponge. I grasped at the power and pulled. I wanted it all with a burning, insatiable greed. I wanted to unleash it from within. The wind squalled around me in an instant, sounding like a thousand trumpets being blown at once. The elven girl stopped in her tracks, turning to look at me. I smiled; all pain in my body was now replaced with malicious retribution. Her eyes glowed red; I could feel an arcane hum stir from her. The Ravynari man near me stepped back quickly, almost stumbling. I saw Nova take off again with as much of a sprint as he could manage while being in pain. He was just a few yards from the Ravynari girl before she pivoted her attention back to the incoming attack, knife in hand, readying to strike Nova. I felt power flow into me like fuel to an infernal kiln. I willed that voice to help me, begging the nudge at my back to do something, drawing it in. From where I still lay on the ground, I reached my hand up towards Nova. I had to do something, anything, to save him from the clutches of death. The Ravynari, who had brought the knife back, was winding up to swing it just as Nova leaped off the ground. I yelled a strained sound, almost leaving me in a raspy gurgle, causing the Ravynari girl to lose focus for just a moment. Then I felt it leaving my body quicker than wind could travel, pouring out of me like the very lightning striking overhead.

My hand remained in the air as a strand looking like that of a thread extended from my entire arm. I pushed even harder. "Give. Me. More." I ground my teeth, whispering the words under my breath in demand. I heard the words respond. "I am here". The strand glowed in the overcast's darkness, in the same way the light of a dim candle would glow. It reached Nova in an instant. Before the elven girl even had time to blink, Nova was engulfed in flames. Large wings of ruptured hellfire manifested themselves from his back, fire trailing through the air behind him. The elven girl tried to turn back and tripped, falling to the ground in the mud. Nova landed on top of her. Biting down to rip her cloak, the woman let out a piercing scream of panic as some of her clothes caught fire. She threw Nova off, but he didn't go far. I wasn't sure if he had it in him to hurt the girl. I think he was just trying his best to help us. No, he needs more. It was a necessity that she should no longer live. I willed the voice to come help, opening the channel through me. Again, I felt the power leave me quicker than lightning, followed by a crackle through the air like a whip snapping. The Ravynari girl's eyes burned bright red as she hummed with arcane energy. She was trying to focus her heinous magick on me. I felt a smile escape my lips as I realized her attempt would be in vain. Nova was already leaping through the air, aiming to land on top of the Ravynari again. My will reaching Nova again before the Ravynari girl's heart could beat, a helm of ice encapsulated the poodle's entire head and face. Coming down over his snout with long, sharp fangs made of burning blue ice overlapping each other. Where he might not bite to attack and kill, partly being too sweet, I could help with that and take the burden. I willed the helm open as Nova landed atop the girl; the cavernous, iced helm jaws snapping shut with a thunderous clap, drowning the air with the promise of death to come. The elven girl lay there on her back as she screamed and writhed. I opened myself to the power, wind coming from so strong around me, it lifted me to my feet. I realized as I stood, I was levitating just above the ground, partly engulfed in flames. I willed the flaming iced jaws on Nova to open, extend, and then snap closed with the force of one ton of steel hitting an anvil, closing on the girl's throat, leaving only gore and carnage. She let out gurgles as she tried to scream again, bubbles of blood leaving her mouth and throat. I let it pour out of me as I watched the flames crawl from Nova's legs, setting the Ravynari ablaze. I saw to my left one of the Ravynari men racing towards me. I turned in his direction, the fire and ice leaving Nova to recoil back to me through the strand like a fluid spring. Nova ran back to where Kenric had lain, now pushing himself to his feet. I didn't know how to react to the man rushing at me. Time seemed to stand still as I burned in the surrounding flames. I could hear my heartbeat in my ears, feel it pounding in my chest, feel the length of my wet hair slamming down to whip against my skin in the wind. I drew upon the seething anger within, a burning coal in my chest; flames rolled up my body from my feet with longing to consume. Then came a subtle flash of light to my left before I had time to do anything; I darted my eyes in that direction only to see a little shimmering through the air in the storm's overcast. Then, a small shimmer caught my attention back at the man running in my direction. I saw a blur of something moving back and forth rapidly, then a soft blinking light appear on the other side of the Ravynari. All I could make out was a series of steps in the mud and water as the shimmer twisted and changed. Without a moment's notice, the Ravynari man clasped his hands to his chest and throat, blood gushing and viscera spilling as he fell to his knees. Another blink of light and a shimmer rippled into being; the shimmer then appearing behind another of the Ravynari elven, their features briefly obscured. They too fell. Of the three remaining, one turned to run and two drew their weapons in a panic. With a blur around one, his arms were severed, falling to the ground, his severed hand still wrapped around the hilt of a blade. A second later, his legs were severed, and his body fell over onto the ground with a solid thud. His legs fell in opposite directions. I barely saw another shimmer of light before another Ravynari fell to the ground, clasping their throat with their hands as the cloak they were wearing fell to the ground. The top of their head, which was scalp and skull, rolled onto the ground as the body made contact. The final Ravynari was still running, a respectable distance away now. I saw a shimmer where the one elven had just fallen, then a physical shape of a human started taking form close to the fallen body. I saw a little streak of silent light soar through the air, hitting the cloaked Ravynari across the back, leaving a gash from the top left of his torso angled down to the bottom right, blood leaking out and bone exposed. He slowly stopped running, falling face-first a few steps later. No light soared after the Ravynari plummeted, only the soft shimmer surrounding the human form. The shimmer intensified at his hand as the familiar gleam of the Syreth blades became visible. "Eryn!" I cried out his name almost hysterically. He turned to smile at me softly, blood covering his entire face. The Syreth blades were put away before I even noticed. He gave an enormous bow in my direction with a wave of his hand in front of him in a gentlemanly manner. "Miss Octavia." I saw Kenric standing to my right, now holding his sword, with Nova beside him. I started crying even harder. We were all alive. Somehow we survived the attack. I realized I was standing with my feet firmly on the ground now, no longer on fire, rain hitting my face. I looked up into the clouds as lightning struck across the sky. Pain ricocheted through me from my injuries as I caught my breath. I suddenly felt weightless as I eased my tense body, blackness taking over.

Chapter 13: Responsibility and Respect

I woke to two voices speaking near me, having a serious undertone to
their conversation. I opened my eyes, blinking a few times to dampen
the abrasive dryness. It was two women having the conversation. I
recognized one voice, Lady Alsendra. I exhaled a slow breath of relief
before glancing around, realizing I was in a type of makeshift tent. A
simple, yet large, natural cotton cloth held up with a few large sticks
assembled together with a type of twine or rope, strong enough to
hold the cloth up. The tent was small, just large enough for the bed I
lay on and maybe one more person. I moved my neck, the incredible
stiffness making any movement slow and strained, but I wasn't in
agonizing pain like I had been in before passing out. I heard the
woman talking with Lady Alsendra raise her voice in an annoyed
tone. "If the girl is indeed who you think she is and capable of what
you believe, you have brought us far bigger issues that need attending.
I don't need to tell you to navigate this with extreme caution and
apprehension, Alsendra." Lady Alsendra let out a puckered smack
before speaking. "I cannot see what path needs to be taken, and it is
absolutely maddening!" "Come off it, Alsendra, you mean you're in
the very same predicament as every other person on earth this one
time?" "Althira, what I brought you may very well be of little or no
concern after you face what others will bring. I have seen the way this
can shift the very weave of fate. If word gets out about Octavia, her life
won't be the only one in danger." There was a pause between them
before Lady Alsendra continued. "You are the most capable person I
know to help hone her skills. Without proper guidance and protection,

I will be forced to strip her of her abilities sooner rather than later. You know what kind of verdict the Council would agree on if given the full details and the chance to intervene; therefore, the less they know, the better. I'm telling you the full truth so that you can understand the gravity, but Althira, if we can't keep this under control... you know where this progresses." She paused again. "Welcome back to us, Octavia," Lady Alsendra said the words loud and clear. I didn't dare speak up; I feared getting myself even deeper into trouble. Slowly turning, I groaned, pushing myself up on my feet, each stiff muscle protesting with sharp torment as I forced them to cooperate. I lumbered my way to the door of the tent, which was just two pieces of cloth meeting in the center to make a tall slit. Blinding daylight assaulted my eyes, making me squint hard in protest. A moment later, after my eyes adjusted, I looked around outside.

We were in a sort of clearing, with small trees and tall grass scattered throughout. Vantor and Draven were parked not too far from the tent. The mysterious veiled coachwoman in all black sat atop the coach the beautiful Friesians were attached, her posture perfectly straight and proper as she clasped the reins. I saw Eryn carrying some sticks and limbs in his arms from the woods, for what I suspected was fuel for a fire. I glanced to the left of the tent. Lady Alsendra and, what I presume to be, Althira Thorne, based on the conversation I overheard, were sitting together. They sat on wooden crates, with the long ends up to make temporary stools. Underneath their entire ensemble was a large cloth, maybe a blanket, flattening the grass around where they sat. Lady Alsendra looked similar to how she had when we last saw her. This time she wore a festive-looking navy blue high-low style dress, shorter in the front and longer in the back. Her full neck and chest were covered by the dress, which stopped at the arms. Her legs were crossed as she sat straight up, silver strapless heels on her feet. These heels were shorter than I had seen her in prior. Althira sat on the right side, opposite her, on a crate. Althira wore a wine red high slit dress, more fitted than Lady Alsendra's. The top had a deep V-neck shape, cutting down over her decolletage area, stopping just above her bosom. Little straps wrapped around each shoulder, perfectly balanced by the two high slits up each leg clear to her hips. Her legs were crossed in the same way as Lady Alsendra's; the little flap of fabric between the two slits flowed down between her legs to just touch the cloth on the ground. She wore black heels with leather uppers, straps wrapping to just above her ankles. I almost couldn't believe how good she looked. She had to be Lady Alsendra's age, but her legs were stunning. She had almost the same shade of nearly flawless porcelain skin as Lady Alsendra. However, Althira had black hair with only a few grays to be seen on the sides. She had it tied up neatly in a round, ornate bun on the crown of her head, with an ornamental piece of silver metal wrapped around the circumference of the bun. She glowed from within with resplendent grace. With a critical eye, Althira assessed me from head to toe, then lifted a fine teacup, the clinking sound delicate against the quiet, and took a sip. I just noticed that both she and Lady Alsendra held teacups and saucers. I must have made a face, because Althira asked, "Do you have something to say, girl?" Did Lady Alsendra nearly just snicker? I shook my head, barely moving. Althira spoke again, projecting some of the same power into her voice as Lady Alsendra carried. "So, you are greeted good morning by my dear friend Alsendra here, to which you say nothing. You come out here with an ugly look upon your face, again not saying anything. You do not introduce yourself despite knowing who I am. So, I ask once more, do you have anything to say?" I fumbled over my words as I tried to speak, only to stutter before I stopped myself, concluding I would just hold my hands out to the side. Althira pursed her lips together, turning back to Lady Alsendra. "Dear gods Alsendra, is she physically capable or just mentally hindered?" I blurted out, "Pardon me? You don't have to go around being nasty." Althira glared at me with burning vitriol. "Nasty?! I don't think I've ever had anyone refer to me as... nasty. Let's see what you think of something worthy of being called nasty." I thought I briefly felt a low hum of arcane from her as she flicked her finger.

Nothing happened for a moment until I felt something crawling on the back of my neck; I reached up to flick it off. It was a spider. Then, something on my leg; I glanced down to find maggots crawling up to my knee. I looked at the other leg; there were hundreds of spiders clamoring over each other to make their way up that leg. A high-pitched squeal escaped my lips as I stomped and thrashed, my arms and legs flailing, trying to dislodge the filth that was clinging to me. Eryn was at my side in an instant. "What is going on?" he asked, as if he did not know. I pointed at the bugs as if they weren't obvious. He shrugged, looking at Lady Alsendra and then back at me. By now, large roaches were crawling up my left arm, going into the sleeve of my tunic to crawl around my body. Then I saw a snake, thin and black, crawling up my right arm from the wrist, making its way to my shoulder. It coiled back, ready to strike at any moment. I screamed and jumped back as the snake struck at my face. I fell backwards onto the ground. I opened my eyes from where I now lay on my back, noticing the snake was now gone. I collected myself as I realized it hadn't bitten me. The bugs were gone now, too. Althira sighed. "Alsendra, have you brought me an invalid?" Eryn stood over me, looking down before reaching his hand down to help me up. I accepted. Upon standing, I took a quick look at the two women. Lady Alsendra, looking rather amused, sipped her tea. Pinky in the air. Althira continued after a moment. "This is the girl you said had abilities, the Octavia girl?" Lady Alsendra tilted her head forward, closing her eyes with the movement. "This is indeed her." Althira sipped her tea before speaking. "Yet she couldn't thwart a simple old trickery illusion." Lady Alsendra inhaled deeply with obvious frustration. "Observing this girl's performance at the Rights would have, I believe, significantly enhanced your opinion of her." Althira arched an eyebrow. "Interesting." She took another sip of her tea. "I aim to find out for myself; perhaps I won't find the results as disappointing as this." She held out her hand to signal that the "this" she spoke of was me. I heard a couple of whinnies coming from behind me. I turned to see Kenric leading our three horses by the reins, tying them off not too far from Vantor and Draven. Nova was trotting along behind him. I was so relieved to see that they were all alive and well. I noticed as Mareion turned, the hair was missing in a few places along his side, but he seemed in good health otherwise. Sylareth had a few scratches on her chest. Virelen had a few superficial scrapes on her side near the saddle. I glanced at Kenric and Eryn; they both seemed completely fine, as did Nova. I wondered how we all healed so quickly. "Wait a minute, what was I hit in the back with when Sylareth and I got thrown to the ground? Why did those Ravynari attack us? How am I not seriously injured, or any of us for that matter, and where are we?" All the questions came spilling out at once. Nobody answered until Althira sipped her tea unnecessarily loudly before speaking.

"Well, I say, Alsendra," a sly smile playing on her lips, "the girl isn't dense enough not to reason, I suppose." Eryn offered me his arm in escort, leading me to the cloth blanket Lady Alsendra and Althira sat on. He dropped his arm as we reached the blanket, dipping away for only a moment before bringing back a wooden crate like the ones Lady Alsendra and Althira sat on. He sat the crate on one side of the blanket, gesturing for me to have a seat. I did just that, looking around at the two powerful women in front of me. Oh, gods, take pity on me. I was between them.

Lady Alsendra spoke up first. "Let us be sagacious enough to discuss one subject at a time, my dear. You suffer from unfortunate, involuntary logorrhea. On any account, it would seem the one Ravynari girl possessed arcane abilities. Exceptionally rare as it is, especially for a Ravynari, she was rather gifted. Pity she was... well, what she was." She followed the words with a tsk tsk tsk before continuing. "Even so, her powers allowed her to launch a completely unexpected assault, catching each of you off guard. Incapacitating Eryn in an instant, with him going down and being your main line of defense, gave them the upper hand momentarily. Although we are unsure whether she knew Eryn's actual capabilities or if she was wielding her powers with careless abandon. Perhaps she got lucky taking Eryn and Kenric out the way she did. Eryn atoned for his brief lapse in judgment in the end." She looked at him with a flat-lipped smile, Eryn returning a soft smile back. "The reason for the attack was unknown, but they were the Ravynari, so it doesn't take much speculation to surmise their intentions and reasoning." "She said something about me being a 'little arcane wielder' or along those lines. I remember that before she kicked me in the face." Lady Alsendra and Althira sighed in unison. "Yes, it would seem she somehow picked up on that. I suspect it was something you're responsible for, giving it away when you first ran into the Ravynari. Something Althira here will soon teach you how to avoid." Althira nodded in agreement. "Moving on from that. As for your injuries, you can give thanks to Althira for that. She has always had an affinity for the art of healing herbs and medicines. As for asking where we are, that was a rather foolish question, but I will disregard your folly. We are only a short distance from where you were attacked last night, just in the woods outside Thalmyr's Cradle. Eryn and Kenric got you here during the storm. I sent word to Althira immediately upon seeing what I did through the connection of the necklace. I wasn't sure which of us would arrive first; fortunately for you, it turned out we were not needed, as it were." She stopped to sip tea again, pinky out. "What you have conveniently failed to bring to attention is your vulgar use of power during the attack. That is certainly a question worthy of consideration and scrutiny." Althira chimed in before Alsendra could continue. "You mean what is 'claimed,' she did." Alsendra made no acknowledgment of her words, continuing. "You are only just learning of your abilities; you do not know what you are capable of or how to wield the arcane. You could very well have fried the poor beast." Alsendra flicked her hand towards Nova. I shook my head. "No, I would never hurt him. I had to do what I did to protect them." Lady Alsendra cut me off with her booming voice. "What you did was reckless and could have killed all three of them and yourself. You are full of arrogant ignorance to think you have any control over what you do not even begin to understand. You cannot fathom the consequences of wielding the arcane — yet." She paused with a deep inhale. "I can assure you with great zeal, Althira here will train you to have the responsibility and respect you currently lack."

"In any event, you have progressed more than halfway to Liraquor; at most, a day and a half of travel remains. Unless Alsendra here provides a generous escort for you herself." Lady Alsendra looked over at Althira with pursed lips. "Merciful heavens, Alsendra! You are intentionally toying with my patience and good graces." Lady Alsendra tittered under her breath, seeing only her chest move as she tried to conceal her amusement. "Well, nevermind that then, dear, it seems you will pick up where you left off with Eryn and Kenric." With a final, contented sigh, she tipped the teacup, savoring the last drop of the fragrant tea. "Now that we have finished our tea, I believe it is time Althira and I take our leave." They both got up, equally graceful as they were elegant, dresses flowing in mesmerizing cascades of fabric behind them. I had to wonder how they wore heels walking through grass, rocks, and dirt. That couldn't be the most practical choice they had available. Eryn and I trailed behind the two of them. Kenric was still tending to the horses. Eryn opened the door of the sleek black coach, pulling down the foldable step before giving Lady Alsendra a hand in, firmly shutting the door behind her. The two beautiful Friesians neighed in excitement as they tore off, both in the same unison clip-clop I remembered. It looked like they were going far faster than the coach should be able to travel, going out of sight a few moments later. Althira remained standing by us, turning to me and Eryn. "I will see you in Liraquor tomorrow. My building is the only Hall of Arcane Mastery and Excellence in Liraquor. I trust that finding it is entirely within your reasonable capabilities." "We will be there." I told her, trying to sound confident in my reassurance. I looked around for a moment, realizing I didn't see her coach. "I don't see your coach around." I said with questioning confusion. "Coach?" She scoffed the word out. "Honey, I wouldn't be seen in something as mundane as a coach." She grinned wider than I had ever seen Lady Alsendra smile. It wasn't big or particularly warm, but it was a smile, nonetheless. Proceeding in a direction opposite to that of the departing Lady Alsendra, she moved forward along the path. Althira snapped her fingers, and a large white horse appeared out of nowhere as if it were running out of the woods, pulling behind it a lavish chariot. The horse was huge, easily the size of a Clydesdale, with a slender neck and a solid, brilliant, shimmering white coat. It sported a long mane and tail, hair feathering around the legs, with what appeared to be a long, gray, spiraling horn coming out of its head. Blue eyes on the gigantic creature gleamed. All four hooves were gray at the top, before transitioning into black at the bottom, all four oddly uniform and equal. The chariot was ornate, painted glossy white with golden art and decorations affixed on top. Faces made of gold metal adorned the front of the chariot. One face laughing, one crying, one looking as if it were in agony or anguish. It pulled up beside Althira, never stopping but only slowing, Althira hopped on in one swift and elegant maneuver, grabbing the reins and lifting herself onto the back as it rode by as if she were weightless, she made the act look smooth and effortless. Althira let out a series of shouts: "Yee! Yuh! Yee! Yee!" as she flew off down the path in a spectacle, the fabric of the wine red high split dress flowing in rhythmic folds on the wind behind her like a dark brocade river, in stately ripples of old-world grace. I thought for a moment I could make out white feathered wings flapping off the gigantic horse as it barreled away, leaving a trail of dust in its wake. I could hear Althira cackling maniacally as the chariot went out of sight. After a moment, I turned to look at Eryn in utter confusion and dismay. "I'm sorry, but what in the nine realms of hell did I just see? Was that a unicorn?"

Chapter 14: Perseverance

I got the last of my belongings packed into my little handbag once
again; it was worth the trouble of unpacking everything to get myself
properly groomed and presentable. I felt human again, like myself.
Nova appeared at my side, sitting like a perfectly sculpted and
picturesque statue. He looked up at me with those big brown eyes,
backed by intelligence more human than animal, giving me that same
oddly almost human grin before pressing the side of his face and head
to my leg. I reached down with both hands, squeezing his head
against me as I rubbed his ears. "I'm happy you're okay too, big boy." I
crooned. He sat back once again and thereafter sprang up to run off in
a flash. I smiled; he was such a lovable being. I could see what Kenric
saw in him, and I partly suspected Kenric played a large part in
Nova's sunny disposition and cheerful personality. Kenric was folding
up the cloth from the tent neatly, Eryn snapping the sticks that held it
up before chucking them off to land where they may. Now that I got
my little sack of belongings up on Sylareth, I looked the horse over
more closely, rubbing my hands over the scrape on the front of her
chest and shoulder. Flashbacks came to me, of us tumbling to the
ground, the sound of her whinnies, the lightning crackling overhead,
the feeling of immense pain as I collided with the ground. I jolted back
to the present when I realized Kenric stood beside me, now speaking.
"Don't worry about the horses; I've been keeping a close eye on them
to ensure they heal well. They don't have any major injuries aside
from flesh wounds and some good bruising. Although I suspect they
will be skittish and suspicious of different things for a while, which is

completely understandable. We just need to give them a little more grace and understanding." Kenric leaned in, pressing the top of his forehead to Virelen's head. She closed her eyes, giving a few low snorts. "They don't understand why they were hurt the way they were, especially when they did everything right. If that Ravynari who hurt them wasn't already dead, I would repay her treatment of the animals tenfold." He shrugged before going back to packing up the rest of his things. He spoke the words I felt. She deserved the same treatment these poor creatures got. Eryn approached us, putting a handful of things in the saddlebag of Mareion, moving to pat him down the side. Mareion shook his head, swishing his tail. "Let us get going then."

We all hopped up on our horses without another word further, taking our assumed formations back on the path. In a way, it was nice to be back at our semi-fast riding pace. The sound of the horse's hooves clopping along in a soothing, melodic fashion eased some knotted tension inside me. I noticed Kenric sped up a bit to get closer to me. "You know, I wanted to thank you for not letting Nova get himself killed." I looked at him, feeling like I hadn't done enough. He continued. "Nova's smart enough to scare away someone hurting those he loves, but not smart enough to understand it's not worth putting himself in harm's way. He's always been so selfless like that, loving to a fault. He wouldn't have been able to hurt those Ravynari, not really; he doesn't have it in him to bite to draw blood, much less to kill." Nova ran up beside Kenric, letting out a bark as if he was part of the conversation. Kenric smiled at him. "That's right boy, you tell her." I let out a long breath before speaking. "When that Ravynari had the knife in hand ready to strike Nova, I didn't know what to do. I did what came naturally, which was to save Nova from being stabbed by that Ravynari at that moment. However, I think we should really thank Eryn. I would've been attacked by one of the Ravynari myself, had Eryn not appeared there, striking him down moments before. I froze, everything going in slow motion before deciding I should burn them all, but I don't even know if I would have been able to do that. I don't really control my abilities like that." Eryn, overhearing our conversation, slowed to get closer to us. "Don't give me more credit than I deserve, Miss Octavia. I nearly allowed all of us to get killed, or worse. The blades channeled extra energy to me, granting me isil-tyelle without extra need for my arcane. They reacted to the situation, heeding the call for help and answering with lethal ferocity. I merely assisted them." "Yeah, right, Eryn, stop being so stupid and just admit you're a killing beast wrapped in a suit." I rolled my eyes. He gave me a soft smile and laughed. "I am nothing of the sort, Miss Octavia. I told you I'm just good at a brief fight occasionally." Ugh, his overmodest position was so annoying. "Good at a brief fight," — as if he didn't cut down five Ravynari in just a minute or two without one of them having even the smallest chance to fight back. If I could do what he did, I'd never shut up about it. The thought of Ophelia just crossed my mind. She isn't ever going to believe what Eryn did or what he can do without seeing it. Part of me wishes she could have been with me to witness everything, but I was also relieved knowing she wasn't there for the attack.

We traveled on for a while, several hours I suspected, only slowing momentarily here and there to let the horses cool down and catch their breath. We were out of the wooded areas, now riding across grass-lined hills with rocky outcrops scattered throughout. There was a fork in the road ahead. Eryn stated that the scenery would remain the same if we turned left, but the horses would find the path easier to navigate. He said the right path would reward us with grand views, but warned that some sections were dangerous for the horses. He said both took about the same time to get to Liraquor, so that wouldn't be a deciding factor. He seemed fine with either, noting that coach or chariot would be forced to take the left path while we were free to do as we wished. I asked Kenric what he wanted to do since he hadn't spoken up, to which he expressed indifference, leaving the decision up to me. I finally decided we should go right. If we were going to take the same time either way, then I would rather see prettier scenery. We could give the horses time to traverse the terrain carefully if we needed to. All this was new to me, but the more I got to see, the better. So, we set off down the right path, only stopping briefly for Kenric to get Nova on the horse with him again. He said he would rather Nova be with him than run around if we were to go over any potentially hazardous terrain. After riding for another half hour, I saw a change coming on the horizon. Rocky outcrops lined our left side, talus littering the ground around some of the larger formations. To the right had been mostly flat grassland, with only a few rocky patches along the way. The closer we got to the strange-looking terrain, the more I realized it was an enormous cliff. There was no land I could see on the other side at all. We had been hearing roaring and rumbling noises for a while, but it just now dawned on me. I blurted out, "Is that water?!" Kenric and Eryn both confirmed it was, acting surprised I hadn't already come to that conclusion. Well, I didn't expect large waterfalls and the like in this type of terrain, but I had also traveled nowhere near here either, so I didn't know what to expect. We got close enough to the cliff face to see what was on the other side; my mouth dropped as the full effect of what was on the other side hit me.

It was the sea; I couldn't make out anything but dark blue water as far as the eye could see. The sound now came into full clarity. The crashing and roaring were most notable as the white-topped waves rolled in, caressing the cliffs before washing back out with a bubbling and gurgling exchange. Splashes and a faint slapping could be heard between the waves hitting the cliff face. A breeze started blowing a little stronger from the water. I closed my eyes as I inhaled; the air was remarkably clean, covering my senses in a sweet and salty essence. The air was cool and crisp, periodically catching the scent of mineral and seaweed undertones. This was a happy place. "Eryn, Kenric... I know this sounds strange, but I feel like I could remain here for days." They both laughed low before Eryn spoke. "I'm afraid many a person has felt the same way, falling victim to the sirens before leaping to their death." "Sirens?" I said the word with extra emphasis at the thought. "Yes, indeed, Miss Octavia, the waters like this here are their home." "I wouldn't say that to the selkies. They may think differently about who truly inhabits this area," Kenric interjected. I snapped my head in his direction. "Selkies live here? I only just met a selkie at the Rights a few days ago — well, several selkies — and you're now telling me I'm in their homelands?" I found it hard to believe; I could scarcely believe everything that had transpired in such a short time. The thought crossed my mind again: were all selkies as beautiful as those at the Rights? Were the ones I met from here or somewhere else? Eryn spoke up, breaking me from my thoughts. "There is a beach between here and Liraquor. It's a bit out of the way for our trip now, but how about we make a trip there soon after we're settled? We can spend the day on the sands, hunting for shells, and maybe meet some selkies if we're lucky." I know I beamed at him like a silly child, but that sincerely sounded amazing. I have never been to a beach, much less had someone who cared about me enough to take me. Ophelia and I were always too busy trying to survive on our own to take a trip or do anything, such as going to the beach. I don't think either of us ever even considered it. Now that I sat here in this spot, overlooking the water and smelling the crisp air, I wondered what else my older sister and I had missed out on. I think we needed to have a serious discussion about our lives after this mess was over, and I hoped it would eventually end, because I realized in this moment... I have many things left to see. I felt a new sense of fervor wash over me. It was time to reach Liraquor at once, to do what I needed to do to return to a normal life. "Let's go!" I yelled, taking off on Sylareth with a full sprint run, the wind gushing around us as we rushed by cliff-side and rock in a blur. Eryn and Kenric trailed behind me, yelling for me to slow down so Eryn could get ahead, but I didn't have the time for that. Althira Thorne was awaiting my arrival.

Chapter 15: Relished Ingress

The path we were on eventually made its way onto a larger path again, one more suitable for the travel of coaches or chariots like the one Althira rode on. I still wanted to know more about that. I had seen nothing like it or the horse pulling it. Or was that indeed a unicorn? I wasn't sure those even existed, but I believe I saw one with my very eyes just hours earlier as Althira rode away. We could clearly see the view of Liraquor coming up now, the cobblestone path we traveled going up an incline with large hills to both sides. Noticing Liraquor was almost hidden by the hills around, the town itself sat on a large, raised stretch of land with valleys on each side. The path made its way up, across a small stone bridge with a small stream traveling through a valley below before making its way through the doors of a massive stone gatehouse. The width of the gatehouse was great enough to span from valley to valley. Flanking towers at each end sat at the edge of the steep declines, overlooking everything around for what I suspected was a great distance. Spanning the top from tower to tower was a walkway. A wall standing about half the height of a human could be seen along the front. Expertly crafted crenels sat atop the low wall of the walkway. Massive ironclad wooden double doors were now partly closed as we approached; long ribbon banners of some sort draped down the walls of the gatehouse to each side of the doors. The banners were ruby red, with a design around them in dark yellow. A two-headed lion sat at the center of the banners, facing inwards towards the door on both sides. One of the lion's heads appeared to have goat's horns, while the tail of the lion's body looked to have the head of a snake at the end. Several men adorned with gleaming armor stood around the entrance. One guard on each side of the large wooden doors, just under the large hanging banners. There were several guards scattered about on the walkway above, wearing different armor, which looked to be chain mail and smaller open-face metal helmets sitting atop their heads. Each of the guards overhead carried crossbows, most being slung over their shoulders from what I could make out. We made our way up the cobblestone path at a slow and steady trot, not wanting to create any cause for concern. My curiosity got the better of me after a short while. "Eryn, why is there a lion with two heads and a snake for a tail on those banners?" He glanced between them before answering. "That is the Chimera, Miss Octavia. The creature of multiple beings in one body. The creature's lion-like attributes manifest as significant strength, fierce aggression, and assertive dominance. The goat part of the creature makes it cunning and unpredictable, as well as having the agility of both cat and goat. While the snake part makes it venomous and quick to strike. The creatures cannot be approached without their knowing it beforehand, as they can see in all directions at once. Their terrifying and ferocious nature makes the creature almost impossible to defeat. They are the embodiment of chaos, the impossible coexistence of incompatible elements working together in unison. They can even breathe fire, or so the stories go. I've never seen one myself." "They're real?!" I almost spat the words. I thought Eryn was talking about myths and legends, not a real animal. He let out a throaty laugh. "Yes, they are said to be real, but also unbelievably rare. It is said one has been seen in the very spot where Liraquor now stands, hence why you will see the creature on banners and tapestries around the town. You should ask Althira about it at some point. I believe she might have a relevant perspective to share." "Halt!" One guard demanded, all three of us coming to a jarring stop just yards from the gatehouse doors.

"Announce yourselves! Names and intent!" The voice was monotonous and harsh. Eryn, being upfront, spoke for both me and Kenric. "My name is Eryndor Roswyn, Chamberlain to Lady Alsendra of the High Council. We were ordered here to have an audience with Althira Thorne. These two people behind me are part of my constituents, and that is all you need to know." The words, imbued with power, left Eryn's lips, strong and resonating. It almost sounded as if Eryn dared the guard to question him further. You could hear a few of the guards talking low or whispering to each other while the one who originally addressed us cleared his throat. "My apologies. Welcome to Liraquor!" He barked orders for the guards to open the gate doors and make way. As we passed through the gatehouse, I looked above us, noticing a thick iron portcullis hanging just inside of both the first set of doors and the second. Archers peered through the murder holes overhead. They set this place up to trap and kill anyone who shouldn't be here. While it was clever, it was also a little concerning. Who was Liraquor trying to protect itself from with such a profusion of fail-safes and lethal force? Could there be some other reason, something I haven't considered, or that's been kept from me? Exiting the gatehouse, the full scope of Liraquor came into view; the sprawling city stretched before us, a symphony of sounds and smells rising from the bustling marketplace. The effect of its sheer size and majesty hit me with full force. This was more like a city than a town. Well-kept and clean, Liraquor had buildings of all shapes and sizes lining the unnecessarily wide streets as far as I could see in any direction. Even the cheaper looking wood frame buildings were well constructed, some even adorned with fancy and intricate carvings or paintings, all appearing flawless. Taller, more towering buildings made of stone popped up between the lower buildings, reminiscent of the way mushrooms might spring up from a forest floor. As they moved, the residents strolled along the pathways, going toward various locations. The people here were dressed in everything from the darkest black to the brightest, vibrant colors. I could see a plethora of races, ethnicities, and styles. This was so much more diverse than anything we saw back home in Faladorn. Everyone here felt equal, and that was certainly a change from the social status norms with the prestige expectations placed on wealth that Ophelia and I had become accustomed to knowing. After I had a moment to take it all in, I noticed Kenric was trying to get my attention to follow him and Eryn. Eryn proceeded down one street situated to the west. I nodded in acknowledgement to Kenric before nudging Sylareth to move after them.

There weren't many horses, just a few here and there, their hooves softly thudding on the path. Of those, a fair number were

Liraquor guards carrying javelins and spears. A few smaller carriages and coaches were parked along the sides of the street, in front of unique buildings. One building had beautiful orchestral music coming from it. Another building had butterflies of various blues, reds, and oranges fluttering all around the front along a small grass patch between the building and the street we rode on. Everything was so stunning here, vibrant and mesmerizing. I kept looking at the assortment of different shops and storefronts as we rode past, seeing how each one was different in its own way. Some were magical, while others were more mysterious. I stopped, unable to believe what my eyes saw in front of me. There was a large window across the front of a stone building with a large wooden floor platform built on the inside. In the window stood a tall elven girl. She was on the slim side while maintaining curves and wide hips. She had beautiful brown skin, light hair with white highlights in the longer sections, and... nearly naked. A far-too-small triangle of cloth attached with two strings barely covered her groin. Her breasts were out and bare, with only something that looked like small leaves covering her nipples, the outer perimeter still peeking around. The medium-height heels on her feet covered more skin than the rest of her nonexistent clothes. She was stunning, with an otherworldly quality about her. She stood there eyeing me intently as she danced, swaying her hips back and forth, bringing her arms up to caress around her head before letting her hands slide down her body sensually, giving me an alluring smile. I know my eyes were bulging out as my mouth hung open, but I had never seen such a display publicly. Here, in front of everyone walking by, at that? Kenric turned, scolding me to join him and quit my staring, but I simply pointed with remonstration. He looked at the girl and then back at me. "Would you like to hire her?" He asked as if he were being serious. I snapped my head around fast enough to feel a jarring. "Hire? Whatever for?" He sighed in exasperation. "Well, stop gawking with such interest, or we can go hire her to come along. She is a courtesan; this is what she does, being hired when she catches someone's eye. I imagine she has good wealth at that, seeing as that type of work is well respected and governed in Liraquor. She will be hired primarily by wealthy patrons to serve them in an array of ways. Intellectually, socially, and most notably sexually. Unless she prefers to be hired only for specific reasons, but that is up to the discretion of each individual courtesan." I almost gasped and had to catch myself before I allowed my mouth to fall open again. Kenric snorted. "That isn't even the most shocking thing in this town, so you're sure in for a treat." He turned away snickering as I saw Nova's tail flapping back and forth excitedly from his right side. Eryn spoke up loudly from just in front of Kenric. "Come along, Miss Octavia, the hall is just ahead." His words hit a nerve in the pit of my stomach, making me realize I was nervous now. I did not know what to expect. I drew a deep breath and nudged Sylareth to move on once again.

Eryn slowed before coming to a halt in front of a stone building. It was large, but not exceptionally tall. A single metal door stood at the entrance. The door was tall, but not overly grand or ornate. A canopy roof large enough for a small group to stand under stretched high above the door. I suspected both were more practical than aesthetic. I saw a plaque hanging just above the door overhead, "Hall of Arcane Mastery & Excellence". The words under the name read "Althira Thorne–Magister, High Council". Why hadn't I noticed before that she was a member of the High Council? I figured out she was some sort of teacher, so magister made sense. Part of me wonders how close Althira and Lady Alsendra really were to each other. What information did they have, and what confidential things are they keeping hidden from everyone, including private matters about myself? I had no way of knowing, but I aimed to find out anything I could from my time here. Eryn knocked on the iron door. His knuckles made a pinging noise against the metal that reverberated. After a few moments with no response, Eryn knocked again. A noise that resembled keys or some tools contacting the metal on the other side of the door could be heard. The lock on the door clicked a few times from the inside, opening immediately after. All three of us stood there waiting for someone to greet us or make themselves seen, staring into the innards of the hall. Eryn pushed the door, stepping in with one foot as it swung back. We heard a noise that sounded like a cry as the door bumped into something. We all peeked around, trying to see if anyone was there, when out of nowhere a short mass jumped out from behind the door screaming. It took off running right at us, going for Kenric's leg. Nova flailed around in Kenric's arms, barking up a storm in protest to get down after whatever that moving mass was. Kenric reacted faster than we had time to think, kicking the thing running along the floor. It went rolling and tumbling, letting out squeaking cries, until it came to a stop. All three of us stood there in silence as we watched with curiosity. The creature slowly got back on its feet. It couldn't have been any more than a foot tall, wiry and faintly humanoid. Its skin was something between deep violet and smoky charcoal; the skin smooth like onyx, while little hairs made themselves present at random. The creature's ears were tall, rigid, and pointy. "Eryn," I said with some concern, considering the creature, "is that a goblin of some sort?" The creature squeaked some fast chatter at us before it spoke actual words: "Your mother... was a goblin." I shrugged. "She probably is." Eryn and Kenric were nearly crying from bellowing with laughter. I didn't find it particularly amusing. I crossed my arms while waiting for them to recover. The little creature moved closer to us at a good pace. Its body seemed to blur around the edges as it passed through shadows and dimmer light. This creature — it was certainly different. There was an unnerving quiet as it moved, not appearing natural. Its little fingers were long and clawed with sharp nails. As it got closer, I could make out that it was wearing a necklace and bracelets. I held my hand to my mouth as I realized his jewelry was made of teeth and bone. The creature noticed my reaction and paused, a wild grin spreading across its face, displaying rows of needle-like teeth. Its eyes were narrow and gleaming with silver-white light. Eryn and Kenric stared wide-eyed at the thing. "That is no goblin." Eryn looked as confused as I felt about what the thing might be. Although the creature stood shorter than a child's knee, it possessed an undeniable and imposing sense of danger. A voice came from directly behind us, breaking the silence and making us all jump.

Chapter 16: Dubious Salutations

Althira stood directly behind us. "I see you have met Vexil." The little creature, Vexil, I guess he was called, was laughing at us in an assortment of squeaking noises. Barely five minutes into our arrival, and I was already a bundle of nerves, my composure utterly shattered. Althira looked at Vexil before rolling her eyes lightly. "Don't mind him; he just likes to enjoy himself. Though Vexil is not a goblin. He is far more useful and cunning than any goblin." Vexil let out a whistle when Althira said that. She continued. "He is a gremlin. A shadow gremlin, also known as a Duskkin, if I'm being precise. He is my loyal servant." With a strange tut-tut, Eryn's lips formed a sound of disapproval. "Servant? You imprison the poor creature?" Althira cackled. "Imprison? Heavens no, and there's no need for the self-righteousness hun, it's not a good look on you. I've tried to get rid of him. He comes right back." After we all stared at her for a moment without speaking, she clicked her tongue. "Are all of you equally dense? What kind of charity is Alsendra running in Faladorn?" Kenric spoke, but Althira held up her hand, not too different from the way Lady Alsendra does. "Let me clarify this one time so that we can move on with more important matters, seeing as how all of you are going to be hung up on this unimportant trivia. I am Althira Thorne, Magister of this hall. Do you understand what that means?" "That you are like a teacher?" I said questioningly. She continued. "Is that the only thing you think I am? Don't answer that." Her hand swished as she spoke. "I don't want to know. While I am a teacher of sorts, that is true, I am much, much more." She grinned facetiously. "I am the Magister Mortis

Velum, also known as the Death Veil. That makes me a master of illusion, shadowmancy, necromancy, and secrecy. So yes, indeed, I can teach those gifted enough in the arcane to study my craft. Aside from that, Duskkins like Vexil are drawn to someone as fluent in the dark arts as I am. He is also incredibly useful, as I mentioned previously. He excels in managing curses, extinguishing light, and silently removing any unwanted guests from my sanctum without leaving a trace." Vexil giggled at that. The thing was still unsettling. "He will follow my instructions, but he is also utterly amoral. To him, there is no right or wrong; there is only do or do not. It would be advisable not to test him or to act foolishly. He will also start playing tricks if he gets bored, so notify me at once if he acts out too badly. Now that we have that out of the way, can we proceed?" We all nodded in unison. "Finally! Right this way." Althira turned in the blink of an eye, her high-slit dress flowing around her legs as she did.

We followed her down a corridor. The building had cosmetically appealing wood floors, dark and dented in the center from years of walking in high heels, I suspected. Stone arches crossed the corridor from side to side, spaced apart at satisfying equal spacing. Torches were positioned on either side of the arches, with a few in between. Even though the sun was almost down, I could make out meticulously detailed stained-glass windows overhead. Althira stopped as we entered a large room with a rounded ceiling above. The room was rather plain, almost uncomfortably bare. The walls and rounded ceiling were completely bare, save for the dark wood floor that creaked under our feet. "This is the resonance room." Althira's voice echoed loudly in the capacious air around us. "This is a place that will echo the arcane around inside, giving the wielder the ability to master incredible illusions. Creating illusions they would otherwise not be capable of creating." "I don't think I can do anything like that," Althira cut me off. "That is for me to find out. As you are right now, I'm surprised you can walk bipedally without falling over. Come along now." She started walking off again as we followed, soon taking a turn behind her as she went through a set of double swinging doors and down some stairs. "There's another level underground?" It might have been a foolish question, but I had seen nothing like it. Althira made a nasal noise. "A level? Who's to say there aren't many?" All three of us glared at her, unable to tell if she was joking or being serious. She didn't elaborate as she moved through a couple more turns. We reached another door. This one was heavy-duty and steel. Althira stopped just in front of it. "Vexil, if you would be so kind." The gremlin stepped forth, blending into the shadow made by a stone pillar in front of a torch. Vexil became nearly impossible to see — no, nearly invisible as he blended in to become one with the shadows. For a fleeting moment, once or twice, I thought I saw the shadow moving but couldn't make out anything distinguishable. A moment later we heard a noise on the other side of the door, like keys or tools against the metal, then the door flung open. Vexil walked out without a sound, with a wide grin on his face. Althira headed through. When we reached the other side of the door, we stood frozen, seized by awe and disbelief. We were standing in a cavernous underground room, possibly even a cave made into a type of room. Dirt was on the floor below us, vines crawled up various walls, and tree and plant roots hung down through the ceiling above. This room was far darker than the others we had been in. I could just make out something on the walls that looked like sigils made of iron. The air was cool, far cooler than it was above ground, smelling metallic, as if tinged with dry blood. I could also make out the scent of several dried herbs. The beam of Althira's torch cut through the darkness, illuminating only a few yards in front of us; the air was thick with the smell of damp earth and decay. In the place where the light left to become darkness, a fog seemed to roll in just inside the light before dissipating. I swore for a moment I could hear whispers in the air, but disregarded them. Althira spoke up, giving me a start. "This is the vivisectum. It is a multipurpose room. Used for necromancy, both normal and forbidden, as well as secrecy. Part of practicing the forbidden is knowing how to practice secrecy." Eryn let out a "hmph" but didn't elaborate. I wondered what had perturbed him. It was possibly the necromancy talk, or the mention of the forbidden. I'm going to ask him about it later when Althira isn't around, unless I forget about it. Althira spoke again as she was moving toward the door with us following behind. "There are a few other rooms we may use for your testing and training, but these are going to be the two we start with. I need to see where to take you from there." After leaving the vivisectum, we came to a hall with several doors on each side and a set of doors at the end. "This will be where you sleep for now; you can pick any room you like. The showers are at the end of the hall; you can thank the natural hot springs running through this place for the warm flowing water. I do not have any other students at this time, so you will have the dormitory to yourselves. Clean linens are in the cupboards at the end of the hall, the small door on the right before entering the double doors to the showers." "Where are the other students?" Kenric asked with a raised eyebrow. Althira shrugged. "They didn't make it." She continued on without missing a beat. "I will make sure the horses tied up out front are brought around to be properly stabled and tended to." She turned to Kenric. "And make sure that beast doesn't soil my hardwood floors. Vexil would have to get rid of the poor thing if that happened." She said it almost laughingly. "Now, I suggest you get yourselves a good night's rest, because tomorrow is going to be a trying day for you. I finally get to find out for myself what you're really made of, my sweet." She said the last part with a small smile. "Let us hope Alsendra is correct about you, or you could come out a little worse for wear." She walked off cackling to herself. We all got ourselves ready for bed, picking a room. They were all the same as far as I could tell, so I just grabbed the one next door to Kenric. Eryn picked the room on the other side of me at first, then moved to a room closer to the entrance at the end of the hall. He seemed to think he would be better able to protect everyone from there should there be any unwanted arrivals during the night.

My eyes jerked open as something startled me awake. I could feel a small weight crawling over my legs, making its way up the bed. I kicked my feet up in the air screaming, not able to see anything, but hearing a thud on the floor near the bed. The door burst open, Kenric coming in behind it, Nova on alert right behind him. Kenric held a torch in hand. I looked around in a panic, trying to find what woke me, only able to point at the end of the bed and then at the floor. Kenric seemed to understand, moving towards the end of the bed to look around the other side. Without warning, Nova went into a frenzy, barking and yipping. I pulled the blanket up to my neck as I still sat straight up in bed, ready to cover my face if something popped out of the darkness. Then Nova shot out the door at breakneck speed, nose to the ground and tail high in the air. There was a commotion in the hall outside. Kenric moved to look out the door as we could hear Nova running down the hall at a full run. Nova let out a couple of yips of startled excitement from down the hall. I got out of bed to stand by Kenric, trying to see what was going on. I hear Eryn from down the hall by the entrance. "What in the name of the gods is going on down there?" Kenric and I both looked at him and shrugged. Without warning, we jumped as Nova took off, coming back down the hall at a barreling run as if something was after him. Kenric stepped out into the hall to calm Nova, or at the very least to see what was after him. As Nova got closer, shooting past us in nearly a blur of movement, we heard a squeaky laugh of hysterics going by with him. Then I saw it; that unsettling little gremlin was holding onto the poor poodle's tail as they ran around in unbound chaos. "Vexil!" I yelled while pointing. Eryn moved as Nova approached him. Gods, he was quick. Eryn grabbed Nova by the collar, causing both to spin around from the momentum. Eryn slapped Nova's tail with one swift movement, Vexil flying off as the Duskkin flew to land several yards away. He lay there, making squeaky, groaning noises. Just then, Althira burst through the entrance of the dormitory hall. "What in all the realms is going on down here, and why is there enough noise to wake the dead!" She sounded vexed as she stood there in a beautiful cream-colored silk gown, torch in hand. Her hair was braided to one side, draping over her shoulder with a soft caress. We all looked at her before pointing to Vexil, the gremlin now standing with a mischievous smile on his face. "Bah!" She bit the sound out. "This meaningless nonsense roused me from my beauty sleep?!" She almost had a look of scorn. "Vexil, OUT!" she yelled the word with such power; the very walls resonated with the sound. "One more outburst and I'm going to banish you to the nether!" He took off at a sprint for the door, chattering to himself nonstop as he went. Althira turned back to us. "Seeing as how all of you are up and so eager to start the day, I will see you in precisely thirty minutes in the resonance room. We might as well get an early start." She spun around with a scowl, leaving without another word. I turned to look at Kenric. "Great, now we start our day with her in a bad mood." I sighed.

Chapter 17: Rationalization, Intelligence, and Discernment

As we entered the resonance room, Althira was standing in the center of the room with her hands lightly touching fingers as she held them in front of her in a nonchalant, yet elegant demeanor. She was wearing a fitted, all-black dress. It was a one-shoulder dress, wrapping around over her right shoulder. The dress was fitted down to her hips, from there draping down in a cascade of flowing fabric. There was one high slit up to her hip on her left side, opposite the fabric over her right shoulder, giving the dress an overall oddly satisfying A-symmetry. She stood with the left leg bent out of the slit of the dress, showing she was wearing silver sparkling heels under it. What is with Lady Alsendra and Althira always dressing so formally, while wearing the most uncomfortable-looking heels? I really felt like a peasant around them. She didn't speak until we were all standing before her. "Eryn, Kenric, go find yourselves something to do. The kitchen is down the corridor in the center, then to the left. You are welcome to help yourselves." They hesitated, causing Althira to get testy. "If you do not want food, you are welcome to go stand outside twiddling your thumbs if you otherwise cannot occupy yourselves. Now go!" The words echoed around the round room before trailing off. Eryn and Kenric made their way out, Nova trailing behind. Althira said nothing for a long while as she stood there looking me up and down, as if trying to determine something. She broke the silence, this time speaking more softly. "Gods, what has Alsendra burdened me with?" I attempted to speak back, but she held up her hand just as I opened my mouth. "This is a time for you to listen; you are to speak only when spoken to and then only in answering a question." I nodded. "Now that we have that established. Alsendra said you are untrained and uneducated — that part is painfully clear, but do you understand the risk Alsendra puts herself in by bringing you to me? Therefore, putting myself at risk. I very much hope you can make it worth our efforts, at least try not to disappoint." Again, I bobbed my head in a brief nod to show I was listening. "Now, before we begin, I want you to understand the fundamentals of the arcane. To successfully wield the arcane with confidence, you will need to remember three things: rationalization, intelligence, and discernment. Remember it as R.I.D. If you forget, you can ask yourself, 'How can I rid myself of this enemy?' You must rationalize the scenario, meaning you must determine in any instance the best course of action and the most effective ways to wield the arcane. Then comes the intelligence. This requires you to know how to use that rationality, how to appropriately react, and when to be on the offensive rather than the defensive. That is where discernment comes in. You must be able to judge the surrounding dangers based on your conclusions from intelligence accordingly. Ask yourself, 'What should I react to first in this moment?' That could very well be the deciding factor between life and death." I nodded before she continued. "Alright, let us move forward."

She walked around me slowly in a large circle, as if she were a wolf to prey. "I would naturally assume that when you performed your Rights, as someone previously uneducated, you would have used some sort of focus point?" I nodded again. "That was a question. Answer." "Yes, I used the purple candle and focused the flame before that devil came to life." She stopped. "Purple?" I nodded. "Lilac or indigo?" I thought for a split second. "Indigo, but darker, possibly." "Interesting. Maybe you have potential. That remains to be seen, however." She continued her slow walk around me, posture straight. "Tell me, what was your desire when you willed the being into existence?" I shrugged. "I'm not sure if I'm being honest. I felt the nudge at my back, and the voice came to help, so I opened myself up to it." She stopped again before screeching out. "Voice?!" She paused before speaking in a calmer manner. "Alsendra failed to mention that. Has the voice made itself known to you before?" "It has, but never in that way. I've always been able to hear a faint voice on the wind or have an uncanny knack for intuition, but what happened at the Rights was something altogether different. It told me a series of words to repeat, which I did. Then fire from the candle went up one arm and down the other before a poof and that thing roared to life." I held up my arms in exasperation. I didn't know how to explain what had happened. Her eyes were wide. I tried to read something behind her expression, but I couldn't make out anything specific that would be telling. She slowly made her way back to stand in front of me before speaking again. "Do you know why the Rights are performed, why the ceremony is called The Rights, and why we started it all in the first place?" I shook my head. I truly did not know. She continued. "The Rights were instituted to discern those capable of wielding the arcane with such fluency that it may take form and manifest in some tangible way. Many people are born with the arcane, but we needed a way to weed out the special from those who can merely light a candle. The extraordinarily capable are few. However, when those select few are identified, they are inducted onto the High Council after properly honing their abilities. This is the reason every member of the High Council is exceptionally gifted in at least one area, sometimes multiple areas. That would also be the reason so many families with influence strive so hard to get their kids through the Rights. Having a child as a member of the High Council would be something to boast about and fuel egos. From that, the Rights were born. Not named rites in a ritual sense, but for granting one's birthright — that being their earned claim to commune with the arcane, thus granting you the entitlement to the gift of the Arcane. That naming choice was meant to prevent any lack of clarity or mix-ups. Alsendra was put in charge of hand-selecting the participants and overseeing the Rights because of her affluent gift of sight. She can see those with potential and the potential outcomes. That is why you were chosen. However, it would seem she often has a rather difficult time seeing what you will conjure up with your arcane, as well as missing occasional details surrounding you. That has led her to believe you are one of the Mortis Velum. Alsendra has the same reactions to me, so she's well accustomed to the signs. Seeing as how I am the only Mortis Velum Magister in existence, you were brought here before me to find out that very thing. I am currently the only Veil on the High Council. If you are indeed one of us, and you can already manifest flame and fire with no prior education, I fear Alsendra's assumptions about how dire the situation is would be correct. For that specific reason, the situation demands immediate attention." There was a pause where neither of us said anything before I asked a question. "What exactly is the Mortis Velum?" She looked at me as if she were dumbfounded for only a moment before answering. "A Mortis Velum is what I am, what I have already told you I am capable of, and what I practice. We are the Death Veils. Masters of the dark arts, as some would call it, but we are mostly referred to as the Veiled because of our mystery, trickery, and secrecy. The velum, or veil, refers to the same thing, but when referencing the velum, you would be speaking about what a Mortis Velum practices and the shadows they surround themselves in, and so on and so forth. The words are used interchangeably by most mages. I've always liked the way Mortis Velum rolled off the tongue, personally. We Mortis Velum move in shadow, breathe life into death, turn life into death, all while also possessing the ability to curse. Some of us can have their arcane take many forms through their illusory abilities." She smiled facetiously once again. "How about I stop this chatter and show you what a Mortis Velum truly is so you can fully understand?"

I felt a sharp gust of wind blow by me just a moment before Althira's hair fluttered up, then down again. It felt as though the pressure in the air of the entire room changed, threatening to take my breath away. The air was thick, making each breath feel labored. Althira held up her hand, gave one quick snap, and then she was gone. Vanished without a trace. There was no light or sparkle; she was just gone. I looked around in confusion, where thereafter, without warning, I was surrounded by six Althiras. All identical, I had no way of knowing which one was the real one or if there even was a real one. They held out their arms; dark smoke rolled from them in the same way smoke would roll out of a choking chimney. The smoke surrounded me with a spiraling twist, spinning as it engulfed me, obscuring my vision like being inside of a nightmare. The smoke went up my nose, making me choke. As I opened my mouth, the smoke rushed in; I was gasping for air as I clawed at my neck in panic. The smoke wrapped around my arms, pulling them down, away from my throat. I thought I could make out hands made from smoke and shade, grabbing me from within the smoke. I tried to scream, but I couldn't get enough air. Then I heard a noise from what I thought was the direction of the entrance to this room. The smoke pulled out of me, whipping away like a coil unwinding. I was on my knees as I recovered my breath. Althira was nowhere to be seen as I looked around, then at the door I spotted someone coming into the room. "Ophelia!" I hollered as I jumped up in a sprint. Just as I got a few feet from her, she stopped. A hooded person stepped up behind her, their arm reaching around her as it held a knife to her throat, blood seeping down the front of her gray top.

Chapter 18: Dissimulation and Subterfuge

I cried out in horror as Ophelia stood there, eyes wide, her hands on
the arm around her neck before she stumbled forward, but the entire
room went black. I held my hands out in front of me to feel around, not
even being able to see my arms, moving in what I thought was the
direction Ophelia had been in. Then I heard her crying for help from
behind me. I swung around, running at full sprint into the complete
blindness towards where I heard her cries. Everything stopped as the
air felt stale. There were no movements or sounds to be heard. The
blackness in the air thinned out as a couple of forms took shape near
me as it cleared. Ophelia was on her knees, knife still to her throat,
blood running down from the corners of her mouth. I felt cold as ice as
I saw what stood behind her. The Ravynari man from the attack, the
one who stood over me sniffing and wagging his tongue. I shuddered
to my core. The Ravynari had a smaller blade to Ophelia's throat,
bending down to sniff her hair as the thought left my mind. He
grinned at me, his disgustingly filed teeth making themselves visible.
The Ravynari reached down, grabbing a fistful of Ophelia's beautiful
hair, twisting it around as pieces pulled out from her scalp. She cried
out. "Stop!" I yelled as loudly as I could, but he just grinned again. The
Ravynari pulled her up by the hair until she was standing in front of
him. He leaned in from behind, breathing in her scent, and then his
tongue darted out to lick her neck and ear. Ophelia jerked, trying to get
away as he held on to a fistful of hair. He grinned at me again before
hissing out his words. "Don't worry. After I make sure she's dead, you
can watch me have fun with her body. Then you can have a turn." My

stomach turned with revulsion.

He took the blade of the knife, running it along Ophelia's chest, leaving behind a cut trickling with blood. "I'm going to enjoy cutting this one up, nice and slow." Ophelia screamed an ear-piercing scream as he cut her side. I felt a wrath ignite in me so hot and fast; I had to focus on pulling in jagged breaths from the surrounding air. Wind swirled up around me, making my ears pop and ring. All I could see was red. I was engulfed in flames. I heard the voice from a fiery chasm belch, "Your wrath burneth." I looked up as the infernal devil stood over me once again, just as it had the night of the Rights. I saw the Ravynari man bringing his arm back to position the knife at Ophelia's throat. She cried out in a squeal of panic, "Octavia!" I let the wrath flow from me, unbridled and unchecked. I swung my arm. Something that looked like a sword of flaming ice and ember cut through the air, taking out the Ravynari in one clean swoop. He still moved, which meant he was still alive. I pulled the power into me. That voice above spoke, "Giveth thy desire, Master." I willed my strength into him with everything I had. I was going to make sure this scum of the earth never hurt another person again. The infernal devil let out a bellowing war cry, bringing the large wings down to flap. Fire and ash rushed out from under us in every direction. I saw Ophelia get up, flashing with what looked like a mirage before standing directly in front of me. In the blink of an eye, Althira stood where Ophelia had been. "Octavia, stop this at once! It was merely illusion and shadowmancy. Dissimulation! A subterfuge! None of it is real!" I saw more red. She played these cruel tricks on me to make me get upset? She was about to find out what upset looked like. I reacted without thinking, hurling plumes of hellfire and ember forward at Althira. In a split second, she raised her arm, positioning it in front of her face with graceful ease. Black smoke and shadow engulfed her body. She pushed the black smoke outwards into the flame, taking the form of an enormous snake's head. I shut my eyes tightly as the snake struck right at me. It hit me, knocking me back through the air, sending me to land on my back.

I opened my eyes; the unsettling little Duskkin was inches away from my face, his long, skinny fingers and claws poking at my lips. I jerked up, hitting the thing with my head, causing it to tumble back. Althira stood close to me, with the same pose she had when we first entered the resonance room. "Glad to see you're back." She shifted her weight slightly. "Congratulations, hun, you have failed miserably. If we have learned one thing today, it is that you are indeed ignorant and in grave need of training and education. Alsendra was correct about that." — "Now that you are done with your cute fire tricks. Let us go back even further. Tell me... do you know why the High Council was created, long before the Rights existed? Do you know what their duties and responsibilities are?" I shook my head. "That was a question, speak!" The power in her voice sent an icy chill down my spine. Vexil flinched, his pointy ears pulling back in response. "You already said the Council created the Rights to find the most powerful arcane wielders, or something like that, so I would assume the Council was created to be an all-powerful governing body?" Althira scowled. "You indeed suffer from involuntary logorrhea, as Alsendra said. There is no shortage of idiosyncrasies coming out of your open mouth." I rolled my eyes. Quicker than I had time to see what was coming, I glimpsed a solidified smoking object hurtling right at me. I tried to jump, but it was too late. With a rush, the object slammed into my leg behind the knee, buckling it and forcing me to the ground. What had hit me looked like a long, thick rod of smoke, coming from Althira's arm as it slowly dissipated in front of me. "Do not roll your eyes at me when I am here speaking the truth, girl. I am here trying to give you invaluable knowledge that not everyone is fortunate enough to get. If you were in control of your arcane, that would never have touched you." She clicked her tongue.

"You should've learned this information before you even learned of your arcane; however, I have no choice but to overlook that, seeing as how that ship has long sailed." She paused for a moment, appearing to mew at her jaw. "The High Council is many things. Authority, governing, protector, and wielder. The High Council did not create the law; we only listened. We listen to the voice of the arcane when it speaks. The voice is not that of a god, nor of a spirit, but it is the pure manifestation of the raw consciousness of the arcane. The Council members are not rulers; we are stewards. We heed the call of the arcane. We are the protectors, healers, and watchers. But we never rule. A primeval arcane force communicates with rare individuals. Some hear it through fire or water; you hear it on the wind, it would seem. Only the humble or the worthy can hear it. They are chosen to protect, not to control. The High Council is formed from these; they are known as the First Listeners. Originally being six mages to hear the voice first, they came together to create the High Council. It was later realized that every mage who heard the voice possessed incredible control over the arcane. Far more adept at wielding the power than a regular arcane wielder, because we can channel the purest, raw form of Arcane. Every one of the High Council members has heard the voice; that is why there are so very few of us. And I'm afraid this is just the beginning of what you will come to understand, but you need to get a grasp of the basics before I can hope to help you. You understand?" I nodded, reeling at the abundance of information. "I didn't know any of that." I said the words with some confusion behind them. "Well, obviously, just look at you," Althira motioned at me with her hands as I still sat on the ground. "Get up; your lesson is far from over."

Chapter 19: Vulgar and Licentious

Althira resumed pacing around me as she proceeded with her teaching. "Alsendra was correct in stating your blatant and foolish display of power. You do not know what it means to commune with the arcane, the gift that has been given to you. You cannot wield power such as yours with reckless abandon. You will end up killing someone by mere accident, potentially yourself. You indeed possess the gift of shadowmancy; to what end remains to be seen. The fire trickery you use is nothing more than an illusion you manifest, but it is no less lethal than a veritable devil of fire and flame. It will burn and incinerate all the same. You can manipulate the surrounding elements to take the form of whatever you need at the moment, but you only know what first came to you." Althira stopped pacing in the surrounding circle. "Vexil!" She yelled the gremlin's name. He popped up in her shadow before her. I hadn't seen the creature walk up or where he came from; it was as if he had corporealized from the shadows themselves. He made some singsong chatter before Althira spoke. "I believe we are in need of your assistance. Octavia just advanced to her first lesson in curses and binding. How about you help us teach her a lesson in defense?" The Duskkin grinned wildly, turning to glare at me. Goosebumps peppered my skin in response. He giggled maniacally for a moment before halting. Vexil progressed into some type of chant that sounded like singing a pleasant song, swaying back and forth, then with no time for reaction he spat on my leg. I gasped in disbelief. Althira stood by observing, seemingly unfazed by what had happened. I noticed the spit burned my leg. I raised the leg of my now tattered cloth britches; the spit had gone through the pant leg to my skin. Where it touched my skin, the skin blistered and wrinkled, oozing around the perimeter of the wound, skin puckered into taut ridges around the edges, like that of an old map. I panicked, ripping at the leg of my britches. I tried to use the fabric to wipe my skin, but it was futile. The damage was done, and it was as if there was nothing there causing the burning. As the wound continued to burn, I groaned in a frenzied panic. Watching in horror, black lines spread from the wound, traveling up my leg, as if they were worms burrowing through the innards of an apple. I could feel the burrowing under my skin. I grabbed and clawed at the skin to stop it, only for it to spread further. Althira stood there, same posh pose, unmoving.

"Octavia, rationalization, intelligence, and discernment. You learned this just moments earlier. What are you going to do to stop this, or are you going to allow a simple curse to consume you?" A nudge at my back as I heard the voice speak. "Child, we are one." I opened myself up to it; I instantly lit up in surrounding flames. Althira stood, not moving or showing any expression. I couldn't think clearly, not with my leg melting in front of my eyes with agonizing pain. My panic consumed me in a flurry of emotions. Fear and anger at the forefront. I acted instinctively; I'd fry the gremlin doing this to me. That would stop this. As if knowing what I would do before I did it, the Duskkin stepped back quickly, getting between Althira's legs. Vexil glanced up at Althira with a bunch of chatter, pointing at me. Althira glanced at him, but didn't react. I felt the burning almost to the top of my thigh. Panic and fear soared through me in a double dose. In a burst of aggression, I unleashed a fire and ember attack, originally targeting Vexil; however, the flames mistakenly engulfed Althira. Once again, black smoke and shadow seemed to swallow her, acting as a shield for her and the gremlin. I could hear Vexil inside cackling. My anger grew into furious wrath in an instant. I lashed back out, and a piece of the scorching devil above, resembling a blazing arm, descended towards them. As the hand slapped over Althira, ash and ember flew in every direction, but nothing happened at all. The smoke and shadow shield remained. It cleared around Althira slightly, just enough to see her face. "Are we done with the childish outbursts now, hun?" My thigh was throbbing with relentless agony. I glared ahead. Althira pressed my buttons in the worst way, and she knew it. That made me even angrier. It was fuel to the flames, real or not. I felt the flames, a fiery embrace, pulsing in plumes, starting from my feet and moving up my body. One pulse, then another, leaving the top of my body to fuel the infernal devil standing above me. Althira rolled her eyes. She stuck both arms straight out to her sides, throwing her head back. She lifted off the ground slightly, appearing to float weightlessly, mere inches above the wooden floor. Then, with the tiniest of poofs, she was gone. Now, standing where she had previously stood, was a dragon. It was all white, scales the color of the brightest light you can imagine, light shimmering off the scales with a gold tone over the entire being. The texture of the scales reminded me of a porcelain vase. It wasn't particularly large, but it was terrifying. The dragon shook its leathery wings; the fine scales underneath shimmered in the light as the gold tones evoked the memory of a burning autumn sunset. The dragon gave one powerful flap of its wings with a whoosh before ascending through the air. As it flew, catching my attention, I saw the dragon clutch something in its claws. It was Vexil. I cried out in pain as my leg was now unbearable. He laughed and danced at me in taunt. I caught my breath as I felt the pain now working up my hips. In the excitement of panic, I raised my arm, shooting fire at the dragon in an instant. It came erupting from me like a geyser of molten lava. The dragon simply tucked its wings and rolled, ducking down before swooping back up, quicker than any fire could reach it. Then the dragon turned its head toward me, narrow silver eyes drawing my full attention. Holding a familiar, unsettling glint, like Vexil's, I was left wondering how this beast was Althira. I was lost in my observations of the dragon when suddenly it opened its mouth and a frigid, devastating funnel of ice and hail blasted towards me. Once again, sending me flying back and then landing flat on my back.

I sat up, panicked, as I felt the curse wiggling its way up my abdomen, almost up to the sides of my chest by this point. I spared a glance around. Althira stood in the center of the room, once again looking at me with a look of burning vitriol. My heart skipped a beat, but she did nothing. I saw the Duskkin at her feet, grinning wide with malice. Althira spoke, "Vexil, drop it for now." The gremlin did another chant that sounded like a song, and I could instantly feel the curse leaving my body. Althira still looked fuming mad. "Do you see why you fail? You think you can flaunt raw power when that does nothing to help you. The way you wield your gift is vulgar and licentious. It is disrespectful of your gifts to whore them out in this way. You hear the voice of the arcane; I give you that much." She paused before bringing one arm up to rest a finger under her chin, as to concentrate. "Twice now you have stood here before me, given the opportunity to show me why Alsendra placed so much faith in you. Yet both times you have as good as spat in her face." "Well, it's not as if I—" "SILENCE!" Althira almost bellowed the word, the walls shaking with the reverberation. Vexil ducked behind her legs. "Do not mistake my casual benevolence for tolerance. You indeed have a problem knowing when to speak. If you can't intelligently and methodically use your abilities to save your own life from a simple curse or to see through shadowmancy illusions, you may very well be lost to me. This concludes our session for now. We will resume tomorrow morning. I need time to contemplate." She twirled, making way to the door without another word. I slowly pushed myself to my feet, checking my leg where it had been burning, only to find it looked like it did before the entire ordeal. My back and butt had to be thoroughly bruised after the two times Althira had knocked me flat today. I'll certainly feel that worse tomorrow. I glanced around the resonance room as I made my way out, wondering how, with everything that had happened, the room still looked the same. There were no burn marks or damage, no large marks on the wood floor, and no broken walls. I wondered if it had been built with something sturdier. I exited the resonance room to see Vexil zipping down the corridor, cackling and chattering with a grin on his face as if he was off to have the time of his life.

   I heard voices speaking after exiting the room, sounded like Eryn and Kenric were having a conversation. I figured I would go find them; I was done with Althira for the day, and my mind was too weary to consider anything else. They must have been down the corridor where Althira told them the kitchen was located. I followed the sound of their voices until I reached the doorway where they were located. I peeked inside, my head slowly appearing as I rounded the corner. Eryn's guttural laughter echoed through the room as Kenric, squatting on the floor, waddled like a strange creature, playfully jabbing at the air with his sword, the metallic clang adding to the absurdity. I concluded it must be a goblin Kenric was imitating. I walked through the door, Eryn taking his hat off to bow to me as I entered with a "Miss Octavia." Kenric hopped up and gave me a smile. Nova was sitting on what looked like a large blanket of some sort, chewing on something. It looked as though it might be a bone. My eyes about left my face when I saw what was on the table. In a large basket with a red piece of linen were rolls. My mouth watered just glancing at the big, fluffy pieces of bread. I ran to grab one. Eryn chuckled. Wait until she finds the pot roast stew. I whirled around with the buttery roll half in my mouth. "Stew… like with beef?!" I mumbled the words out over the bread. Kenric and Eryn laughed softly. "Why don't you take a seat, Miss Octavia? Kenric and I will get you a warm bowl". I sat down, grinning like a fool. Now this was the pick me up I needed. There was nothing that could lift my spirits like a good hearty meal, especially with all the fresh injuries I sustained from the day. Eryn sat the bowl in front of me only moments later. Steam wafted up from the brown gravy to hit my nose. Letting the delicious meat juices and spices tease my senses, I breathed in deeply. I sat there like that until I couldn't stand it, digging into the stew in what I know must have been the most unladylike way possible, but I didn't care. After I had finished, I sat back, wincing as my sore back contacted the hard wooden chair. Eryn, noticing my wince, asked how my studies had gone and if anything of importance had happened. I gave him a quick rundown of the events, leaving out some of the more concerning parts. After that, it was getting dark. We hadn't seen Althira yet, but I suspected she was still in a broody mood. I suggested we go get ready for bed, because I needed the warm showers and to allow my body to recover. Thus the day was concluded, and we were carried into sleep's quiet realm.

Chapter 20: Unbecoming Visitants

"How are you feeling this morning, Miss Octavia?" Eryn was always
so mannerly and chipper, no matter the time of day. I groaned before
answering. "I'm doing surprisingly better this morning, considering
how sore I was last night. The tea and tincture that Althira had you
bring for me before I went to bed were remarkably helpful." Althira
had told Eryn to have me take the herbal medicines, with the promise
that it would have me fully recovered by morning. While I wouldn't
say I was fully recovered, I would say I was almost miraculously
better given the circumstances. Kenric walked past where Eryn and I
were standing in the dormitory hall, Nova trotting alongside, as a
smell caught my nose. "Is that coffee?" He giggled and took off at a jog,
holding his cup carefully. "This is mine, go get your own!" I grumbled
and groaned, but decided I would begrudgingly head to the kitchen for
coffee, possibly getting a bite to eat if I could find anything. "Would
you like to come?" I asked Eryn, seeing as he didn't appear to have
made it to the kitchen yet. "Don't mind if I do, Miss Octavia." Eryn
gave me his arm to lead me down the hall and then down the small
series of corridors to the kitchen. As we got closer, I noticed something
smelled divine. I walked faster the stronger the smell reached me. As I
rounded the door to the kitchen, I saw Althira sitting on a tall chair in
front of a pub table that was positioned in front of a stained-glass
window. There were no designs on the glass to be seen, but the colors
were brilliant. The reds and greens shone over Althira's hair and skin
like the northern lights over a night sky. She wore a dress constructed
from countless strips of fabric, with open sides that offered a subtle

flash of skin at her waist. The dress was black and royal purple. Black looked good on her. Her heels, black and mid-length, were propped on the bottom rung of the chair; though a little plainer in design, the elegant curve of the heel still caught the light. She was sipping tea from a delicate-looking teacup, with a matching saucer resting on the tabletop. I discovered the source of the amazing sweet smell drifting on the air. "Cinnamon buns!" I almost yelled; I was so excited. I grabbed one, taking a bite as Eryn handed me a cup of freshly poured coffee. I sat at the low, casual dinner table. I took a sip of my coffee and then another bite of the cinnamon bun, not realizing the ill-mannered moan that escaped my throat until it was too late. Althira sat her teacup down with a solid thud against the saucer. "You do that again, it may very well be the last sound you make." I turned to look at her, seeing how her eyes were burning into me. "I apologize; I didn't actually mean to make it." Althira looked as though she had lost her appetite, pushing her teacup and saucer back on the table. "Not only is she uneducated and primitive, being a floozy comes at no thought to her." She left the room in a flash, not giving us time to process her words before leaving. Eryn looked at me, giving me one of his gentle smiles, and shrugged. She could call me whatever she wanted, because this coffee and cinnamon bun was all I cared about right now.

As we finished eating our delicious breakfast, a sense of renewal and vigor washed over me. We passed Althira in the corridor shortly after leaving the kitchen. She paused briefly. "I need a little more time to think. Meet me at the vivisectum in about an hour." She was off without giving me time to answer. I noticed Vexil as she walked away, sitting on her shoulder, giving us a toothy grin as they went. The thing was still so unsettling. Eryn and I continued our casual stroll, talking as we went. "Eryn, I've been meaning to ask, why did you seem upset or annoyed yesterday when Althira was showing us the vivisectum? Was it regarding the necromancy or the mention of the forbidden? Also, what do you really think about the shadowmancy Althira said I have the gift for?" Eryn wrinkled his forehead just the slightest at the question, making me even more curious about what was going through his mind. "Well, Miss Octavia, in part yes to both of your first questions. Necromancy is not something to be taken lightly. Unless he who wields the arcane has enough capability and power to control what he creates and manifests with necromancy, it is something that should be left buried in the earth. While it can have its uses and benefits, I fear for your well-being if you attempt such practices. Now, as far as forbidden necromancy is concerned, it's not actually forbidden per se; it is immoral and inhumane in most situations, therefore making it highly frowned upon. However, should the forbidden necromancy being performed go devastatingly wrong, there will be heavy and dire punishments for the ones responsible. At the hands of the High Council, no less. The repercussions of what Althira has planned for you are yet to be seen." He paused. "As for the shadowmancy, I have no qualms about it. It is a powerful form of the arcane. If you possess it in the way Althira is leading me to believe, you are most likely the next Mortis Velum. It's not very often one comes along, so you will be a bit of a big deal to the High Council and those who find out about your unusually rare gift." I thought about that for a moment. "Does this mean I will be inducted onto the High Council without choice?" I wasn't opposed to the idea, but I at least wanted a say. If I really have the abilities Althira described, shouldn't I at the very least be able to decide what I wanted? "It is too early to know anything for certain, and you remember Alsendra has taken extra precautions to keep details about you from the High Council. To add to that, you have now learned how secrecy plays a large role in Althira's powers as a Mortis Velum. You will possess the same aptitude for secrecy and the dark arts as she does. Where your journey takes you will be interesting, to say the least, Miss Octavia." I thought about that while furrowing my eyebrows. Eryn echoed some of my own thoughts. If I were to be inducted regardless, why the extreme measures and secrecy? Seems like unnecessary actions by both Lady Alsendra and Althira, and if I was to be part of the High Council as one of "The First Listeners," wouldn't the Council themselves offer some sort of protection for me without all this need for secrecy? This ultimately leaves me with unanswered questions. I snapped out of my thought as a ruckus of chattering and squeaking hurtled past Eryn and me at our leisurely walking pace.

Vexil was running off at full speed, headed towards the front of the building, as it would seem. A few moments later, as we neared the end of the hall we'd been on, I could see Vexil fiddling around with the large metal iron door at the entrance of the hall. He opened the door after what seemed like a significant amount of effort on his part. Slowly, making his way around the open door to look around. He let out a singsong noise that sounded a lot like "yooooo-woooo." From outside the door, a scream of excitement filled the air. A shoe came through the opening of the door. Vexil went tumbling backwards, rolling until he came to a stop. With loud squeaks and groans, he rolled over, finally ending up on his back as he lay there on the floor. The door opened a little wider. I dropped my arm from where I had been holding Eryn's arm as he escorted me. We both tensed up a bit in anticipation, not knowing if whoever was on the other side of that door meant trouble for us. A feminine voice on the other side spoke. "Oh, I am so sorry, you poor thing. I didn't mean to hurt you. You gave me such a fright, I about died." That voice... It was so familiar to me, but I couldn't quite place it. Then I realized to whom the voice belonged. "Gabrielle?!" she came bustling through the door, a large bag over her shoulder. She was in a simple, light peach-colored dress. Fitted, but not tight, flaring out around the bottom from the hips. The footwear she was wearing consisted primarily of gray sandals. She beamed at me as she opened the door, exactly as she had the night we met at the Rights. "Octavia!" She stopped to look at Eryn, with a look of uncertainty and apprehension on her face. "Oh, this is Eryn, chamberlain to Lady Alsendra and my current chaperone." I said confidently to reassure her. "Chaperone?" Eryn asked in amusement. "Well, isn't that what you are? I mean, I'm just not sure what else to refer to you as?" Eryn gave me one of his soft smiles. "No, that is perfectly fine, Miss Octavia." With an air of curiosity, Gabrielle stood motionless, her eyes carefully examining us in that moment. "Where are my manners? Please come in. Althira is around somewhere. I assume you're here to see her?" I couldn't imagine why she would make the long trip to Liraquor unless it was something important. "No, silly, I am here to see you!" "You are?" I hope I didn't sound rude, but I couldn't imagine why she would come all this way to see me when we had only met for the first time less than a week ago at the Rights. "Of course I am!" She gave a wide smile where her eyes almost closed. "Lady Alsendra came to me and asked if I would come. She didn't really give me a lot of details other than it was super important and she strongly advised me to come." Eryn and I looked at each other.

Althira was walking up from one of the long corridors, her heels tapping against the hardwood floor. "Who do we have here?" She asked in an almost annoyed tone. "I am Gabrielle!" Gabrielle beamed at Althira, Althira giving back a grimace. "Do I need to ask what you are doing here, standing inside my chambers?" "Oh, I should have told you that to begin with. I apologize for that. Lady Alsendra sent me. She told me, 'You have a role to play; it is of the utmost importance for you to make haste to Liraquor and make yourself present' or something close to that. And so, anyway, here I am! Hi!" Althira almost curled her lip. "Alsendra would. She and I really need to discuss her sending me all these wonderful, unbecoming visitants. I can only handle so much elation at one time." Heavy sarcasm coated her words. Vexil started throwing a fit, squeaking and squealing. He spoke to Althira, but I couldn't make out anything he said from where I stood. Althira snapped her gaze up to Gabrielle. "What do you have in that bag, girl?" Gabrielle dropped her smile. "Well, you see, Lady Alsendra sent me with." "I asked what it is, not why. Answer directly!" Althira's voice echoed around the entrance of the hall. "How about I just show you?" Gabrielle opened the top of the bag. A head popped up at us over the edge of the bag without another moment wasted, startling us. Althira gasped. Vexil went mad, cooing and crowing in an array of singsong sounds. Eryn glanced at me. I shrugged in response, not knowing what to say. Althira spoke with scorn in her voice. "Alsendra and I need to have a discussion indeed."

Chapter 21: Veil of Mourning

I stood there wide-eyed, unable to form words for a few moments as I
took in what peered at us over the bag Gabrielle held. A green, moss-
coated head revealed it was the Leshy. Vexil was squeaking and
ranting at the Leshy before giving it an obscene gesture. The Leshy
responded by jabbing its stick arm in the air a few times with little
whoops. "This is the Leshy from the Rights, as I'm sure you see. Lady
Alsendra thought I should bring him along. She gave little explanation
for that either, but he seemed happy enough to come along. At least
until we arrived here. He didn't seem to have a name as far as I could
tell, so I named him Spriggle." Gabrielle appeared pleased with herself
for naming the little tree man, grinning widely at us as she revealed
the information. "And you thought it a good idea to carry a tutelary
deity of the forests around in a mere peasant's handbag?" Althira
scolded with anger backing her words. "Do not answer. It was
Alsendra who told you. I'm aware. Now go take it out of that bag and
put it in the dormitories away from Vexil before we end up with a
homicide. I do not wish to find out which of these creatures would be
the ultimate victor." Gabrielle, with a look of innocence, getting
scolded, nodded to Althira quickly. "I'll take you to your dormitory,
Miss Gabrielle, right this way." Eryn held his arm out for Gabrielle to
grab. She beamed at him before grabbing on, and they were off
without another word, departing to the sounds of Vexil's rapid
chatter. Althira watched them travel down the corridor for a moment,
a look something akin to a sneer fixed upon her face. "I have made my
decision about your studies today. I believe I tried giving you

objectives too advanced for your current aptitude. I overestimated your abilities at this time based on what Alsendra previously told me about what you possibly possess. I realize you are not ready to control the arcane with any significant amount of respect or grace. Or rather, I misjudged your character and the fortitude you possess, given that you have abilities with such potential. We will start slower and ease into your studies at the vivisectum today, then I will reevaluate your studies as we move forward." "Thank you." I said the words with more relief behind them than I wanted to reveal, but if I were being honest, I didn't think I could take another round of us going at it like we had yesterday. "Get yourself prepared and meet me there. I need to grab a few items before making my way." She turned and was off with an air of bravado and speed. I had little to prepare, and the anticipation made me restless; I grabbed another cup of coffee before we started. Something told me I could use the extra energy.

Althira was standing outside the vivisectum. The heavy-duty iron door behind her closed tightly. She nodded in recognition of my approach. Vexil was sitting on her shoulder. Neither of us exchanged words; instead, we waited as Vexil hopped down to disappear into the shadows, appearing a moment later as he opened the door from the opposite side. As we stepped into the vivisectum, the same smell and sensations from the first time I entered this place reached me again. "Since you have a knack for fire illusory, we are going to start there, with something suited for schoolgirl age. You can't possibly mess this up." I noticed she had a small bag of things with her when we entered, from which she now grabbed a black candle. "We will work on the very basics. You are going to perform a whispered candle ritual. I want you to use this as your first step towards communicating with the spirits. This is a powerful, straightforward, and low-risk way for you to channel energy. There are three results I aim to get from this practice. One being spirit scrying. I will then have you detect hauntings. Then we will move on to the voice of the flame. Only after you have successfully completed one, will you move on to the next. Simultaneously, however, you're going to learn how to perform the veil of mourning. I will not elaborate on that, as it is already something you know how to perform. You just aren't aware of what it is yet." Althira pulled out a small jar of something to rub on the black candle. "This is ash from a cremated corpse. I will keep the details to myself as your knowing the details may corrupt your results. Tell me, Octavia, do you know why I have chosen a black candle for you?" I thought it over for a moment. "Not specifically. I'm not educated on what colors are beneficial for, but I would assume black pertains to death and necromancy? Or perhaps Shadowmancy?" She gave me a subtle smile. "People always assume black to be death or lack of something. If something is black, it must be sinister or referring to the shadows." She said the words with thick sarcasm. "However, that couldn't be further from the truth. You weren't too far off in some of your assumptions, though. Black is going to absorb and channel the energy of death and shadow. Here is the part you may not know and what I would like you to pay attention to. Black represents the void, mystery, and the unknown. It is a powerful tool and weapon to the Mortis Velum, as the veil itself is shrouded in shadow and secrecy. You will soon find all of this out if you succeed. Last, but certainly not least, the black in this candle will be used for summoning echoes of the dead and protection. Part of the black being a powerful tool to us includes being able to be used as shadowmancy to protect ourselves while performing necromancy. This can be as simple as communicating with a volatile spirit to raising something from the dead that cannot follow orders. At some point you will need protection or to protect someone else; that is why we start here." She handed me the torch, the light reflecting off her face as she moved to place the black candle into a heavy-looking candleholder before slowly placing that into a bowl of black liquid. "After your failures yesterday, I have determined we need to start with defensive skills. Your display yesterday with that minor curse from a Duskkin was an embarrassment to the Mortis Velum. You were in a panic and frenzied, idiotic rage; therefore, you died." I nodded to show that I was paying attention. "Now the ashes I rubbed on the candle will help give you an extra boost to commune with the echoes of the veil. This charcoal water beneath the candle will serve as your Shadow Bowl. You will use the reflective surface for scrying when the flames reveal messages that cannot be heard."

Althira took the torch from me before continuing to speak. "Now I will tell you the steps you are going to follow, so I want you to pay attention as I go over them. You will start by kneeling before the candle. I want you to close your eyes and focus intently on the silence and stillness. Vexil and I will remain here, but in the shadows. You will be unaware of our presence. Next, you are going to light the candle with deliberate and strong intent. You will listen to your instincts, saying a chant. This chant is to be recited three times, each time speaking the words softer than the last, as if the words themselves are drifting off into the void. After you have successfully completed those steps, you will return your attention to the flame. The candle's flame will become the 'voice' for the dead. It may flicker unnaturally, bend towards an unseen presence, or crackle to give a response. Determining the responses accurately will be up to you in the moment. Then, after you feel you have succeeded with your tasks, you will close the veil. Open communication between the dead and the living cannot remain open. You will snuff the candle out in the correct steps to sever the connection. I will not go into details on how to close the veil, as that should be second nature to a Mortis Velum. That will be an excellent test for me to gauge your progress as well. My words of advice and the key to your success are this: 'The veil is shrouded in shadow.' Now let us begin." With a swift movement I could barely perceive, Althira snuffed out the torch just after I kneeled, the smell of extinguished fire filling the air. It turned out that she was indeed correct about her being undetectable in the shadows. While I knew she stood just a few feet from me, I could not see or sense her presence at all. The darkness was absolute; I couldn't see a thing, not even the outline of my hands right in front of me. That was incredibly eerie, sending shivers down my spine. I found the candle by feeling around in the dark delicately. I held a hand on either side as I concentrated on fire and flame, focusing intent on it as calmly as I could until I entered a state of near-meditation. I pictured the sparks and glow, the warmth, and then I felt an actual warmth between my hands. I opened my eyes. The dim light from the lit candle a few feet around me was the only vision I had. I glanced around the vivisectum, but Althira was nowhere to be seen. Either she was standing in the dark somewhere out of sight, or she had a cleverer way to conceal her presence. I suspected either was a real possibility. I remembered Althira said to chant by following your instincts. I closed my eyes almost immediately, going back into the meditative state I had been in previously. I heard a brief whisper of a voice from what I thought was from the flame, but it was too hard to tell. "Repeat my words." There followed only a long moment of silence. Then, a sharp, popping spark shot from the candle, followed by the eerie voice speaking again. I spoke as it did, word for word. "By flame that bends, by breath unseen, I call the whisper, soft and lean, through veil of dark and hush of tomb, speak through the shadow, grant me your gloom, ash to ash, and sigh to sigh, let the candle's flame be the dead's reply." I spoke the words as surely and calmly as I could. Repeating the chant three times as Althira said, letting it trail off by the third. The flame sizzled. I thought I heard a whispering voice coming from the flames. I leaned forward, concentrating intently. "Release me." The voice was faint and raspy. I stared into the black liquid, humming lowly to myself to let my mind remain blank. I jumped at what appeared, my heart pounding in my ears as I gasped for air.

The face that appeared in the liquid was not human — well, not the living kind. Chunks of its skin were breaking away, revealing the rotting flesh beneath. Bone and inner deteriorated tissue exposed. One eye was gone while the other remained, with no color or life behind it. "What do you want, spirit?" I asked slowly and sternly. "Release me from these confines." The voice rasped out, bugs spilling out of its mouth as I saw my reflection grimace in the dark fluid. Without warning, the spirit's reflection stood directly behind me. I let out a startled scream. The spirit smiled. I watched as it brought a hand up over my head, bones visible through the skin, to reach down and grab a fistful of my hair without hesitation. It yanked hard, pulling my head. I fell backward, lying flat on my back. Panic seized me as I grabbed and groped, my fingers finding only empty space. I sat back up quickly, kneeling before the candle again. With no need to concentrate, the flame roared up, burning an almost eerie black color. A voice from the flames spoke. "You light candles for the dead, but who will light one for you?" I gasped, taken aback by the threatening tone as the disfigured face blinked in and then out as I stared into the dark fluid. "Let me speak to a benevolent spirit." I figured it was worth a try to get something nicer. The same raspy voice responded. "They do not wish to speak to you, but I do. Would you like me to show you what awaits under your skin?" The voice trailed off in a sadistic laugh, chills running down my spine. "Why are you so angry?" The instant I stopped speaking, the flame flickered violently, its light transforming to a dark burning black that cradled a deep royal purple within. "You light a flame, but shadow owns you, girl!" Then I remembered Althira's words of advice. "The veil is shrouded in shadow." This spirit saying the shadow owns me couldn't be a coincidence. As the revelation hit me, I saw the spirit in the reflection. Two hands shot out, encircling my throat, a crushing pressure that stole my breath, a terrifying sensation of suffocation. The words came to me; I now knew what I needed to say. I willed with all my might to force the words from my throat, clear and strong. "Weep, oh shadow, for the breath of life, weave my heart in grief and strife, from sorrow's cloth a shield is born, I hide within this veil of mourn." With staggering speed upon the words leaving my mouth, a dark shadow engulfed me. The spirit let out a blood-curdling scream, releasing its hands from my neck in an instant. "The veil is shrouded in shadow." Now it made sense. This was the same smoke and shadow I had previously seen Althira use in the resonance room. I looked around, realizing I could now see around the pitch-black room better than I could before this shadow was around. The flame of the candle roared up once again, whipping back and forth with a gust. I remembered Althira's last steps. "Close the veil." I felt the weight of the ancient voice at my back now, a presence like cold stone. I knew all I needed to do was open myself to the power, to do as I was told. I did just that. Repeating the words, "By flame and ash, I break this tie; no spirit stays, no shadow nigh. I seal the dark, I claim my breath, begone, return to silent death!" Now I was to snuff the candle. I placed my hands around the flame, realizing the shadow seemed to protect my skin from burning. I focused, willing the shadow to close around my hands tightly, snuffing out the candle a moment later. The room fell silent and became black. A strange sound echoed behind me, and I whipped around, eyes straining, but found only impenetrable blackness. A spark ignited, blinding me momentarily with its intense light, and then Althira was there, the flickering torch in her hand casting dancing shadows. Vexil was on the ground at her feet. She placed the torch in a holder near where she stood. She looked back at me. I froze, wondering what her response would be to this. She gave me a genuine smile and clapped. "Congratulations, hun, you have learned to use the veil of mourning. Veil of Mourning is what we Mortis Velum call the protective shadows we shroud ourselves in. Called so because it was first used by a Mortis Velum during a great time of grief and mourning. It was later realized that the shadow veil is used and manipulated by the arcane wielder's emotions. The stronger the emotion, the stronger the protection. You can use this to make yourself untouchable, but more than that, if you possess the emotions and strength, you could use the shadows to protect yourself and someone else. Even a small group. The extent of your abilities remains to be seen. At any rate, for the first time since being in my presence, you have achieved something that wasn't utterly disappointing and embarrassing. You displayed self-control and respect." Althira grabbed the torch, turning to walk back to the door as I followed. She stopped briefly, turning her head only slightly to the side to speak to me behind her. "You know, perhaps there remains hope for you yet."

Chapter 22: The Veilwarden

Upon leaving the vivisectum, Kenric and Nova met us at the door.
"What now?" Althira sounded more than displeased. Kenric looked a
little hesitant. "It would seem you have another guest waiting to
speak with you." "Bah! I'm about one uninvited guest away from
putting an impenetrable barrier around this entire place. Who dares
wish to speak to me?" Kenric shrugged slightly. "I'm not entirely sure,
but it appears to be someone with an important status among the
Orriveth elven. Possibly one from the Royal Court, accompanied by
two bodyguards." A look of concern and worry flashed across
Althira's face as her expression fell. "Gods. What has been brought to
my front door now?" She took off at almost a jogging walk, looking as
if she were gliding. Kenric and I could barely keep up with her pace
while trying not to run. As we approached the corridor nearing the
entrance at the front of the hall, there we saw the elven men waiting
for Althira. Judging by his clothing, rich with intricate embroidery,
and his gleaming, ornate armor, the elven man in the front center
must be royalty. He wore deep emerald-green clothing, tailored to fit
him precisely. Gold accents stressed the green color, adding to the air
of royalty. The gleaming gold pieces of armor strategically placed over
his clothing made me wonder if they were functional or merely there
for aesthetic appeal. The two guards behind the man were plainer
dressed; their worn clothing was a stark contrast to his finery. They
wore simple brown and gray clothes, accentuated by shining silver
armor, and somehow still exuded wealth. The elven man in green had
long red hair that came to just below his shoulders. His fair skin was

sprinkled with freckles, his pointed ears peeking from behind hair tucked to one side, multiple gold rings glinting in his one visible ear. His eyes were the color of the clearest spring water, sparkling and bright. His features were exceedingly handsome. He stood there talking to Eryn as we walked up. The elven man turned to us. Upon realizing Althira was walking up, he gave a courtly bow, oddly similar to one Eryn would give. Althira waved her hand in an annoyed dismissal. "Cut to the chase, Rayden. While I appreciate your manners and formality, we both know you would not be here unless you came bearing bad news in some capacity." The elven man, who I now learned was named Rayden, smiled warmly at Althira. "You know I've always admired your straightforwardness to cut right through the twaddle, Althira." Althira shifted her weight to one leg, crossing her arms with a look of anticipation. "You are correct. I'm afraid I come bearing bad news. If it is all right, I think we should speak in private." Rayden cast a look around the room at the rest of us. I wondered for a moment where Gabrielle was as I glanced around. I figured she was in the dormitories with the Leshy. Althira clicked her tongue, a sharp sound that cut through the air, motioning for Rayden to follow. He took off following her, then halted abruptly, his eyes locking onto Eryn. "It was nice catching up, Isiltyan." Eryn wrinkled his face as Rayden walked away. After they were out of earshot, I asked Eryn, "Isiltyan?" He looked pensive. "That is what the Orriveth know me as. Isiltyan means moon-stepper. The name given to me because of my ability with the syreth blades." I wanted him to elaborate, but I got the feeling he didn't want to, so I let it go.

Althira appeared in the corridor minutes later, as we were all standing around discussing my studies of the day. "Octavia, Eryn, come with me. This involves you, and you will not like it." We followed her down the corridor and into a room. The general theme of the room was the same as that of the rest of the building. Wood floors, stone arches, and stained-glass windows running the distance of one wall overhead. This room looked as if it were set up for holding meetings, as a large wooden round table sat in the center. "Take a seat." Althira ordered us; it was clear she wasn't giving us an option. I sat on one of the wooden chairs with a ruby-red cushion, Eryn sitting down beside me. Rayden sat across from us. Althira sat between us, crossed her legs, and straightened her posture. "Rayden here brought us even more trouble than we already had, so I will just let him tell you about it." Althira sounded like she was about to explode, her voice tight and trembling, but doing everything in her power to stay calm. Rayden tilted his head forward, closing his eyes before speaking in what seemed like an attempt to get his story together. "It may go without saying, but I'll start with the trivial details for Octavia's sake. I am of the Orriveth, royalty by birth and title. I am a Veilwarden, also known to my people as the Elaria Silthien, which means Emerald Star in your language. It is my honorary duty to oversee the shadow and the veil. Therefore, I am the custodian of the boundaries between life and death, should someone be arrogant enough to think they can tear open the weave between the realms. It is my responsibility by birthright to stop anyone who tries it, to maintain the boundaries." Eryn mumbled something to himself. Rayden continued. "I work closely with gifted seers and scouts. Those who can see, hear, and otherwise gather information that will alert us to any impending dangers that may need attending. Within the last day or two, one of our seers alerted me to something alarming, but I disregarded it as it didn't directly affect the Orriveth. However, now one of our scouts has brought back information far more alarming, and this will not go ignored." Rayden inhaled deeply before sighing, then continued. "It is believed the Ravynari are calling for the murder of the one who killed one of their rare arcane wielders. The Ravynari girl was apparently exceptionally gifted with the arcane among their people, considering that those who can wield the arcane for anything useful are exceedingly rare among the Ravynari. They claim she was slaughtered and left for them to find her body torn to pieces. The Ravynari are preparing to wage a full assault, possibly even go to war, over their prized arcane wielder being killed." I felt my heart pounding and my stomach sinking as he spoke. I reached up, grabbing my chest. Eryn noticed, placing a hand on my shoulder. "I come here to tell you they may come to Liraquor to find you, but we do not know how much they know. It is unclear whether they even know where you were headed. Let me say this, however. I could find out who killed the Ravynari girl without too much difficulty. If I can find you, I suspect the Ravynari may not be too far behind in finding out the same information." Althira smacked her mouth. "It's always some kind of trouble that I get dragged into. I'm getting too old for this...

poppycock!" Rayden looked as if he were trying not to burst out laughing at Althira's disdain.

Rayden's tone changed, now carrying a serious undertone of warning. "Regardless of how capable you may be at defending yourself, you cannot survive a crowd of Ravynari should they come for you." "She's as good as dead." Althira hissed. "Calm yourself, Althira," Eryn said, his voice smooth, yet I could feel the immense power thrumming through my very bones. Althira snapped her head over to look at Eryn, "Do not make me force you to partake in a battle for dominance. It will not be in your favor." Eryn chuckled. "I've got one hundred gold on the Isiltyan being victorious in that brawl," Rayden chastised through a smile. Althira glowered in response. Rayden's words sparked my curiosity: how intimately did he know Eryn, and what was the origin of their connection? And then Rayden knows him well enough to recall his people have a special name for Eryn. What secrets was Eryn keeping, and what were the limits of his abilities? I was getting the impression that Eryn was capable of far more and far more important than he would have anyone believe. "Back to the task at hand, I think it would be wise to prepare yourselves to the best of your abilities for the Ravynari to attack. Or maybe put Octavia into hiding somewhere for a while," Rayden finished. "Hiding will not stop the Ravynari. They will just kill, maim, and rape hundreds of innocents to get to one. You know better than anyone how they operate, like the disgusting filth they are!" Althira bit each word out. Rayden nodded in acknowledgement. "Indeed, I do. I'm merely offering any ideas I can for a solution where everyone remains alive and healthy." The room fell silent as we all sat there taking in the full weight of the situation before Althira broke the silence. "This is Alsendra's doing. She set all of this in motion with that ridiculous seeing gift of hers. By trying to prevent what she saw, she set the very thing in motion by sending you here. Had she left well enough alone, you would've been fine. The Ravynari would still be alive. Alsendra couldn't see you killing the Ravynari girl for whatever reason, but doing just that has now led us down the very path she saw leading to devastation." We all turned to stare at her. Althira indeed knew far more than she had told any of us. What else did she know? "Oh, gods, Alsendra. That is why she took so much effort to keep your gifts and whereabouts as secret as possible. If the High

Council knew the extent of what you are, and then now added the Ravynari wanting to rage war to get to you, they would either be forced to go all out to defend you or be forced to turn you over as a peace offering to the Ravynari. It would be put to a vote." Althira sat looking wide-eyed at me. "I need to send word to Alsendra at once. She needs to know what has been set in motion. Hopefully, her sight offers us a solution to this mess. Or she causes even bigger issues." She trailed off. "To add one last thing, Althira. I am here to pass on the message that should the Ravynari start a war that would aim to slaughter potentially thousands of people, the Orriveth will see fit to step in. We will see it through to the final blow." Rayden paused for a moment before continuing, his words clear and powerful. "We will not escalate the situation," he spoke his next words more sternly, "but if they dare cross that line, they will face our full, unyielding force. And Althira, we will expect your participation considering it was one of your pupils that started this." Althira scowled with fiery passion in his direction. Rayden appeared unfazed, continuing. "I also do not need to remind you of how incredibly powerful the abilities of a Mortis Velum are during times of battle." The look Althira gave Rayden made me a little concerned for his safety. "I want to make this exceptionally clear, Rayden, so that you can relay my message to the Court. I will not obey any orders. If I cooperate, it will be because I did so of my own accord. You'd do well to remember you have no authority here. You are my guest while in this sanctum. Should it come to conflict with the Ravynari, I will do what is right." Eryn dramatically let out a breath of air. Althira stood up to leave. She stopped at the doorway, turning to speak to Rayden one last time. "I truly hope it doesn't come to a senseless battle, a meaningless fight with needless casualties. I know death all too well." Eryn spoke up. "Miss Octavia, please give Rayden and me a moment alone? We have some things to discuss." I appreciated the graceful manner in which Eryn brought our interaction to a close. I respectfully got up to make my leave, setting off down the long corridor.

Chapter 23: Seeding Death

I didn't see anyone as I made my way back to the dormitories at a
leisurely pace. As I got to the underground hall, I saw Nova running at
full sprint after a ball. Kenric was at the opposite end of the hall,
whistling for Nova to bring the ball back. Nova grabbed the ball,
bringing it to me immediately upon seeing me enter the long corridor.
This sweet creature had a way of lifting my spirits; his presence alone
was enough to bring a smile and take my mind away from the terrible
things in the world. That he was ridiculously adorable was a
delightful bonus. I took the slobbery ball, petting Nova on the head
before chucking the ball as hard as I could down the long corridor. I
was satisfied with how far it went. It hadn't quite reached Kenric, but
it made it clear to the other end of the hall, regardless. Nova bolted
down the length of the hall in a barreling run, sliding several feet as he
reached the end, the ball rolling on the floor in front of him. He and
Kenric ran circles around each other after that, playfully fighting over
who would have the ball. I heard what sounded like a female voice
arguing, almost at a shout. I realized the one voice I heard for certain
was Gabrielle's, her voice coming from not too far down the hall to a
door on the left. I decided I'd go see what the commotion was about; I
wanted to check in on her, regardless. We haven't had time to speak
much since arriving here, so I welcomed a moment to catch up with
her while basking in her happy aura. I got to the door and heard her
yell, "Get out of there right this minute!" Despite my knocking, I
suspect she did not notice, as she was enveloped in her hysterics. I
opened the door just a crack to speak. "Hey Gabrielle, is it all right if I

come in?" To which I heard her reply, "Of course it is, silly!" I walked in, closing the door behind me gently. She glanced up, smiling widely at me while she bent back over, picking up pieces of clothes, scoffing and huffing the entire time. "Is everything all right? I heard you from the hall, sounded like you might have had an argument?" She huffed. "Well, you could say that. Spriggle got into my bag and threw out all my clothes. Now the stupid thing is over there wearing my undergarments!" She pointed towards the bed, but I didn't see the Leshy. I walked over closer to the bed, looking around. Spriggle was on the other side, standing on the floor. It looked like he was dancing, or something like a dance, while wearing a pair of Gabrielle's bloomers. He was standing in one leg opening of them, with the rest of the bloomers wrapped around his shoulder and torso, in the same fashion as a toga would be worn. He saw me and yelled in a tiny voice, then he extended a piece of fabric from the bloomers, as if it were an expensive gown he wanted to show off. "I see." I couldn't think of anything else to say because the situation was undeniably odd.

We talked for a moment. Gabrielle told me she believes the Coravelle is indeed her arcane familiar now. It just showed itself to me for whatever reason. "Does that mean you're a spellcaster?" I guessed that much, though I didn't ask. She nodded with a slight tilt of her head to the side. "I think so. That is what Lady Alsendra seems to think. She said my abilities could be helpful in something that was to come, but I can hardly see how that's possible when I can't do anything except manipulate silly emotions from a distance." I thought about that for a moment, thinking how that could be useful in certain scenarios. She could take away fear, anger, or even extreme grief if she could control it well enough. I wonder... "Gabrielle, do you think you can cause someone to feel fear or a similar emotion? Strong enough to manipulate their behavior and decisions?" She crinkled her nose, thinking about it, and then shrugged. "I guess so. I've never thought about it in that way, but it should work. Manipulating emotions is the same whether taking or giving different feelings." "You should work on developing your control over the arcane. Not that you asked, but think about all the good things you could do with such a gift. Not to mention you could stop someone from attacking you or save a child too fearful to save themselves from the edge of a cliff ledge." She thought about that for a moment before beaming at me. "I've never thought about it like that, but that is true! Thank you; that gives me a little incentive to try harder." I just smiled back at her, lost in thought over all that we've been through with my own gifts over the last few days. A knock on the door jolted me back to the present. It was Eryn. "Miss Octavia, are you in there? Althira requests your attendance immediately." I rolled my eyes and sighed. Of course she does. "My apologies, Gabrielle, but we must put this conversation on hold." As I walked out, I heard the Leshy making grunts followed by Gabrielle saying, "I have never!" I could only imagine the trouble Spriggle would be to her. It made me curious why Lady Alsendra said for the Leshy to be here, but why did she send Gabrielle. While I was happy that she was there, I also felt that it was inappropriate for her to be here if she was going to have to stay locked away in her dormitory babysitting Spriggle.

"She asked you to meet her at the Vivsectum." Eryn's voice was smooth and almost too calm. That made me wonder how his conversation with Rayden had gone. "Are we going to have a study session this late in the day? She said the one this morning went well." "I suspect Rayden's news has stirred up a sense of urgency in Althira. If that's the case, she'll most likely be pushing you to the height of your limits." I didn't even want to think what that would look like coming from Althira. I told Eryn I was fine making the short walk to the vivisectum on my own, even though he was adamant about escorting me. There was no need when the room was such a short walk away. I saw Althira standing in front of the door awaiting my arrival, Vexil on the ground at her feet. She looked agitated already. I huffed and let out a sigh. I had a feeling she would not make this session easy for me with whatever was to come. "Since you did well this morning with the Veil of Mourning, you should be able to progress into this next practice with little tribulation." She motioned for Vexil to open the door before continuing. "First, we are going to start with death weaving. And then you are going to find out how to ghoulcraft once you have learned the basics of death weaving. Seeing as you have the gift of the Mortis Velum, you will use this technique in ways no other mage can. Considering the recent news of a possible impending Ravynari attack, it seems prudent for you to learn it sooner rather than later." Vexil popped the door open, coming out at a trot with a huge, toothy grin across his face. "You learned this morning how easily we can use shadow and shade to shield us and others, but you can also use it as a lethal weapon. Where you can create manifestations through shadowmancy, you will also be able to summon death itself through shadowmancy, using the veil in a multitude of ways." She handed me the torch, holding her hand out to motion for me to proceed. "I know you had to use a chant to summon the Veil this morning, but a trained Mortis Velum needs no such preliminaries. It will become redundant when you can channel the essence of life and death; the voice of the arcane you hear will provide you with the push to weave the threads through both sides of the veil. I will now explain to you the steps to death weave, and then I will demonstrate before you proceed. I would normally let a student figure it out the hard way, but we do not have the time to dilly-dally." She stopped now, holding up her hand for me to halt behind her. "Death weaving, aptly called so because we can weave thread through the loom of life, so to speak. A Mortis Velum can take the threads of life and death, occasionally even plucking a thread from lingering spirits, grave soil, items with sentimental value to a deceased, etcetera. Threads of shadow can be plucked for use from places of terror and horror, dark corners of the world, moments of intense fear, trauma, or deep secrecy. You'll learn that much later. We weave and stitch that thread for our own use and benefit, mostly. This in its entirety is the fundamental required for learning necromancy. The complexity of these weaves can take hours or mere seconds. When using such an ability for battle or to defend yourself, clearly you are going to use a method that takes seconds, preferably a method that doesn't require you to use your hands." Vexil started squealing and laughing hysterically, giving me chills down my arms. He was still so disconcerting. Althira made some large gestures with her hands, waving them around in front of her in a wide circle, then making a pattern with them. It seemed to be sigils from what I could make out. A moment later, a long and narrow bone-white object with a deep purple shadow essence appeared in her palm. "This is an arcane needle; some mages refer to them as shadow needles. With this, we Mortis Velum can stitch death into reality."

"Before we begin, a definitive understanding of death weaving and ghoulcraft is crucial, so I'll go over a few things once more. A better understanding than just touching the surface of what these are. We've established that ghoulcraft is necromancy, which deals with the manipulation of death, decay, and disease. It is fueled by decay and rot, bone and flesh, and the residual essence of the spirit left after death. It can also be used for good sometimes, such as creating complicated healing salves or finding out who killed a long-deceased corpse. We can cure diseases and curses. After the way you handled the minor curse from Vexil, it would benefit you to pay extra close attention during your studies on this matter. Moving on. We can give the dead a voice to speak, although most uses for ghoulcraft are not for such benevolent usage. Death weaving, in contrast, is an ominous entity, unlike anything else. I want to clarify what I said previously regarding summoning death with death weaving. While that is true in a way, we cannot create death from nothing, but what we can do is guide it. Death already exists and looms over everyone, so it isn't hard for us to pluck the strands. We can plant the seed of death to take root. This is where we can choose to end suffering gently or cause agonizing torment that would lead the victims only to wish for death. Did you know that with the knowledge of death weaving, we can preserve a dying person? It is temporary, but it can be an incredibly useful tool to stabilize a dying soul long enough to be healed or rescued. Sometimes long enough for dying souls to deliver a last goodbye or an important message. Despite this, it becomes apparent once more that most death weaving is well suited for malevolent uses. An example might be ending a life in an instant, silently, ensuring no one sees it. We can manipulate the strands of death so acutely that we can even cause a person to suffer long-term insanity at our hands, eventually leading them to their demise. We can take the cruelty further by binding a soul to a particular place in a strand, resulting in forcing that person to relive their death many times over, driving them past the point of madness, but they will never reach the actual precipice of death unless we would allow it." Althira took a moment to gaze off into the surrounding darkness, bringing her eyes back to me before continuing. "If you were curious about what Rayden does exactly as Veilwarden, part of his duties is preventing us from taking death weaving too far. He keeps anyone with abilities similar to ours from losing all morality. When the Mortis Velum can easily possess an army of undead constructs, while cutting down our enemies with no need to enter physical combat, and then being able to shield ourselves within the shadows, I believe you might now start piecing together why we are regarded by others so warily. I'm hated just because people fear me, but those are the gross little sewer rats that don't concern us. It is also why you will have those, like Rayden, show up to get us on their side. Sometimes with threats, but that rarely turns out well for them. Rayden doesn't fear me, but he lacks respect. A folly that will teach him a lesson in due time." I saw a smirk on Althira's face just then that made my heart flutter. I had the feeling she made sure that some of those with threats were no longer among the living. "I trust you will learn a great deal from our lesson, but I want you to remember above all else never to be tricked or coerced into something you know is wrong. You can stop it before it starts, and it is imperative that you remember you wield such power. So, in concluding this lengthy segment, we are the only mages to exist that can shape both body and fate, therefore controlling the path, the destination, and the aftermath. Our abilities are limited to directing and changing what already exists; we cannot bring life or death into being from nothing. In time, you will learn your strengths and weaknesses in this area. I know this sounds redundant, and much of what I have said has sounded like a repeat of what was already discussed, but I can't stress enough the importance of understanding these abilities before practicing. Remember how we spoke of forbidden necromancy? Well, when you don't understand how things involving necromancy function, you get horrendous results. We would both be accountable for the repercussions if our practices didn't go as planned. Putting it bluntly, I lack the energy to handle this issue right now, so tell me now if you grasped the concepts we discussed, or if I should provide further clarification? The moment to voice your thoughts is now, if you wish." I really couldn't think of much to ask. Sure, I had a lot of questions about how a lot of this stuff worked and the details, but that wasn't what Althira wanted to know in this moment. I was trying to follow along and understand what I could with my limited knowledge. "I suppose my only question would be how we keep ourselves from becoming victims of death weaving while performing it?" Althira let out a long exhale, almost sounding like one of relief. "A reasonable question, and one you will soon learn the answer to."

Chapter 24: Death Weaving

Althira motioned to Vexil with a flick of her hand. "Fetch the Isiltyan."
I felt my eyes widen a bit with the realization that she meant Eryn. I
wondered how he might help us in relation to a lesson about death
weaving. Althira held the arcane needle in her hand, waving it about
here and there with what seemed like an intentional pattern, all the
while keeping her eyes closed. I stood in silence while observing. A few
moments later, I heard Vexil's chattering coming from somewhere in
the vivisectum's darkness. Eryn trailed at a respectful distance behind
him, only coming into view after getting closer. He gave a small bow
and smiled in my direction. Althira continued what she was doing
with the arcane needle before turning to speak to Eryn. "Octavia and I
are here to begin her first lesson in death-weaving. I believe I have
explained the fundamental principles well enough for her to proceed
with caution. Now, with that said, I need an assistant and someone
who is... capable of helping with this lesson. I would appreciate your
help with this, seeing as how I am limited with who I can trust right
now and you being who you are and given your —" "Absolutely! I
would be honored to assist Miss Octavia in any way I can," Althira
certainly noticed when Eryn abruptly cut her off mid-sentence. She
furrowed her brow, but said nothing. I couldn't help but wonder
what prompted Eryn to interrupt her, particularly since I had always
relied on Eryn's courteous and gentlemanly conduct. There is certainly
something he's not telling me, and I plan to get to the bottom of it. I am
far too nosy and invested to let this go now. First, the suspicious
feeling I had about Rayden and Eryn, and then now this — it was

causing an itch I would have to scratch. The thought crossed my mind of enlisting Gabrielle's help with my covert detective work, but I was concerned about the possibility of this being something sinister, and what if Eryn was attempting to keep it a secret for a reason, something that he preferred to remain unknown to others? I would have to think about it and tread around the matter carefully. Althira spoke up after a moment of silence, breaking my chain of thoughts on Eryn. "Take a stand there in the center." Althira pointed to a dimly lit spot in the center of the vivisectum, with dimly lit candles scattered around in a messy circle. Eryn followed suit without hesitation. "First, you need to learn two of the most important necessities required for death weaving. You need to see the strands of death and life, the threads that are attached to every living soul. You will also need to learn to summon your own arcane needle, as it will be of great help to you while practicing." She motioned for me to stand beside her. When I reached her side, she took a piece of cloth and wrapped it around my face. I jumped back at first, startled by the action. She scoffed to let me know I needed to relax, which I did. "Now, I have taken your physical sight. With that, your third sight will now be easier to focus, therefore becoming stronger. Do you remember how you were able to perform the Veil of Mourning? You are going to use the same energy for this lesson, just altered as you will see."

"Alright, by now you have learned how to get results. You have learned that when you manifest something with shadowmancy, it brings your creations to life. You have learned how to implement the Veil of Mourning. You learned shadowmancy on your own by naturally having it; therefore, you have learned that we can wield the shadows to be both our battle axe and shield. With that said, you are going to take everything you have learned from this thus far and create an arcane needle. You saw the one I created moments earlier; now you will do the same." I considered how much more comfortable I would have been performing this task had my vision not been obscured by a blindfold. I put my hands in front of me, palms up, very similar to how I held them before me when we were working on the Veil of Mourning candle. I pictured a large needle crafted from the darkness of shadow and shade. I felt a breeze brush around my shoulder, but the vivisectum was otherwise eerily silent and still. I could smell musty soil in the air. I imagined the pointed end of a needle and how a needle is used with thread. Just as I finished thinking about that in my mind, I felt a slight weight in the palm of my hand. I inhaled sharply. "What is that? Is that a needle?" "What have we discussed about asking foolish questions, girl?" I could hear Althira huff with annoyance. "Now that you have that basic skill figured out, we're going to move on to the next step. Similar to how you did with the Veil of Mourning, I want you to use the same energy and emotion you used to create the surrounding shield to sense and see your surroundings. When you focus properly, no object will ever be unseen by you. No amount of darkness or blindness can obscure the true sight of a Mortis Velum. Remember how I knocked your feet out from under you while we were practicing in the resonance room? How I told you if you had control over your arcane, I would have never hit you? That applies here and in learning this. When you master this, you will see things coming at you in all directions, whether or not you are looking with your eyes. Now focus, without waiting for the arcane to guide you, and take control of it to create the surrounding Veil." I did exactly as Althira said. Remembering how I did it the first time. The words spoken, the emotions felt, the way I felt with the energy whirling around me. I couldn't explain why, but after doing something for the first time, it became exceedingly easier every time after that. It was the same as when I had manifested the infernal devil. I can now do it far more easily, and I suspected I could do it without much thought with a little more practice. Moments later, I felt the same energy around me. I smiled, knowing it was the same shield of protection. "Very good. Now that you have done that, I want you to concentrate on pushing the energy within the Veil outwards away from you, but without pushing the shield of the Veil itself." I tried to do that, but I didn't feel like anything had happened. I thought about how candlelight would light up the room, or maybe the way shadows would move through light, but nothing happened that I could tell. "Let me assist you." Althira sounded as if she said the words with a smile. Without warning, there was a violent shove to the side of the shadowy shield surrounding me, almost knocking me over as it hit. Then, I felt something cold and damp touch my leg, and I immediately began yelling in panic.

I jumped and shook my leg, thinking of all the awful things that could touch my leg, my imagination taking over all rationality. I felt something quickly wrap around my ankle. I shrieked. I was almost certain now it was a snake; it felt cold and scaly as it slithered around my ankle. Without thinking, I grabbed at the arcane, that now familiar voice on the wind, and I pushed my will into the shadowy veil around me. I felt a surge of wind and energy circle and whirl around me with a crackle. Moments later, I could feel the thing around my ankle get yanked away as I willed the surrounding shield to remove anything from my presence. "Very well done, Miss Octavia!" Eryn said with a proud tone, I imagined through a smile. "Silent! You know better than to disrupt my lessons!" Althira smacked her mouth at the end of her words. I swear I could sense Eryn's smile even while blindfolded. "Let's proceed without further interruption. Now that you realize you can direct your power and energy into the surrounding shroud, all you have to do is modify it to use to feel and see around you. In the same way you just used it to repel, use it for sight." I did just as Althira said, channeling the energy around me, so I focused on trying to "see" around me. I pictured where I thought she stood, pictured where I last saw Eryn standing, and from the direction I last heard his voice. While at first I couldn't exactly see, I could feel their presence. Vexil was the strongest presence I felt in that moment. I focused on him, seeing a purply dark haze around him in the shadows. I saw a solid object next to him. I realized a moment after seeing a tall heel that the object was Althira's leg. I saw an odd strand coming up from Vexil. I could only describe it as a faint line, dancing in a floating way, like a delicate hair swaying in the wind. I heard Vexil coo and giggle maniacally. "Mm-hmm, see you are learning." I saw a hand with an object in it grabbing through the air, realizing a moment later that this was Althira. "I told you I would first demonstrate, so pay attention as I will only go over this once." Althira moved the needle in her hands through the darkness and shadows around us, in a manner that wasn't entirely human or natural. The unnatural-looking hands reached for the strand floating in the air, carefully caressing it with one hand while the other, with the needle, moved in. As she deliberately guided the needle around, the strand snapped, the sound echoing softly. Vexil laughed with his mouth open as he watched. It occurred to me just then that he could see what was happening. I wonder if Duskkins can always see this way; that would make sense with the way Vexil disappears and seems to become one with the shadows. I will have to ask Althira a little more about that when I get a chance later. "You see how I now essentially have control over his life by controlling this thread? I can guide it to do as I wish." She moved her hands in one sweeping motion, picking up the thread and then tying it into a knot using the needle. "Having completed this action, I have now brought his life strand under my control." Vexil had a string of saliva dripping from his chin as he gazed up at us. I could tell that he was completely captivated by Althira and the way she used death weaving. With his having such a lust for the dark arts and seeing it firsthand, I can now see why he stayed around Althira. The little gremlin was truly obsessed; this was like a drug to him. Althira then made a large zigzag pattern with the hands she controlled. The string faded out for a moment before floating back up through the air as it had before, now with the knot no longer in the strand. "Now it is your turn. You will practice with Eryn." My body tensed at her words. "Eryn? No, I can't..." "You WILL do as I say! If you kill him, then that is something you will have to learn from. That would be your burden to live with, so it would be wise to proceed carefully."

I knew Eryn stood not too far from where Althira and Vexil stood, but I couldn't quite see him through the shadows. I knew all I had to do was pull in the arcane, just grab at that voice on the wind to get a small amount to do what I needed. I realized I could now do it instinctively and without difficulty — a far leap from where I first started without even knowing I had these abilities. I thought about leaning into the surrounding shroud of shadow, pushing towards the center of the cavernous room. I felt the veil slowly inch its way in the direction I knew Eryn to be. Before long, I could see his body slowly coming into view, exactly the same way Althira had. His energy felt different seeing him like this. After his whole body was within my sight of the veil, I looked for his strand. It had to be something similar to what Vexil had, but I couldn't see it. I pushed harder to gain some clarity with the sight. I still could not find it; perhaps Eryn's was thinner and harder to find than Vexil's. I inhaled deeply, held my breath for a moment, then released it. As I refocused, I glimpsed something: a flicker in the dark, much like a firefly's glow. I shifted my focus to where I saw the flicker, now realizing the energy was different. That is why I was having difficulty locating Eryn's strand. Now that I knew what to look for, my vision sharpened and the details came into focus. When I saw Eryn's strand, which shone with a vibrant gold hue, my expression shifted. Slightly translucent, almost as if it were emanating a light from the center, and yet altogether different from Vexil's. Contrary to what I had first expected, it turned out to be something else entirely. "Now that you have located the strand, proceed with weaving the thread to become one with the needle." I paused, skeptical of what was being asked of me. My hesitation didn't go unnoticed. "On with it then! You will learn this whether or not you cooperate in this moment, so it would be in your best interest to do as instructed while in this beneficial learning environment." At first, I struggled to move the hands around as I was moving my corporeal hands in front of me before I realized that the action didn't make the incorporeal hands in the veil move much. I had to do what needed to be done through thought and concentration. I intently focused, moving my right hand with the needle in towards the strand. As I reached the strand, slowly pushing the needle through, the strand snapped to the needle, now truly becoming a thread to be woven. A thread of brilliant, rich gold. "Now weave a knot." I froze, horror overcoming me as I felt my body become overwhelmed with anxiety. Sweat was beading up on my forehead, the feeling of my underarms becoming damp now noticeable. "I will not do this if it will bring harm to Eryn." "Then fortunate for you that no harm will come to him if you do everything correctly." I had to relax my shoulders a bit; they were burning with fatigue from being so tense and holding my body too rigidly. I thought about it for a moment and realized that what made the most sense to me was to let the thread drape over my left hand as I took the right with the needle, bringing it around, then pulling the thread back through itself to create a knot. I dropped my left hand, pulling the needle out with my right to tighten the knot. The energy and brightness of the strand suddenly changed as the knot was pulled taut. I heard Eryn catch his breath, then complete silence. My heart sank into the pit of my stomach. Oh gods, what have I done?

Chapter 25: Death Woven

Althira sighed heavily, her patience wearing thin. "You are indeed ridiculous. He is fine. If you placed any faith in him, you would know it would take much more than something as simple as that to kill the Isiltyan. Isn't that correct?" "Indeed, Miss Octavia." I wasn't sure if Althira was just saying that to reassure me or if she was being truthful, but it was good to hear Eryn's voice, regardless. A small sigh escaped me as I allowed myself to relax slightly. "Now that you have bound his life's thread to you, I want you to find a place in the thread where it is significantly weaker. All you will have to do is widen your vision and then look at the length above as you give it a tug." I found myself able to do this rather effortlessly, I think in part because once I figured out how to see and use the veil, it became second nature. It made sense why Althira could wield such abilities with ease and grace; she had decades of practice and knew exactly what she was looking for. In time, I suspect I will wield and control my abilities similarly. As these thoughts went through my mind, I spotted a short length in the thread that appeared less vibrant than the rest of the strand. It dimmed significantly before continuing on as the thread had initially. "I believe I found a place like you described." Althira released a throaty hum, the sound rumbling in her chest. "Do you believe, or are you certain? Remember, there is no room here for mistakes or guesses. I will neither confirm nor deny whether you are correct in your assumptions, as it's crucial for you to discover that yourself. For your next instructions, if you are certain you have found the correct spot, the spot where the thread is thinner is a place in Eryn's life where he experiences near-death. If we so choose, we can make certain that death comes for him at that place in time or we could repeat the spot and cause him to live a traumatic event over again for as long as we wish, but we are not here to learn that or deliberately kill him today. Rather, I would like you to focus on strengthening this area. Give him less of a near-death experience. Do this by working the strand to be thicker in that area, making it more consistent with the rest of the strand." I focused, reaching out with the hands to caress the thread as carefully as I could manage, bringing it together slightly with a gentle tug. When I released it, the thread went back to exactly how it had been. Well, that let me know I needed to do something more than just pulling the threads together. I caressed the thread again, as gently as I could, tugging the more vibrant parts of the threads closer together. Except this time I focused my energy into the thread, intentionally willing the strands to close together. After several tries of this with nothing happening, I changed tactics. In order to achieve the outcome Althira desires, it was necessary for me to concentrate and apply myself with diligence, and frankly, I was also pleased to be of help to Eryn. I know I can do this; I just had to find the correct method or way of doing this without causing harm.

The thread remained caressed in my hands as I stood staring at the long piece. Althira and Eryn remained completely silent and unmoving. The only sound that could be heard was Vexil breathing heavily and panting similarly to how a dog would when hot. The thought came to me: I could use the needle to stitch the two pieces together to become one solid and consistent piece. After pondering for a while, I tried it—it was the most rational option, and I couldn't think of another idea that wouldn't put Eryn in danger. The thread remained caressed in my left hand as I manifested the needle back to my right hand, bringing the needle to the thread to pierce it just as I did when I tied the knot beforehand. The thread snapped to the needle with a little ting that rang through the silence of the shadowy veil around us. I paused for a moment to contemplate my next action. Seemingly, the way to connect the thread to shorten this near-death experience would be to bring the needle and thread just to the other side of the dimmer piece. I slowly brought the needle over to pierce the thread, opposite the side the needle was already hooked in with. I held my breath as time seemed to stand still around the vivisectum. I exhaled slowly, my vision clearing after a moment of holding my breath, and brought the needle to the thread. Nothing happened, so I continued pushing the needle through the thread. The strand buzzed with a low hum, and I felt a faint vibration, leading me to believe this was the expected result. As the needle was almost completely through the strand, I let go of it for a moment, bringing the hand back up to grab from the opposite side so that I could have a better grip on the needle. As I pulled it through, the string jerked taut. Without warning, the thread that was still attached to the needle pulled back, yanking the needle from my hands. The needle got flung back to the thread I had just pulled it from before tearing back through it. Everything happening around me caused me to let out a small, stunned sound. The needle had cut the incorporeal hand in the veil; I took note in the moment that I could feel the cut in my corporeal hand in front of me. Before I could react or realize what was happening, Vexil screamed a high-pitched scream. I turned to look, hearing Althira say, "Watch yourself, girl!" as my head was mid-turn. The thread blazed with a light more intense than the sun, a blinding flash that seared the vision. I yanked back the veil out of sheer instinct, pulling away from where Eryn stood. All of this happening within a split second, I didn't have time to think. The blinding flash hit the shielding outer walls of the veil I shrouded myself with. I was hit with the blunt force of a mule at full sprint, the veil shielding me from the impact. It startled me enough that I dropped the surrounding veil entirely. Almost immediately after that, the light that caused the flash reached me, and I was sent hurtling through the air. I hit something solid, but not as hard as a rock wall, feeling the back of my head hit as I then slid down. I felt consciousness leaving my body as I collapsed to the ground.

I came back mere moments later, realizing Eryn was kneeling in front of me. I heard Vexil giggling; I moved my head up from the damp dirt of the vivisectum floor to see Althira's high heels standing a ways back beside Eryn. "Miss Octavia! Miss Octavia! Are you with us? Are you all right?" Eryn sounded almost panicked. I groaned, reaching my hand up for Eryn to take, helping me sit up. Sitting up now, I reached up to feel the back of my head, but it was only mildly sore, noting that there was no blood. I turned to look at the wall behind me, only to see that it was several meters away. What did I hit? I looked for a pillar, but the nearest pillar to me was several paces to the side of where I landed. I looked up at Eryn. His appearance was identical to how it had been before we began, with not a single hair appearing to be out of its proper position. Althira burst out in deep laughter, sounding almost sinister. Vexil was at her feet, sing-songing along with her laughter. Eryn directed a nasty look towards her, which then caused me to look at her in a state of confusion. After she had finished her brief laughing episode, she returned to her poised and stern stature. "Well, I am certain you won't do that again." She said it while raising an eyebrow. That made me partly furious. She was so smug and sarcastic, but she was also correct. I would not make that mistake again. "What even happened? What did I hit?" I wanted to ask more, but I would start with the basics first. Althira was the one to speak first. "I would say the Isiltyan took action to defend himself in this situation." I glanced up at Eryn. His gaze shifted to the floor as he actively avoided making eye contact with me. Why would he attack me? "It is not his fault; it was instinct and reflex for someone like him. Now, as for why you were thrown across the vivisectum, that is no one's fault but your own. I told you when we started to keep yourself shielded closely. I even made you increase the strength of the surrounding barrier. Your letting that fall and forgetting such an important basic is your own folly, and I hope you have learned from it. While this time you only got sent back, the next time could very well be your last. If you forget that, then my teachings have unfortunately failed you. As for why you landed here, I used the veil to catch you midair. I already told you we can use the shadow and shade to shield ourselves, as well as others in some circumstances. This is precisely what I was referring to when I spoke about performing actions in this manner. You will learn to do the same. We still have yet to learn what you are capable of, but we will see soon enough." Eryn was now standing. I moved to get up; he reached a hand out in an offer to help me up. At first, I thought about reaching up to knock his hand away. I was mad that he looked guilty and mad that he sent me flying, but Althira saying it wasn't his fault was the only thing keeping me from being absolutely livid. I didn't want him to think I didn't trust him either, because I honestly still did. Between his sincere gentlemanly ways and his loyalty to Lady Alsendra, I felt I could trust him with my life. I grabbed his hand, and I felt the strength in his grip as he pulled me to my feet. I would, however, stay more wary around him until I found out exactly what information was being withheld from me. "Get yourself together; we're far from finished."

"Back to positions. We are not stopping until you learn this one technique." Eryn stood still, bringing his head up after a moment to look at Althira. "I'm not sure that is wise, my lady. After what has already happened, I don't want to bring any further harm to Miss Octavia if it can be prevented." "I wasn't asking. If you do not want to be helpful to us during this lesson, I can find a suitable replacement. Perhaps the Highborn, no?" Althira spoke the words with a threatening tone, covered in sarcasm and malice. "I don't have to tell you how lethal that would be for him, or that you would be responsible for his death. I would hate to see what happened to the person responsible for a Highborn's death. I can only imagine what Alsendra would have arranged for you should any harm come to either me or Miss Octavia. Now we both know you are smarter than to harm Kenric, and we both know you can not threaten me, Althira. For you to have the ignorant gall and audacity to stand before me attempting to threaten someone like myself proves how far you have fallen in your disgrace. You will stop the disrespect and passive-aggressive bullshit. Now act accordingly! I will not repeat myself. Do I make myself clear?" The words rolled off Eryn's tongue with heavy venom and power, bellowing through the vivisectum air like a war horn in the dead of night. This differed from the power that Lady Alsendra spoke with and was still different yet from the power Althira spoke with. This oozed out of Eryn's very pores. Before him, I felt a powerful urge to hide and retreat, with the possibility of removing myself from the situation momentarily flashing through my thoughts. While I had only observed occasional glimpses of this side of him before, I had seen nothing nearly as significant as this. A surge of energy pulsed out of Althira, hitting me in the stomach like a fist, with a large plume of black smoke rushing out in front of her, taking the shape of a snake coiled back and ready to strike. Eryn didn't flinch or even change his breathing. Vexil ran behind me, clinging to my leg while pointing and chattering nonsense. I bent down, grabbing the creature with one quick swoop, fully prepared for us to make a run for it. After a moment of complete silence, Althira then withdrew the smoky, demonic snake. After it was cleared away enough to see her face, I could see that she was… smiling? Surely she didn't think this was a joke. "Well, I'm glad to see you haven't completely lost what made you respected and likeable in the first place, Isiltyan. I thought perhaps your playing housekeeper for Alsendra all this time had made you soft." Eryn made his annoyance clear as he almost hissed at her. "Anyhow, if we are done with this little pissing match, shall we get back to it?" Althira quickly turned without waiting for an answer, the fabric of her dress flowing with dramatic flair as she went. This time around, I found Eryn's strand quickly, ready to end this entire ordeal and to move away from the tense energy between Eryn and Althira. Although this time, Althira stepped in and helped guide me after blindfolding me. She let me take control of the strand, also noting that the knot I previously made was now gone, pointing out how it would be useless and I now had no control to claim with his strand. Althira made motions with her shadowy hands in demonstration, then told me to do as she did. What I had to do was take the strand with the needle and make a small type of knot that fully tied up the thinner piece that would have been Eryn's near-death experience. After that, Althira showed me how to roll the thread gently between the hands, gradually smoothing out the knot until it was no longer visible. Once we had spent a little time working on it and moving energy around perfectly, she was happy with what we had done, and we wrapped things up for the night. I headed straight out of the vivisectum without delay or a word spoken. I kept far ahead of Eryn in order not to speak, and Alsendra took a different direction back to her room. I made it to my dormitory room in record speed, quickly shutting the door behind me. I didn't have the energy to speak to anybody. I collapsed onto the bed, the exhaustion of the day washing over me as my eyes closed before I could process it.

Chapter 26: Predilection For Apathy

When I woke the next morning, I was lying on top of the comforter, fully clothed. Confusion hit me until I remembered briefly collapsing onto the bed and falling asleep almost instantly. My mouth was dry and gritty, my eyes squinting as I tried to focus and adjust to having them open. Nova must have heard me opening the door, as seconds later, I heard his paws click-clacking on the hardwood floor at a full run before sliding to a halt in front of me. I rubbed the sides of his head and ears with both hands; he gave me one of his grins with his tongue half out the side. I loved the dog, but right at this moment, what I needed was a warm shower and to brush my teeth. I quickly made my way to the showers, craving how refreshed I would feel after basking in the natural hot spring water. It really seemed to have some healing properties. Luckily, I didn't see anyone as I made my way. I suspect I woke up late, and the aroma of breakfast signaled that everyone was already up and busy. After finishing my shower, I peeked out of the door into the hall while still wrapped in an oversized linen towel, not seeing or hearing anyone directly from the corridor. I forgot my clothes in my rush to get to the showers, so I would have to make a run for it. I started sprinting, heading towards my room while ensuring each step was deliberate in order to avoid slipping and falling. About a third of the way back to my room, Nova ran out of the room he and Kenric now occupied, running along beside me and jumping up and down, all the while grabbing at my towel. "Stop that now; it isn't playtime, you silly boy. Go on now." I was talking to him in a hushed tone so as not to draw attention, but he didn't understand;

the loving creature just wanted to play. I was almost at the door of my room when I heard a door open, followed by footsteps. I spun around, the sound of footsteps ringing in my ears, to see who was behind me. Standing there, silhouetted in the doorway, was Kenric! I whipped around and ran at full speed, dipping through the doorway with Nova at my heels. I hurriedly shut the door in haste, closing Nova inside the room with me. I stood with my back against the door for a moment, partly embarrassed, partly elated that I had made it to my room so quickly and without dropping the towel. With any luck, Kenric would simply overlook seeing me in a towel. Maybe he didn't even have time to notice. I looked down at Nova. He was sitting in front of me like a perfectly chiseled statue, looking at me with his head tilted ever so slightly to the side. "Stay there. I have to get dressed." He sat there watching me like a hawk, with his all too intelligent eyes. I felt strange being naked in front of him; it felt like a person was watching me. Maybe my modesty was getting the best of me. There was a knock at the door. Nova barked and ran to the door, sniffing before wagging his tail excitedly. "One minute! I'm indecent!" Kenric's voice answered back, smooth as always. "I was just checking to see if I could have my dog back or if you were intending to hold him hostage?" Nova barked a couple of times, almost seeming to respond to Kenric. I tugged my top on, pushed my damp hair away from my neck, and then rushed to the door, pulling it open. Nova bolted out, taking off down the hall in a prancing run. "Thanks, I would hate to think I had to negotiate for his release." Kenric said the words so dryly that I wasn't sure he was joking at first, but he smiled before turning to walk away as his long hair swayed behind him. I shut the door to finish getting ready.

After I was fully presentable once again, I made my way to the kitchen and dining area. I was hellbent on having a cup of coffee and a cinnamon bun, and I was just praying to whatever deity wanted to listen that there were cinnamon buns. I smelled coffee in the air before I rounded the corner of the doorway where the dining area was. I walked through the door, seeing Althira sitting in what was apparently her spot in front of the stained glass window. Sitting straight and tall with her legs crossed, as usual. I glanced around, looking for cinnamon buns. I was so hungry I could eat a horse. I saw Gabrielle sitting at the table where food often sat; I spotted a basket with a gingham linen draped over the top. My eyes widened. Cinnamon buns! I skipped to the basket, pulling back to see some kind of light, flaky pastry. I was disappointed if I were being honest, but this would have to do, whatever it was. I picked one up and noticed the quivering jelly in the middle, heightening my anticipation for a bite. I stuck it in my mouth as I poured my cup of coffee, deeply inhaling the earthy aroma. I grabbed the soft pastry in my mouth, biting off a large piece as I took it. Oh, this was delicious, too. It was puffy and perfectly flaky; the jelly or jam in the center was some kind of orange filling. The taste of the citrus perfectly balanced with the sweetness, neither being overbearing in the delicate treat. I was extra cautious not to make a sound or moan in front of Althira; I don't think I could listen to her contempt towards my behavior; I know she would be more than certain to have an issue with it. I ate my pastry with my eyes closed, taking in the coffee and sipping between bites. Gabrielle seemed to understand that I was still half-asleep and not in the mood for talking, so she kept silent. I wondered if her abilities as a spellcaster gave her an edge in sensing my emotions even now; it had to be like an extreme form of empathy after all. Althira sat her teacup down with a clank before getting up, her heels making several loud clacks on the wood floor before she came to a stop before the doorway, turning back to speak. "Meet me in the room with the round table when you are finished. There are conversations to be had." I stared back at her, saying nothing, chewing another bite of my pastry. She turned with a twirl, letting out a "hmph" at my apparent rudeness of no response. After a moment, Gabrielle broke the silence with a small giggle. "You know, I think you have a way of getting under Althira's skin." I nodded. "Yes, I believe you are right." Leaning gently against the table, I took slow sips of coffee, and with every moment that passed, I could feel my energy returning and slowly becoming more human. "Hey Gabrielle, have you seen Eryn? I saw Kenric, but I haven't seen him this morning." "I saw him earlier when I first got up, but I believe he headed out shortly after, as I don't remember seeing him since then." I nodded in recognition. I wonder if I should tell her about what happened between Eryn and Althira. Should I tell her my suspicions and involve her? I don't want her to be implicated in the mess I create if it goes south or I learn something I shouldn't know. I decided I would sit on it a while longer while I contemplated what I needed to do. Gabrielle eyed me warily. I suspect she knew I was keeping something from her as well. Should I speak up and tell her I don't want to involve her for her own sake? I couldn't decide what to say, so instead I left. I would just go talk with Althira, keeping my fingers crossed that I have a better time with the upcoming conversation.

I knocked on the door lightly before opening it, my knuckles barely making a sound on the heavy ironclad hardwood door. I pushed the heavy door open. Althira was sitting in the same place she had been the last time we were in this room. She held a book in her hand, promptly closing it and setting it down on the table upon my entering the room. She extended her hand, motioning for me to sit. I pulled out a chair and sat on the ruby-red cushion. "We need to clear some things up. The air between us is fouling, and I will not have whatever toxic energy you have building to impede my teaching and your training. Whatever questions you have pent up and whatever comments you have for me, now is the time to speak them. Speak your truth, and I vow to listen without interrupting or getting upset. Now, whether I answer the question you ask remains to be seen, but I will answer what I find reasonable. This is the only opportunity I will give you for the foreseeable future, because if I'm blunt, these kinds of conversations bore me to no end with my predilection for apathy and lack of concern towards your petty woes. However, in this case, it would seem imperative. So speak." I sat in my chair, unsure where to start. I had so many questions. With so many things I wanted to know, I don't think I have time to ask them all. I considered it, deciding to go with the most recent question that was currently nagging at me the worst. "What is the story behind Eryn? Why did Rayden and he seem familiar, and why do you have such qualms about him? What was that with Eryn yesterday in the vivisectum? The sweet, well-dressed man I know so well was gone, replaced by a different person." Althira pursed her lips. "Right… sweet." I started to rebuttal, but decided I had better hold my tongue in case I actually would receive the answers to my questions. I know she has some answers, but I'm unsure what Althira will truthfully and directly answer. "Eryn and I do have a history of sorts. Did Alsendra or Eryn really not tell you anything about who he is?" I shook my head. "I did not know what he even was until after Lady Alsendra told me she was sending me here to Liraquor to meet you, then only after asking did he tell me he was a spellblade. I didn't know he carried the syreth blades, and I certainly did not know he was called Isiltyan. He introduced himself to me as the chamberlain and right hand of Lady Alsendra." Althira let out a loud, cackling laugh. "Chamberlain is a good one. He and Alsendra are a couple of jestering fools playing at games." She waved her hand in a manner to disregard the train of thought she was on. "I'll start by saying the Isiltyan is no simple chamberlain or custodian of any sort, even if he wants to play as such. He is a royal Orriveth elven, of the purest bloodline at that. He is extremely gifted and truly a powerful weapon if he chooses to be." I felt my jaw drop open before catching myself and quickly closing it. "I will not tell you certain details of his story and lineage, as that is not my information to share. What I will tell you is to stop letting that man fool you into thinking he is a normal, humble servant. Would you believe me if I told you he outranks Rayden in every way imaginable, especially by blood? Eryn has more claim to the Royal Court than Rayden will ever have, and yet he slums around with the likes of us. Peculiar, isn't it?" Althira seemed both genuinely perplexed and slightly intrigued. All I could think about was his being pure Orriveth elven. "But he doesn't even have pointed ears!" I blurted it out in realization. Althira glared at me with a look of distaste on her face. "Do you really think you don't have any mental issues? Perhaps a slowness or a prior head injury? Use your brain, girl! Surely you aren't foolish enough to think all elves look the same? Some are born with distinct features, such as dramatically pointed ears, and then the features skip others entirely. Then you have the Ravynari, who look even different from most elves, partly because of inbreeding, but that's neither here nor there." I held up my hand to stop her. I needed a moment. I was currently overwhelmed by the information she gave me and not sure how to process it.

Wait until I tell Gabrielle about this. And Ophelia is going to pass out when she finds out about this! That led me to wonder for a moment why she hasn't made the trip here yet. Gabrielle had time to make the trip here after us, and it has been a while. Maybe I should send a message to check in with her and perhaps even warn her of the threat from the Ravynari. I put that at the back of my mind to focus on asking Althira the questions I needed while I had the chance. "You said you had a history with Eryn; can you tell me about that?" Althira pursed her lips again. "I will not. That leads directly to the part that would not be my story to tell. You should ask him directly. I'm sure he hasn't spoken about it in years." I thought about her reply. If it's their history and she is involved directly with her side of the story, then how is that not also her story to tell just as much as it was Eryn's? This was getting to me. "Do you know why Eryn serves Lady Alsendra if he is a royal Orriveth as you said? That makes little sense unless Lady Alsendra has something over him or he is indebted, perhaps." Althira cackled again. "You know, occasionally you say something intelligent that surprises me. However, to answer your question, and not to answer your question, Eryn is by Alsendra's side by choice as far as I'm aware. I would not understand why he chose such a lowly life from the royal Orriveth; perhaps you can get that out of one of them directly. I don't care enough to find out for myself." My eyes widened as thoughts ran through my mind, and I connected more dots while simultaneously uncovering even more questions and mysteries. "Lady Alsendra said you and her honed your skills together and that you had as much knowledge as she has… now I know you're still going to keep things from me, that's a given, but what will you tell me about your background together?" Althira wasn't expecting me to ask that, raising an eyebrow in response. "Interesting that you ask that, of all things. There's not much to tell. We were both exceptionally gifted in our areas, and therefore we were both inducted to be taught and trained by the High Council to become what we are today, mostly. Alsendra and I gravitated towards each other naturally. We still do, I suppose. We learned that when we work together, we are an unbridled force to be reckoned with. With her gift of sight and ability to predict the future, and my gift of being able to control shadowmancy around us and influence humans, dead and alive, who can stand against the two of us and succeed? It is not impossible, but it is extremely unlikely. So as you may have concluded, she can tell me what to do and when to do it for us to succeed, when you add my gift of dark sight with the veil to hers, we have been able to achieve things together that no other mages have. I suspect that plays a small part in why Alsendra and I are well respected among the High Council. But they still fear me. I am a Mortis Velum after all." That sparked another question. "You have stated you are the only Mortis Velum Magister, aside from me possibly, but then you refer to the Velum and the veil as we and us, and then speak as if there are more. Is that not the case?" I seem to have struck a nerve. Althira glowered at me, her eyes piercing into my soul. She took a moment, seemingly to calm herself down before speaking again. "I am the only Mortis Velum practicing, and the only one with the aptitude and skill I possess that allows me to be as capable as I am. I will say no more on the subject until you, as one of the Veiled, have earned that information. Now, have we satisfied that sour taste you had for information? Can we move on with a little more trust and understanding? We are not your enemy, and I hope you realize that, because the true enemy may very well show itself at our doorstep at any moment."

Chapter 27: Peasants

I slowly stood up to make my leave, a thousand thoughts racing
through my mind at once. I paused, thinking of a couple more things I
needed to ask now. "I only have a few more questions before I go,"
Althira said nothing; she only flicked a finger up in the air to signal me
to continue. "When you said Eryn defended himself and didn't mean
to attack me in the vivisectum, what exactly did you mean by that
being instinct for someone like him? I now assume you were referring
to his being elven?" "Yes. As you have already been told, with Rayden
being the veilwarden, he governs the veil from blatant negligence;
some of the Orriveth elves have the ability to see within the veil in a
way similar to how we Mortis Velum can. I do not know the full
extent of Eryn's abilities, but I suspect he can see most of what we can,
possibly more, and he can clearly sense when someone is in the
surrounding veil. When you made the mistake with trying to weave
his strand, Eryn, being as powerful as he truly is, his powers reacted
on their own to protect him. I believe what happened is he was well
aware of everything going on the entire time, both seeing and feeling,
so when he felt the negative effects of what you did, his power reacted
to save his life. It is a reflex. In the same way that we can shroud
ourselves with shadow and shade, some of the Orriveth can use light
in a very similar way to shield or protect themselves. I wonder if he
doesn't possess many of the Orriveth abilities. It could also be in part
to the Syreth blades and his bond to them, but I wouldn't be so
certain. The light seemed more like an elven birth ability." I let the
information sink in, heavy as a stone dropped into still water. There

was so much I hadn't known, so much Eryn and Lady Alsendra kept from me. It seemed like everyone was repeatedly trying to keep me from knowing something. I would find out more about this. I thought of one more question I wanted to ask while I had Althira's attention. "When we were in the vivisectum, I saw the way Vexil was enthralled by everything you did involving death weaving. Can he see everything we do in the veil?" Althira smirked. "He is a Duskkin, hun. He walks in the shadows more than he does in our realm. He actively moves to and from the veil at will. He can see everything a Mortis Velum does. I told you when you first met Vexil he could distinguish light and manage curses. He does that by controlling shadows and shade. While he can not control the veil to shield himself in the same way we do, he can effortlessly walk between light and shadow and pluck darkness and curses from the veil itself at any time. The usefulness of the little gremlins stems from that aspect."

"I would assume you will not tell me anything about how Rayden and Eryn's backgrounds are connected?" "You would be correct. Ask one of them if you wish to find out for yourself." I got up, pushing in the wooden chair. "And take the rest of the day for leisure. If I determine we need to have another lesson today after I have had time to think, I will fetch you." Without another word further, I walked out of the room, letting the heavy door shut before continuing. I couldn't believe Eryn, the man that nearly acted like a father to me, the same man that was always so kind and concerned for my well-being, was a royal Orriveth! The thought was almost comical, but it made so much sense. A lot of things that made little sense with Eryn before now made much more sense. A realization hit me. The goblin we encountered on our way to Liraquor knew what Eryn was. The way he bowed down before Eryn and said something about it before Eryn cut him off and made him leave. I rounded the corner of one corridor that led back to the dining area, and just as I turned the corner, I ran right into Gabrielle. "I'm sorry." We chimed the words in unison before laughing it off. "Hey, want to go talk back in our rooms? I have some interesting news." She beamed at me. "Do I ever!" She grabbed my hand, yanking me along behind her as we took off in a jog. Gabrielle led me to her room. Upon entering, I saw Spriggle up on the small dresser to the side of the room. He was looking at himself in the wall-mounted mirror. He was holding out his little stick legs, dancing back and forth while laughing. The Leshy had to be one of the strangest creatures I've ever met; he was nothing like the stories I heard about them growing up. He wasn't terrifying at all. Gabrielle stepped over to him, dropping a piece of bread beside him. Spriggle turned around to look at her, ran to the piece of bread, he picked it up before he hopped down, holding the bread above his head. Running to the other side of the bed where he had been when I saw him playing with Gabrielle's clothes. Gabrielle plopped down on the bed, lying on her stomach. At the foot of the bed, I sat on the little dressing bench, feeling the cool, smooth wood beneath me. "Can you assure me that anything said in this room stays between us? I want your word." "Absolutely! I'll take it to the grave!" Something about her made me believe she would honor that too. "Okay, have you heard anything about Eryn?" She looked at me, a look of confusion pasting her expression. "You mean since you introduced him as your chaperone? No?" Part of me curdled inside at the thought of calling a royal Orriveth elf my chaperone, and he just let me and went along with it. I felt so embarrassed now. I brought my palm up to my face to cover my eyes for a second. "Well, whatever you did probably wasn't that bad." I smiled; she could tell how I felt. "It's not that. I just learned that Eryn is one of the royal Orriveth elven. And I mean super-royal, as in he outranks the veilwarden Rayden in every way, apparently even by bloodline." I spoke low and with purpose. I didn't want anyone outside this room to overhear us, but I wanted to make sure Gabrielle understood everything I was saying. Her face fell, going blank from the expression it had held before. "Surely that can't be. If he were that high in status among the Royal Court, he would never be here with mere peasants like us." She stopped to look up at me. "No offense, but none of us have a lofty position, that's for sure. Sir Highborn Kenric is only a noble himself, and that is a far cry from being among the company of the high-status Orriveth royals. They certainly wouldn't allow him to act as a servant to Lady Alsendra. Actually, the Royal Court would probably consider that as him being more of a slave." Her voice trailed off as she finished her sentence. And even though it was hard to accept, she was correct in her assessment. My mind reeled with questions that echoed in the silence.

We stayed in her room for a while, discussing all the different things this could mean. We tried to work out whether what

Althira told me was even true. Considering she had no motive to deceive me regarding that matter, and assuming her information was accurate, then that would answer some of my suspicions. After I had told her everything I had found out, keeping out a few details, we eventually grew tired of thinking and speculating. "Let's go for a walk around the grounds. I'll grab Spriggle!" Gabrielle jumped up, grabbing the Leshy before skipping to the door, motioning for me to follow. We ran into Kenric and Nova in the long corridor leaving the dormitories. "Would you two like to come for a walk with us? We're just going to take a walk around the grounds." Kenric looked down at Nova, then back to me and Gabrielle with a smile. "I think Nova would say he would love to go if he could answer. Let's go." The four of us walked on together. "Kenric, have you perchance seen Eryn?" "Not since this morning. He was in the shower when I was getting around, and we spoke briefly in passing, but I think he went somewhere after that." Part of me hoped he hadn't left for good. Or that I didn't actually hurt him with the weaving yesterday. If what Althira said was true, I surely didn't harm him at all. Gabrielle spoke up, breaking me out of the deep thoughts. "Which of the blasted corridors leads to the courtyard doors?" I shrugged. I honestly did not know. I had never been to the courtyard since arriving here. "We take the corridor past the kitchen area, and then we make a right. That hall will then lead to the atrium. That's my favorite way to go." Me and Gabrielle must have both given him a look because Kenric laughed after glancing at us. "I know the paths to every outdoor intimately. In case you guys haven't noticed, Nova has a lot of energy and has to use the bathroom several times a day on top of it." Well, that was true. "I was unaware that an atrium was actually present." Since I've been here, my exploration of this place has been minimal aside from where Althira has sent me. Spriggle was on Gabrielle's shoulder, now trying to pester Nova. Nova was making little hops, letting out whines of discontentment. We continued on like that, saying nothing further, following the path Kenric had suggested. When we reached the atrium, I was slightly in awe of the brightness and beauty. While reminiscent of the other corridors within Althira's Castle of a building, this one was unique. This atrium corridor was distinguished by its curved glass roof that gracefully descended, connecting the stone and wood of the walls. The floor when entering the atrium was no longer wood. This turned to a stone path, pea-sized pebbles lining both sides of the stone path lined up to the stone walls. There were oval-shaped areas of soil left open, bordered by bricks to keep out the small pebbles, holding a plethora of different plants. Most of them I didn't know the names of; some I had seen before, while others looked rare and exotic. A few of the plants stood out as being easily identifiable. There were some pineapple plants in an oval area, little pineapples of all sizes growing from the center of the tops. I also spotted things like large monsteras on the outer corners furthest away; various ivy and philodendrons lined the lower parts of the stone walls. Along one wall was a longer area of open soil. The bird of paradise stood there, as tall as a shorter human, lush and vibrant. As we reached the double doors leading to the courtyard, the walls before the door were lined with wooden shelves. These shelves contained many potted plants and herbs. Some pots were empty, containing only moss or bark, or soil. Some plants here were more shaded than those in the open part of the atrium. There were orchids, ferns, bromeliads, and what looked like seedlings of some kind of tree or bush in various small pots. This didn't entirely surprise me with Althira. She seemed like someone who would like to spend time in her garden to reflect. I remembered that Lady Alsendra had quilts on quilt frames, draped in one area of her home. I wondered what hobby I would like when I was their age, assuming I lived that long.

I gazed at the vast courtyard, partly in shock that an area this large was in the center of the large manor I had spent so much time in training. Nova bolted out, prancing and jumping as he went along. This entire courtyard was magical. A large tree in the very center of the courtyard was vibrant pink and white. I believed it was a type of cherry blossom tree. Pink and white petals lay strewn about the base of the tree, their delicate scent filling the air. Nova was running through them, catching one here and there in his mouth before spitting it out and moving along. All around the tree fluttered butterflies. The butterflies were the same as the ones I saw in front of a small shop when we first arrived in Liraquor. I am left wondering whether these stunning butterflies were brought into existence through mystical means, or even if they were genuinely tangible things that were exclusive to the area near Liraquor. Either way, they were a welcome and beautiful sight to behold. Square hedges, meticulously trimmed, lined the perimeter of the courtyard. The entire courtyard area was lined with short, dark green grass and clover. Stepping stones making haphazard paths around, seeming more like a suggestion than to be used. "Wow." Gabrielle echoed my own thoughts, but I was speechless. There were stone and wooden benches scattered throughout. This courtyard held some of the biggest and prettiest camellia bushes I had ever seen, planted in key areas. The edges of each bloom's petals are slightly ruffled, being whiter in the center and deep shades of pink around the edges. In the two far corners opposite where we exited the atrium, there were two raised beds, one at each corner, made of stone. These held large oleanders. I bet Althira had them planted in the raised beds to avoid any accidents with their poisonous foliage. Along the front perimeter of the rock retaining wall holding in the raised beds were tulips of two colors: deep royal purple and black. An actual black tulip? Were those natural? I had to admit they were equally stunning as the rest of the flowers in the area. The black was a true, deep, inky black, reminding me of the selkies from the night of the Rights. Nova came barreling towards us; he looked as if something had spooked him. He slid to a halt behind Kenric, turning to look around Kenric's legs back toward the enormous tree. Kenric looked up toward the tree after seeing Nova's actions, pulling a small blade without hesitation. Me and Gabrielle froze, searching the area for what had bothered Nova. For the duration of those moments, we were motionless as we watched the individual on the far side of the courtyard move from behind the immense tree and into open view.

Chapter 28: Vapid Impulses

Clad in brilliant white, with a mysterious allure, the tall woman who came into view was stunning; her presence commanded attention. She was smiling at us, putting her hands up casually to show she was not a threat. "Well, hello everyone." She gave us a warm smile, showing her white teeth; a smile so large her eyes nearly squinted with the gesture. Without a moment's notice, Nova took off, heading straight for her, tail high in the air as he bobbed back and forth with a prance. Kenric attempted to stop him for a moment before admitting defeat. Nova ran up to her, running in a circle around her while jumping. She gave another huge smile to Nova, reaching down to pat him on the head and rub his neck. Nova ran back towards Kenric with his tail wagging widely back and forth. "She is good. I would trust Nova's judgment of character with my life, and he approves of her." Kenric reached down, putting away the small blade. I hadn't even known he had a blade with him before he pulled it, but of course it made sense for him to always have a blade on him. As the woman stepped closer to us, we also moved closer, walking towards the center of the large courtyard. Details of the woman became clearer as we got closer. She was clearly of some elven descent, based on her looks and short, pointy ears. Her appearance was striking, with a tall, slender physique accentuated by curves and caramel-brown skin. She had short, light-colored hair that was dark blonde, darker towards her scalp. The color that entered my thoughts was that of light nutmeg. There were solid white highlights throughout her short hair, giving the overall appearance of being lighter than it was. The longest part of her hair brushed her collarbone. Shorter pieces were cut throughout, spiking out deliberately in a messy manner, adding a touch of archaic allure. It was striking against her light brown skin. Scantily dressed, she wore a white sheer wrap around her hips, leaving her solid silver drawers in clear view against her skin. The wrap draped down on one side at an angle, with small pieces hanging down, accentuating her long legs. The same sheer fabric she wore around her waist was also worn over her head, lightly draped over the back of her head to fall around her shoulders, caressing her shoulders loosely before descending onto her upper arms. Under the sheer fabric at the top was a thin and long piece of silver fabric, matching her bottoms, wrapped around her chest. The fabric just covered her nipples; the rounded top and bottom of her beautifully perky breasts were clearly visible. Taking in her beauty, I couldn't help but stare; she was truly stunning. I couldn't pinpoint it, but she looked familiar. I was racking my brain trying to figure out if I'd met her before. "How do you do, my lady?" Kenric gave a small bow of respect. She smiled in response, giving him another genuine, soft, and warm smile. I now noticed she had a small silver ring through the center of her nose, not too different from a bullring. It oddly added to her overall ethereal aura, giving the impression of a goddess. "Please don't. There is no need for that, but I thank you for your kindness." Her voice was raspy and sensual. I was taken aback; everything about her provoked carnal desire. The woman exuded feminine divinity. "My name is Jolithae, but you can call me Joli." The words rolled off her tongue with a velvety-smooth rasp. It then hit me — I had seen her before! This was the same courtesan in the shop window I saw when we first arrived in Liraquor. She looked so different here, but that was her; I was almost sure of it. Gabrielle chimed in with her enthusiastic tone. "Hi, nice to meet you. I am Gabrielle. This is Octavia, and this is Sir Highborn Kenric." She pointed to each of us as she stated our names, following up her sentence with, "You're so pretty." Gabrielle flung her hand to her mouth, showing she hadn't intended to say that out loud. "As are you, mira." The lady smiled at Gabrielle as she said the words, with a heavy accent trailing at the end. "Mira?" Gabrielle questioned, seemingly as clueless as I was. "Oh, my apologies. Mira is Errithal dialect, my home clan. It means similar to someone in your language using dear as a term of endearment."

"You are Errithalan? From the same clan near Velasari?" Kenric exclaimed each question, excited about learning the information. Joli smiled warmly again. "I am indeed; that is why I have the accent." "I lived with the Woodwose people near the Velasari Glades for a time!" He was filled with pride, and Kenric's expression was now almost a beam directed at her. "Indeed, I can tell by the markings you bear. It is an honor." In a gesture of deference, Joli inclined her head, then raised it again, wearing a look of bewilderment. "You possess the gift, no?" "I don't possess any abilities, I'm afraid. I just came from a family that provided me with privileged opportunities." Joli raised her eyebrows, followed by lifting her hand in front of her with her palm facing Kenric. A sudden, brief flash of green left her palm, happening so quickly that I might've missed it had I not been watching so closely. Spriggle on Gabrielle's shoulder went crazy, shouting, pointing at Joli while slapping the side of Gabrielle's head. Gabrielle was trying to keep him calm. "Stop that, you pestering thing!" I turned, noticing Kenric's tattoos on his neck and arms. They were now glowing with a radiant emerald green, appearing as if they pulsed with light. The color was very close to what had come from Joli's hand, only far more saturated. Kenric hadn't realized what was happening. I pointed, unable to find words. He looked down, now seeing the tattoos down his forearms glowing. "What in all the realms?" Joli said nothing, shrugging, then walked over to Gabrielle. She reached out her hands with Spriggle reaching up to her, exactly as a human baby would do. She lifted him up, a soft green glow surrounding her hands where she held the Leshy. Spriggle was pressing his head against Joli's chest. She turned around to Kenric, laying a hand on his shoulder, the emerald green dissipating as she did. There was so much happening, I didn't know where to start. "Nothing like this has ever happened. What did you do for my markings to glow?" Joli chuckled lightly with a raspy backing. "I did nothing; I merely fanned the spark for a moment." "Spark? What in the hells is going on?" Kenric sounded panicked now, but the truth was we were all a little confused, I think. Jolithae seemed to be the only one unconcerned as she cooed to the cradled Leshy. "I am surprised you lack so much knowledge considering. Aside from that, however, why exactly do you carry one of the protector spirits? Leshies are to be in the forests, safeguarding sacred land." "Well, it's a long story, really, but he was summoned by a girl at the Rights and then we didn't have time to figure out where to take him before Lady Alsendra sent him with me to come here to Liraquor. She said he would be needed. So we do not know why he's here either, to be honest." Gabrielle gave a very accurate summary. Joli took a deep breath and sighed. "I think you should let him spend some time here in the garden. He would do a wonderful job watching over it for us." She smiled again, this time at the Leshy in her hands that was still not moving and only leaning against her. I did not recall ever seeing the little spirit stay so calm for this long. "Forgive me if this was not known to you. Let me start at the beginning. I am Jolithae the Ashbloom, Ruun of the Errithal elven clan, and now a resident in Liraquor. As a Ruun, I am an elder druid among my people. That's the reason I am here today. I take care of these gardens around us when I'm not otherwise occupied. We druids have a special way with plants and the earthly beings around us. We might not be useful for much, but we can help maintain the beauty of nature. The little Leshy here could sense it in me from the moment I awoke the spark in the marked one. We also move as one with the woodland beings, including these sweet guardians, which allows us to have a special bond. Think of it as druids being able to put roots in the ground to intertwine with everything around us that comes from the soil. That is what it is to be a Ruun. Soon, you will find out the significance of what you saw with your markings today. That is something I can not teach you, but something you will have to find out on your own. It's rather unfortunate you haven't already learned what lies beneath the surface."

We were all taken aback by the sheer volume of information that we were given, and so we turned to each other, our gazes lingering for a moment, before returning our attention to Jolithae. "Plus, Althira compensates me well for my work here." Part of me had wondered if, by compensation, she meant training under Althira. "Are you one of Althira's students as well?" A low, raspy laugh escaped Joli's lips. "I don't believe a druid like me could benefit from many of the teachings from a Mortis Velum. Our areas of expertise are opposing forces: light and shade. I breathe life into the world around, while the death veils manipulate death and decay. If you ask Althira, she will say my abilities only offer vapid impulses compared to hers and that I dress shamefully like a floozy. But a Ruun does not concern themselves with the opinions of things surrounded by rot." I decided at that moment that I loved Joli. She was stunning, alluring, kind and warm, and not afraid to speak her mind. She was grounded, and I always liked that in people. I hope I get to spend more time with her. I have a feeling that we will become good friends. "When we arrived in Liraquor, I saw a woman in a shop window; was that you?" Kenric looked like he was going to scold me for asking. Joli appeared pensive. I wondered if I shouldn't have asked; perhaps it was rude. "It was I. When I am not occupied with these particular tasks, I consider myself to be a courtesan. Now, I don't want you getting the wrong impression and thinking of me as a low-life sex worker. I am nothing of the sort and never would be. Most of the time, I only occupy the window to grab the attention of passersby. The other courtesans usually prefer not to be in public view, and they welcome my ability to bring in well-paying clients. Should I be hired, my clients will provide substantial compensation for my time if they desire it. And if anyone gains the courage to lay a hand upon me without my consent, they will suffer grave consequences because of their actions." A glint in her eyes and a mischievous smile escaped her, letting me know she meant every word. Something told me she was capable enough on her own to make any foe suffer. "What I do and with whom is completely up to me. That's the beauty of being a courtesan here in Liraquor. I get to do what I want while still maintaining my self-respect and dignity. We are not seen as black-market items to be hidden with shame. We get to live a regular life and pay taxes on our income like any other profession. Some people will continue to think of me as a prostitute regardless, and that is their prerogative, but that would be far from the actual services I provide." I had deep respect and admiration for Joli. To take control of your life the way she does, to do as you wish while still being in control. I believe most women strive for exactly that, but she achieved it. She not only achieved it, she owned it. I had met no one exactly like her, but something about her faintly reminded me of Ophelia. Perhaps it was that they both seemed ethereal, with otherworldly grace and beauty. Maybe it was the way they carried themselves; I wasn't sure exactly what it was. I considered Ophelia working as a courtesan in the same way Joli did. I wondered whether she would enjoy that. She certainly had the beauty and features to do it if she wanted. Bearing in mind that neither of us has previously had the experience of meeting courtesans or witnessing anything similar, she would likely be just as intrigued with this as I was. Prostitution was illegal in Faladorn. Its illegality did nothing to stop it; instead, it turned the work into a shameful act to be hidden in the dark. Prostitution often belonged to the ladies of the night, working in back alleyways in dark and dangerous situations without protection. In this moment, however, I was left wondering why Faladorn wouldn't legalize it in the way it was here in Liraquor. This was clearly far more respectable and safer for the women doing it. I had never seen it in this light, where the women working had such reverence and control.

"You guys are more than welcome to enjoy the garden. Do not let my presence deter you from basking in the wonderful company of those rooted around us. They have many stories to tell." She said the words as if the surrounding plants could talk and communicate. Perhaps they were more sentient than I understood. "Don't be silly; your presence made our time here even more enjoyable." Kenric was right; I felt we were better for having met her. Joli had a wonderful personality, and I appreciated the experience. Alongside acquiring an abundance of new information, we also uncovered a rather strange situation involving Kenric and his tattoos. While setting that aside for later consideration, I made a mental note to offer Kenric my help in resolving the problem if he so desired my help with it. "How often are you here? I would love to talk with you again soon." I would be happy for any break away from Althira and her cruel and unusual lessons, especially if that involved talking to Joli again. "I have no set schedule, mira. I come when I feel the plants need my help. The weather plays a part in that as well; it can be quite unforgiving to those who can't always provide for themselves. When my assistance isn't needed, I will probably be at the brothel with the other courtesans or at the grand library. I enjoy the chance to peruse old knowledge. You are welcome to say hi should you find me at either; I wouldn't turn down the company." She smiled at us warmly. A bustle of noise made all of us turn. The noise was coming from up the atrium. Nova barked at the approaching mystery. Moments later, Vexil shot out from behind the doors leading out to the courtyard. He stayed in the shade, not stepping foot into the sun. He was screaming and chattering wildly and pointing. What on earth was he so worked up about this time? Amid his frenzied chattering, I made out the words: "She here." As we were trying to work out what he was telling us, another person emerged from the atrium. It was Lady Alsendra. The only thing I could think to say in that moment was, "Oh." Alsendra already looked annoyed. "Are you all going to stand here without a thought in your heads, or are you going to come with me so we can speak about why I am here?" Well, I believe we have figured out what Vexil was trying to convey. Vexil ran back past Alsendra into the atrium, growling and snarling. She kicked at him, with no aim of contacting her foot. I stifled a snicker before it could escape. It was quite funny to see Vexil's reaction to Alsendra and his obvious disdain towards her when he had the complete opposite reaction to Althira. He never seemed to have a problem with me, but perhaps that was because of me having similar abilities to Althira's. All of us followed Alsendra, Joli staying behind still holding Spriggle. "Should I not take Spriggle?" Gabrielle seemed concerned. "Leave him with me. I will help him get comfortable in this garden before I leave. You can come check on him later or take him with you should you leave. I think you will find he feels right at home here." Gabrielle nodded with an "okay" before continuing on with us. Alsendra paused. "One minute." She spun back to where Joli stood with Spriggle. "You're the druid." It was a statement, not a question. "Indeed, I am." Joli's face had hardened, her words with Alsendra sharper than before. "I will be in touch in the days to come. You have a part to play." With that, our group proceeded through the atrium.

Chapter 29: Fate, A Spiteful Thing

We followed Lady Alsendra through the atrium, down the corridor past the kitchen and dining area, and then on down the series of corridors until we reached the room with the round table. As I approached, I started feeling a sense of dread about the prospect of seeing this room again. It appeared each time we met here; I was forced to learn of things that changed my life for the worse. What could Alsendra bring us now? Before entering the door, Lady Alsendra slowed, turning to speak to us. "Gabrielle, dear, perhaps you should wait in your room until this conversation has been had." Gabrielle didn't say a word, nodding her head with a look of determination on her face before turning to head off towards the dormitories. Alsendra glanced at me, a look of sadness or sorrow glimpsing her face for just a moment before proceeding. As we entered the room with the round table, Alsendra pushing the heavy door open with grace, Althira was already waiting for us in the spot she had been in every time we had come to this room. I was getting the impression that Althira was a creature of habit. Sitting in the same place here, sitting at her same chair in front of the stained glass window in the dining room, and then being so meticulously dressed day after day. Some part of her must be comforted by having some sense of routine. Althira motioned for us to take a seat. We all took our seats, Nova running around the table to sniff Althira, then Alsendra, before running back to take a seat beside Kenric. Kenric sat in the chair next to me, and Alsendra sat opposite Althira to face all of us. "Pardon the abrupt arrival and disruption. Althira, I would not be here if it were not for carrying an incontrovertible need to make the trip." Althira tilted her head in acknowledgement, flicking a finger up for Alsendra to continue. "Let us get the first thing out of the way. How has Octavia been progressing with honing her skills?" Althira glanced at me, a blank expression on her face. "The girl shows promise. However, she is insubordinate, unruly, and petulant. She is emotional and irrational. In time, I will hone her skills to my level, but we have to first break her of the current mindset and attitude." Break me? "I beg your pardon?" I demanded an explanation; an apology would be even better. "See what I mean, Alsendra! She takes everything so personally, and, gods forbid I test her in any one area, she brings her feelings into the situation and muddles my entire lesson!" Alsendra gave Althira a flat-lipped smile. "She reminds me of someone else I once knew." Althira glowered at Alsendra. Was Alsendra implying that I reminded her of Althira? Surely that could not be the case. We may both be Mortis Velum, but we were nothing alike. Althira was well to do, cold, calculated, and she knew she had the power to back it up. I was none of those things.

A knock came from the door. I jumped. Kenric turned his head toward the door, grabbing his small blade out of reflex. Althira glanced at Alsendra. Alsendra nodded, saying nothing as the door opened. A moment later, Eryn popped in through the doorway. His fancy mustache glistened in the light as he came through the frame. He stepped in, taking off his hat and bowing to everyone. I realized now how strange this was, for him as a royal Orriveth to bow to someone like me? Or even Alsendra and Althira. We were all so far beneath him in status that he should barely even acknowledge us according to the Orriveth hierarchy. Regardless of all the thought racing through my mind, it was good to see him again. I was afraid he had gotten upset with me or was intentionally avoiding me. "About time you got here, Eryndor! Did you do as I asked?" Alsendra's words, containing a twinge of rancor behind each one, along with using his full name, led me to wonder if she was upset with Eryn about something. "I did, my lady." Eryn reached into the inner pocket of his fancy-looking overcoat, pulling out something wrapped in cloth. It was a decent-sized pouch, roughly the size of Eryn's large hands. The cloth pouch was of plain cotton linen, dyed a pretty magenta color. He moved around the table to Alsendra, placing the object wrapped in the cloth pouch into her palm. Unless my eyes played tricks on me, I thought I saw something inside the cloth pouch move. Alsendra reached up with her other hand, pulling a small string at the top that cinched the cloth closed. The cloth slowly unfurled into Alsendra's hand. A bright silver chain came into view, light sparkling over the surface of the bright metal. It wasn't dainty, and it appeared long. Althira gasped. Me and Kenric both looked to her, unsure why she had made the sound. "Alsendra, where did you get that? You know the consequences of possessing any weapons made from hushed iron." "Calm yourself, Althira. You know I will do nothing that would jeopardize us. I have seen when the need will arise for this. Between Eryn and me, we were able to pull some strings and have this one made specifically for me. This one is composed of very few, very special additives that have been forged into the hushed iron. If it responds to me, as I believe it will, it will be of more use to us than you can fathom." Alsendra closed her eyes, the hand with the chain on the cloth staying still and unmoving. After a moment, the chain jerked. I jumped again; everything that had happened today had my nerves on edge. Another moment where we all sat looking at Alsendra and the chain levitated in Alsendra's hand. Althira let out an "Agh!" The long chain wrapped around Alsendra's hand loosely before wrapping itself into a pattern above her palm. It stayed there in mid-air, slithering around itself in the pattern it created, looking similar to a trinity knot. "Well, would you look at that? I knew the chances of it working would be much higher when having it crafted specifically for myself. By a very talented Orriveth blacksmith at that. We both know a whisper chain cannot be controlled unless they choose to respond."

Althira slapped her hand down on the table, causing the entire room to look in her direction. "What are you playing at, Alsendra? First you bring me the burden of this girl, causing a vast amount of trouble with the Ravynari while doing so, keeping this girl and everything happening around her a secret from the High Council. I have honored everything you have asked of me until this point, but you are about to have us buried so deep under a mountain of lies and wrongdoings that we are going to suffocate ourselves!" Alsendra scoffed, "Now who is being emotional, my dear?" Althira stood up with a jolt. "Do not test me, Alsendra!" Alsendra tittered under her breath. "You know you won't be able to touch me when I can stay two steps ahead of you." Alsendra gave Althira one of her flat-lipped smiles. "I promise I will not let us fail, Althira. I would not bring something that implicated you in my troubles unless I was certain you could handle it. I trust you with my life, and I'm asking you to trust in me as well. At the first sign of something going negatively for us, I will end it before it takes hold. Fate may be spiteful, but I am even more so." "Alsendra, you know I trust you more than anyone. I would not have been willing to take the girl in or to entertain your mess unless I trusted you, but you know as well as I do that we're about to get ourselves into more trouble than we will overcome." "Be that as it may, we do not have a choice. Things have been set in motion that must be seen through to the end. I'm actively trying to navigate this in the best way I can. The only trouble I have is seeing you and Octavia in certain situations because of that blasted shadow of secrecy that follows you." I had so many more questions. The one that was at the forefront was the chain still floating above Alsendra's hand. "What exactly is a whisper chain?" They looked at me as if I had asked a ridiculous question, but I wanted to know. I had seen nothing like it. Lady Alsendra was the one to answer me. "Weapons such as this, crafted from hushed iron, are powerful. They can only be forged by an extremely adept blacksmith, usually an elven. The words that have to be spoken when forging a chain like this have to carry heavy arcane-powered intent. If the words are spoken too loudly, the chain becomes inert and useless. If the words are spoken in silence or without purpose, a chain like this will become feral and uncontrollable by any mage. That is why its creation is forbidden. Well, one reason. With this, I will wield it for a multitude of uses. As time goes on, the chain and I will learn to communicate as one, providing an edge that is very beneficial to the wielder of magical weapons. Not too different from Eryn's Syreth blades, as you are already somewhat familiar with. We aren't here to focus the discussion on the chain; we have far more concerning matters at hand."

Eryn glanced at me when Alsendra spoke about concerning issues before quickly turning away. I raised an eyebrow in question. Now, what was he hiding from me? I was about out of tolerance for their secrets. "Is there anything you would like to talk about or express before we continue? Any of you? For I feel the mood is about to change for the worse." I looked around, and nobody responded. I had several questions, but nothing I had to ask right this moment, so I would hold on to them for now. Alsendra continued after a long pause when nobody spoke up. "Octavia, I need you to promise me you will remain calm and not overreact to what you are about to hear. It is imperative for everyone's sake that we remain calm and rational; we must do what is best and most intelligent for us to succeed going further." I shrugged. I was already about numb to the constant bad news being brought my way. My life was already threatened, so what would be one more piece of bad news? Unless they planned to kill me or turn me over to the Ravynari themselves. My eyes widened. Surely that wasn't what this was about. Alsendra looked over at Althira. "This is heavy information for all of us, you understand?" Althira tilted her head forward at the words. "Because of some unfortunate circumstances that set off a long chain of events, the Ravynari found out who was responsible for their arcane wielder's death. In doing so, they tracked you back to Faladorn, evidently unable to work out that you had been sent here to Liraquor. Which was my intention in sending you here. The problems that arose with this manifested themselves shortly thereafter. I sent Vantor and Draven along with Nythira to fetch Ophelia as soon as I found out about the Ravynari. Before she could be retrieved, the Ravynari had already reached her." My heart dropped as the realization hit me. Oh, gods, she was dead, wasn't she? But she couldn't be; surely I would know. Ophelia and I were so close; surely I would feel a connection break or a pain. I jumped up, the chair I had been sitting on falling over onto its back. I was going to make the Ravynari pay for hurting my sister. Everyone would know what it meant to come after one of us. I turned to run to the door. Something reached around my throat before I even noticed it was there. It was a hand of black smoke, Althira. I grabbed at it, unable to remove it. My entire body was lifted by my neck, to throw me down into a chair. "Eryn, contain her." Alsendra could make commands all she wanted, but she would not hold me here. Eryn made his way around the table to be at my side, putting his hands on my shoulders to hold me still. I flung my elbow up as hard as I could, connecting it with Eryn's face. He released his grip in order to hold his face. "For crying out loud, how is this one girl so problematic?" With the words barely out of Alsendra's mouth, the silver whisper chain was already airborne and speeding towards me.

It slithered its way around the back of the chair and around my arms, binding them down. I could not move. I flailed my legs, trying to grab at something, anything, tears flowing down my face. Black smoke left Althira's hand, covering my face before going up my nose. I threw my head back, trying to get it away from my nose, but it did nothing. I was gasping for air, unable to breathe. I went still as my vision blurred. Following that, there was only darkness.

Chapter 30: Duplicitous

When I regained consciousness a moment later, my hands and arms were still bound by the whisper chain. "Now, you promised me you would remain calm and rational, and look at you now!" "Do you see this, Alsendra?! This is what I have had to deal with the entire time she has been under my supervision. The girl is utterly irrational!" "We weren't always so understanding ourselves, Althira. Rationalization increases with age and knowledge." Alsendra turned her attention back to me. "Now you are going to sit there and listen since you can't partake in a civilized conversation." I tried to speak, but I couldn't open my mouth, realizing that Althira must be holding my mouth closed somehow. I felt the tears continue to run down my face. I tried to push the tears back to clear my vision. "Now, as I was saying before you decided not to listen and act out on impulse, the Ravynari got to Ophelia before I could retrieve her. She is alive. They are holding her for ransom, expecting you to go after her or for us to turn you over. Of course, we will do nothing of the sort. What we are going to do is get your sister back in one piece. For us to do that, it means for you to do and follow exactly as I say. Do you understand?" I tried to speak, but still couldn't. Alsendra motioned to Althira. "You can let her speak for now." I felt the smoke leave from around my lips and chin. "How do you know she is still okay? The possibility exists that she is currently being subjected to torture, or that she has already been killed." "While it's true that they could torture her, I am certain that she is very much alive and well. I have no problem seeing Ophelia with my gift of sight. That is why it is important that we get her back swiftly and without procrastination. That is also why I arrived here as quickly as I did without warning. We are going after her tonight." Okay, that was good. I didn't have to go fight the Ravynari alone, at least. With Alsendra and Althira helping, I am certain we can get her back. "Are you going to behave yourself if we let you go now?" I nodded, and I would. I looked over at Eryn; a minor cut appeared on his cheek, bleeding. "I'm sorry, Eryn." He smiled at me. Seeing him smile after everything that has happened over the last few days made me feel relieved. "That is all right, Miss Octavia. It has been a while since I've been beaten up by a girl. It was high time." Kenric was giggling to himself behind Eryn. I felt the whisper chain releasing its grip on my arms. It casually floated its way back to Alsendra. "Now that your little escapade is over, let's discuss this and map out our moves around the Ravynari."

Alsendra had Eryn retrieve a large tube she had brought with her from Liraquor. She flipped the top of the tube open, pulling out a long, rolled-up piece of paper. As she unrolled it across the round table, it became apparent that it was a hand-drawn map. "This was delivered to me by one of the Orriveth seers, I believe under Rayden's orders." Althira spoke up before Alsendra could continue. "I'm sure it was by Rayden. Do you know he has already paid us a visit? And that weaselly little elf showed up at my house threatening me with a demand that he would expect my cooperation! I have never! He's lucky I was in a good mood, or he might've been turned into food for one of my ghouls." Alsendra waved her hand in dismissal of Althira's outburst as Eryn was laughing to himself. "Weaselly little elf might be my favorite description I've ever heard of Rayden." "Both of you shut up and focus!" Alsendra's voice boomed, snapping everyone back to focus. "This map is what the seers sketched out of the Ravynari village near Thalmyr's Cradle. There are six entrances, but only two watchtowers. They patrol along this area," she dragged her fingernail across the outer part of the map. "But the patrol is only one group, and they take a couple of hours to make the full loop by horseback. That is something we will use to our advantage. I want us to get in unseen. From there, we will find where they have Ophelia locked up, release her, and get her back safely. I will not have this going askew from a minor oversight, so if there is anything at all one of you can point out or anything you would like to suggest, now would be the time to do that." Eryn stepped up. "I think it would be wise for only one or two to go into the Ravynari village at most. With fewer opportunities for detection, there will be a greater potential for achieving a successful outcome. On the off chance we get caught, it would be better to lose one over four more." He was right, and I knew he was, but his words stung. If one of us got caught, that would probably mean death for Ophelia. If they caught us before we could release her, they would probably kill whichever one of us was caught as an example, or worse. I shuddered at the thought, remembering the Ravynari that attacked us and how we barely survived the attack. They were vile and ruthless; my imagination could just picture the things they would be capable of and want to do if given the chance. And there were far worse things than a quick death. We had to get Ophelia back before anything unimaginable happened to her. My stomach turned into knots at the thought.

"Eryn, I require you to attend to Vantor and Draven without delay. Make certain they are well-fed and prepared to travel swiftly by nightfall. Those boys could be in for a rough time if we run into trouble tonight. Also, make sure Nythira is comfortable. I need the coach ready to move at light speed." Eryn nodded before giving a bow, headed out the heavy iron-clad wooden door to go tend to the coach and horses. A thought occurred to me. "Who is Nythira?" Althira and Alsendra both glared at me, looking perplexed at my question. "You have already met her multiple times, my dear; she is the coachwoman in charge of Vantor and Draven." I felt silly for asking now, because of course I had met her, but I had never known her name. "Oh, I wasn't sure she was even human. I haven't ever seen her face, heard her speak, or even seen her move. It makes sense now that you say that, though." Alsendra sent a tsk-tsk under her tongue. "You are so young and naïve to the world. Who ever said she was human?" I was more confused now than ever before. "So she's not human?" "Nevermind these nonsensical issues and your relentless hounding of never-ending questions. If you want your sister saved, and preferably saved alive, then pay attention to the task at hand, girl!" Althira wielded the words at me like a poison-coated blade. She was not happy with this situation; that was clear. "Octavia, run and get prepared for the trip tonight. We will leave in a few hours at dusk. Meet us in the underground corridor when you are ready." Without another word, I headed straight to my bedroom in the dormitories to get ready. I took a quick shower, got dressed, threw a few things in a bag, grabbed the few things I thought I might need, and took off out the door. I stopped just as I was outside the bedroom door. I turned back briefly, deciding I should bring Ophelia's old dagger with the dragon charm for good luck. She would be proud of me for remembering to bring it. I grabbed the dagger, tucking it into my boot, then I bolted out the door with the wind beneath my feet; my big sister needed me. Alsendra and Althira were standing shoulder to shoulder in the long underground corridor, just outside the vivisectum doorway.

"We just need to practice a few things before we go to make sure you are ready." Althira gave a little whistle and a motion of her hand, hearing Vexil somewhere nearby the door, making a series of noises. A moment later, the door opened. Althira put her hand out, motioning for me to enter before her. Alsendra followed behind me with Althira trailing behind her. We entered with Vexil shutting the door behind me. The atmosphere of this place would never diminish in its eeriness. The smell of stale air and decaying earth hit my nose. "Take a stand in the center." I walked over there as I was told, taking a stand near where Eryn had stood when we were practicing weaving. "Octavia, I need you to hear me and to listen." Alsendra walked around to stand by my side before continuing. "We will do everything in our power to get Ophelia back, and I believe we will, but I want you to prepare yourself for the worst. Should anything detrimental happen, your sister may not come back the same, or even at all." Her words stung like salt in an open wound. I could feel the tears welling up behind my eyes, but I knew she was right. All I could do was nod my head as I tried to control my tears. "Good, then I want you to understand why we are doing this. It is not out of malice, and we are doing it with the best intentions possible." I wasn't sure what she was speaking about. "Doing what?" Alsendra sighed, looked at Althira, and nodded. Althira blinked her eyes slowly before looking at me, making eye contact, "Vexil do it now!" Vexil popped out of the shadow beside me stabbing me in the leg with his long nails, I yelped in pain as I was bending down to grab the wound. Before I could, I felt my body tense, going rigid as a plank of wood. I fell forward, my face hitting the dirt ground of the vivisectum. Alsendra stepped in front of me. "I am truly sorry, Octavia. I find myself unable to trust that you will adhere to the instructions given to you regarding Ophelia. I have not seen one path where you go along and survive. I will not have you messing this up and getting all of us killed by trying to save you. You will be upset about this, and you have a right to be, but I promise Althira and I have a better chance of bringing your sister back safely if we go alone. Should the Ravynari make any poor, unforeseen decisions, the two of us are fully prepared to push back. Eryn is going to stay here and guard the hall in our absence; I will not have you being here unable to defend yourself properly." I tried to scream, but my throat wouldn't work. I couldn't even open my mouth. "By the time you return to normal, we will have returned. Either with or without Ophelia, and I hope it is the former. But you will have your answers," Alsendra looked at Althira. "Go ahead, dear." Althira said a few words. I couldn't make out what she said, only able to see a faint purple glow on the ground from where I lay with my face in the dirt. I felt the soil next to me move as I got rolled over onto my back. I resented not being able to scream in this moment as I looked up, unable to move a muscle. The three creatures standing over me looked like deformed corpses of humans, something straight from a nightmare, faces and bodies contorted, their flesh sloughing off. Some areas had no flesh at all. "Ensure she remains here and does not cause harm to herself, by whatever measures are required. Only Alsendra and I are permitted in this room; all others are to be devoured, leaving nothing but bones." The creatures chomped their jaws in response. "These ghouls will do my bidding; no need to worry about them. Truly, girl, we are both deeply sorry that it had to be this way. We wouldn't do this if Alsendra could see any other way to get both you and Ophelia back safely." As Vexil sealed the door behind them, the room plunged into darkness as they turned together and left the vivisectum.

-To be continued, check back for the upcoming book in the series. Coming soon.

Book 2, Chapter One: Alsendra, The Archmage Diviner

I walked at a faster pace than Althira, partly upset at what we had
done, partly ready to get the night and whatever path it takes over
with. There was only so much I could do to change fate once it started
down one path. After years of fighting it, I have learned when things
are beyond my control or when I'll just make things worse by trying
to intervene. There were times I could only sit back and observe as
what I had already seen unfolded before my eyes. "Be certain you grab
your cloak, dear." I wanted to make sure Althira had her cloak; it
would play a vital part in tonight's secrecy. I reached up to the coat
hook by the large back door of the hall, grabbing my flat, black hooded
cloak. It was a lightweight fabric, but remained warm and opaque. I
swung the door open as Althira grabbed her cloak behind me. Vantor
and Draven were a few steps from the door, my coach waiting to take
us through the dark. I reached into the small sack attached to my
waist, pulling out a couple of stale biscuits. Holding one in each hand,
to give Vantor and Draven one each simultaneously. I didn't want one
getting jealous and worked up before our night had even started. I
stood between the two tall horses, their long manes caressing the
shoulders of the cloak. Vantor and Draven leaned their heads in,
resting one on each shoulder. I brought my arms up to hug their necks.
"I love you two. I need you to do your best for me tonight; our lives
depend on it. And I know you will. You are far too good to me, my old
friends." The boys neighed loudly in unison. They had been with me
for so long; I knew they would understand every word I said. Althira
was standing just outside the coach next to Eryn, waiting to follow

my lead. "Let's get on with it then. I don't want this to take any longer than it must." Eryn gave a hand to Althira as she hopped into the coach. "I still think it would be better to allow me to come along, my lady." His face looked pensive and concerned. "You will do no such thing. What you will do is stay here, keeping this place safe in Althira's absence." He tilted his head with a look of apprehension. "Look here, Eryndor, you will not stay here and sulk about it either. If you would benefit us, I would bring you along posthaste. I have seen what happens in several scenarios if you come along. From what I have seen, your presence with us is unlikely to positively affect our objectives." "I understand." I reached my hand out for him to take as I steadied myself, getting into the coach. "We will be back before morning. Should something unforeseen happen that doesn't involve our return, alert Aeryneth at once. Currently, I place more trust in her judgment than in anyone else who holds a position of influence. Your mother will aid you should the time come." Eryn bowed before shutting the coach door, giving a concession of knocks to tell Nythira it was time.

We rode swift through the dark. Only the sounds of Vantor and Draven's hooves clip-clopping in unison could be heard in the still of night. The moment we departed, Althira cast a shadow over the coach, which concealed us and made it almost impossible for anyone to see or hear us. I was afraid we needed to be as concealed as possible, given the trouble at hand. I pulled the newly crafted whisper chain from my pocket, Althira giving a scowl at the sight. I knew she didn't approve of my decision to have this made, but it had to be done. I couldn't see one path where I didn't have it with me. I made sure the chain still responded to me, thankful that it did. I looked out the window of the coach. In the reflection, I watched a group of Ravynari, three of them. The Ravynari pulled the coach door open, reaching in to grab me by the arm. Althira killed all three of them with one swift movement, sending all three flying away from the coach. I looked down, both of us covered in blood. My eyes widened at the sight. "What did you see, Alsendra?" "Trouble." I slapped the roof of the coach, whispering the words, "Nythira, take an alternate path. The one we're on leads to a small group of Ravynari. Perhaps the one that leads to the easternmost entrance. Keep scanning ahead for the first sign of the Ravynari patrol." The coach lurched right off the next available path as it came up. Vantor and Draven kicked up the speed, able to sense the urgency. "All of this trouble for one girl, Alsendra. You already know we should just let the Ravynari have her. She isn't worth the trouble, and it's certainly not worth starting a war with the Ravynari." "Then, gods forbid one of us should fall tonight." I inhaled deeply before letting the breath escape me to ease some of my troubles. "She may not be worth the trouble; I cannot answer that at this time, but I have seen the way these circumstances will affect Octavia should Ophelia be killed. You know how important Octavia will be in the upcoming days. I cannot have her being mentally crutched as we proceed." "The girl is already mentally incompetent as it is, Alsendra!" I smiled briefly. Octavia indeed had a way of getting under Althira's skin, and part of me enjoyed that for her. Very few people could ever achieve that. "I hope you know what you're doing, Alsendra. You have gotten us into this predicament of your own creation." She was right, and I hoped I could lead us all out of it unscathed. If the gods were on our side, my sight would not fail me when it is needed most.

Vantor and Draven slowed, a sign of our arrival nearing the Ravynari village. If we were being realistic, it was more of an overpopulated camp than it was a village, but that was neither here nor there. The coach soon after came to a halt. "Use your sight and make sure there are no patrols or stragglers between here and the entrance before we exit. If you would, please, dear." Althira closed her eyes to send out her shadow vision quickly and precisely. "There's nothing between here and the entrance for now, unless it shows up when I'm not looking." "Then let us not dilly-dally further." We exited the coach with care. I spoke low and deliberately. "Stay close no matter what we encounter. I will do my best to see what comes, but also keep your sight open for the unexpected. When we get close, use your sight through the darkness to find the girl's location. We should not speak when we're close; we do not know what kind of arcane wielders the Ravynari possess. And keep your cloak up at all times, as you know. Do your best to shield us when possible. Althira, we are more than capable of easing through this." I whispered to Nythira, "Stay far enough away not to draw attention. Vantor and Draven will blend in with the night, as will the coach. Just tell them to stay quiet and make sure they aren't spooked." The coach lurched off with gusto.

We quickly pulled the hoods of our cloaks over our heads, proceeding towards the Ravynari village while staying low. Althira kept us shrouded during our approach. We would not be invisible, but we would remain very difficult to detect. We stayed low, taking each step deliberately and with purpose, not to stumble. As we reached the entrance, it was nothing more than a clearing in a thicket of trees and shrubs surrounding it. I expected a gated entrance, but this was the Ravynari; they likely didn't have the resources or the intelligence to build something like that. I looked at the large fire that was on the left, inside the clearing. In the light of the flames, I watched as we rounded a leaning wood shack inside, slamming into a Ravynari. The entire village was alerted before we sprinted at full speed, only to be surrounded and overwhelmed by at least fifty Ravynari. I snapped out of it. I pointed, showing Althira the building, shaking my head to tell her we needed to stay away from there. We paused for a moment just before we entered the village, giving Althira time to use her sight. She nodded after a moment, pointing in and to the right. We gave each other a nod of affirmation before we crept forward. Another vision of a Ravynari coming from the far right. He ran into us, causing us to stumble and trip, again getting caught. I pushed Althira to the left as I saw the man from my vision coming in our direction. We ducked down along the overhanging roof until he passed. Althira's shadowy veil thickened around us. "We can whisper for a moment. The girl is up ahead, between two of these shacks. They have her in a cage, with a hay bale on each side, from what I can tell. But Alsendra, there's two Ravynari sitting in front of the only way into the cage. We will have no choice but to deal with them." I thought about that for a moment. "I will take care of it when we get to them, just keep the veil up around us."

We moved in, closing in on the location containing Ophelia. We got to a little alley, if you can call it that, between two rundown shacks. The ground between them was muddy and smelled of sewage and decay. I could only imagine what had been put on this ground as I gave a moment of mourning for the high heel boots I wore; they were going to be burned after leaving this filth. Althira put her hand up in front of me, telling me to stop. She nodded and pointed ahead to a space between two of the rundown shacks that looked like the rest. I knew she was telling me that's where they had Ophelia. I nodded once before we began moving in slowly. Althira and I remained shoulder to shoulder. We crept to the far side to get a better view of the opening; I needed to see the ones guarding her in order for me to figure out what needed to be done. The two Ravynari Althira warned about were sitting inside, one sitting on a bucket chewing on something with a bone in it; the other was lying on a bench in front of a bale of hay that was beside the cage. There was a low fire in the center of the opening, not too far from the cage. I scanned the cage, trying to see Ophelia, but I couldn't see her. I gazed deep into the fire, willing a vision to come forth. I saw I distracted the two Ravynari, breaking a wooden board nearby. They caught us before we could get Ophelia out, calling other Ravynari to us. There weren't many, but I wasn't willing to gamble on whether we could handle them. I got Althira's attention, motioning with my finger in a circle to show her to strengthen the surrounding veil. "I can't see a way where I don't have to take them out. I think the best way would be to incapacitate them long enough for us to get the girl and get out. Do you want me to handle it, or would you like to use your ghouls, perhaps?" "You take care of them. I will not risk dropping the veil by doing that." I concentrated for a moment, trying to gain more insight. I realized I would not get any more insight than I already had. I reached into my pocket, pulling out the whisper chain. "Please do not decide to go feral now."

I took only a moment to collect my thoughts, carefully planning out what needed to be done. Raising the chain, I sent it forward through Althira's veil at lightning speed. It silently flew to wrap around the neck of the Ravynari on the bench, strangling him before he could react. He reached up, grabbing at the chain, unable to speak but catching the attention of the other Ravynari. As soon as the first Ravynari was incapacitated, the chain moved in a blur to the second Ravynari, wrapping around his neck with so much force that it sent him stumbling back to the ground. A moment later, he was also unconscious. "Let's go now." We moved in quickly. Althira dropped the veil when we reached the cage. I saw a body lying just inside. "Open this blasted thing." Upon speaking the words, the realization occurred to me: I could use the chain for exactly that purpose. I sent the chain to the metal lock on the door. The chain constricted around the latch of the lock, snapping it in an instant. I pushed the door open;

Althira stepped in before me. I bent over, checking the body on the floor. "Who is this man? It's not the girl." Althira exhaled loudly, causing me to spare her a glance her way. I realized she was standing directly behind me, pointing her finger upwards to the wall to the side of the cage. There, behind one of the hay bales, Ophelia hung from ropes with her feet and hands tied up while all four limbs were pulled away from her body. She was covered in blood, her hair matted to her head with a mixture of dirt and congealed blood. She wasn't moving. I ran over. "Don't fret; the girl is alive. If she were dead or close to death, I would know." Althira said it reassuringly, but the problem remained. Ophelia needed to be conscious to help get her out. A vision hit. We were trying to carry Ophelia out when Althira accidentally dropped the surrounding shroud upon us dropping Ophelia, we were attacked by the Ravynari, Ophelia getting beheaded with a long blade. "No, she must be lucid to get out of here alive. Help me wake her." Before I had time to say anything else, Althira reached out, slapping Ophelia across the face. "Oh, great heavens of old, Althira! There's no need to be a barbarian." I used the chain, cutting through the ropes that held her up with ease. Althira helped me catch Ophelia as she fell. "Fine, here, use this then." Althira handed me a tiny vial with liquid inside. "Why didn't we try this before hitting the girl?" Althira lifted one shoulder in indifference. I pulled the little cork out of the top of the vial, immediately getting a whiff that burned my eyes. "What the hell, Althira!" "What? It's spirit vinegar. You said you wanted to wake her." "Indeed, I do, but this would wake the dead, dear." Althira gave me a sinister smile. "You know, it actually would too if used properly." I waved the vial in front of Ophelia's face, but she didn't react. I brought the vial up to hold just under her nose. She jerked, opening her eyes. "Get it together, my dear; I'm afraid we have to get you out of here alive."

Ophelia sat up, reaching up to her head. I only now realized she had a large gash from the top of her head down the side of her forehead, by her eye. "My word! What did they do to you, girl? Never mind that." I yanked the sleeve off Ophelia's top, ripping it in half lengthwise and then using it to wrap around her head. Althira helped me quickly pull her to her feet. A vision of the Ravynari headed this way from the right. "Quickly! Althira, the veil!" I grabbed Ophelia's arm, dragging her closely behind me. The shroud of shadow and shade encircled us. Althira and I moved shoulder to shoulder with haste, dragging Ophelia directly behind us. "Move left now!" We rounded the corner of the alley, heading forward towards the center of the village, our momentum never slowing. A vision of us getting caught again, this time Althira was gutted before we had time to react. "Left now!" We turned left, ducking behind a tall wall that appeared to be an open area for sleeping. I needed to concentrate on my sight for a moment. I saw four ways out, all of them leading to the death of either us or the death of many Ravynari. Both would be bad. I wasn't allowing us to die, but killing Ravynari would lead to severe consequences, both from the High Council and leading the Ravynari to possibly wanting war. I had another vision. This one allowed us all to survive, but we would be seen. We would have to make a run for it at the last second, but we should be just out of reach if my sight was correct. Gods, may celestial mercy wash clean our earthly stumbles. "Althira, this will not be ideal. We have only one path to take without casualties. A Ravynari with very minor arcane skills will just be able to drop your veil for a moment, revealing us fully. I will tell you seconds before that happens, then drop it and we will run with the wind beneath our feet. After we run, duck to the left; an arrow will miss your shoulder from the right. A Ravynari will try to grab Ophelia from behind, just pull her close and we will be fine. Nythira will wait just outside the entrance with Vantor and Draven at the ready. If we get caught, kill the Ravynari if it comes to that, but get us out of here alive. We will make it; trust me, Althira. Now GO!" We took off in a sprint, Althira's shadowy veil thick around us as we pushed forward. I had Ophelia's left arm, Althira had her right as we forced her to run behind us. I saw the one Ravynari from my vision, the one with minor arcane. I saw the moment she sensed Althira's veil, just as my sight foretold. "Drop it, Althira! RUN!" We took off like lightning through the darkness of night. The Ravynari were momentarily surprised before there were shouts and sounds of metal clanking. "Duck now!" Althira ducked left, an arrow barely grazing the top of her shoulder. I caught my breath as my sight revealed more information. "Shield us behind!" Althira knew what I meant, spinning around without hesitation. She threw up a wall of impenetrable smoke behind us, a volley of arrows hitting moments later. We continued. Althira turned for only a moment as I saw the smoke wall spread out like a low rolling fog before bursting out into a horrifying wave of fire, sending the Ravynari running in fear. Two remained at the entrance ahead. "MOVE ALTHIRA, GO!" The panic from the visions hitting me made itself known, causing me to yell. We pushed harder, using the front flats of our high heel boots to stabilize us in the muddy dirt beneath our feet, dragging Ophelia as we went. "Go right! Now!" Althira headed right without question. I yanked Ophelia left with me. She gave a yelp of pain in response. "Drop them!" Althira didn't hesitate. Hands of shadow and shade that writhed in a mass of black came up from the ground, grabbing the Ravynari at the entrance by the neck, yanking them down to the dirt. We bolted over them. Just beyond the entryway, a small assembly of Ravynari was waiting. They emerged from the thicket at the last minute, my sight not warning of their presence ahead of time. Althira slammed them back with a snake of shadow and smoke; a few continuing on after us, but it gave us time to get to the coach. Vantor and Draven neighed wildly upon seeing us. The door of the coach was already open. "GO!" I yelled before we got to the coach. The boys clawed at the dirt. Althira leaped through the air, landing inside the coach. She turned, grabbing my arm, pulling me up as hard as she could. I turned as I still held onto Ophelia's arm, seeing her feet drag the ground as I pulled. "Alsendra!" Althira screamed my name.

I directed my attention to observing the cause of her distress. The Ravynari patrol had heard the noise of us escaping; they were headed up the path towards us. Their horses were of mixed breeds, not strong, but a few had armor. I yanked Ophelia up into the coach, throwing myself around to the front to sit beside Nythira. I was prepared to do anything I could. We barreled forward, Vantor and Draven moving in unison, a blur of speed. I smiled at how wonderful the boys were; they were so eager to do good. A vision of Draven getting sliced down his side, falling to the ground as viscera spilled, whinnies of pain echoing through my ears. I involuntarily cried out in horror. "I will bring hellfire down on them! Nythira, prepare yourself. We go on the offensive. Spare not one." No sooner had the words left my lips, I heard Althira's voice shout from behind. "Yuh! Yee! Yee!" I turned to see her fling herself from the side of the coach, flying before landing on her white and gold chariot as it pulled up beside the coach. The large, white-winged unicorn at the helm.

Aurelion, gods, the big beautiful beast was a pleasant sight, a spectacle in the night's darkness. Aurelion was taller and wider than Vantor or Draven, and although he was slower with his legs, his wings more than made up for the speed. Althira pointed ahead. I had a vision of her clearing the Ravynari without fail. I gave her a nod. "Slow down and trail behind Althira," I said in a barely audible tone. Althira let out what I could only describe as a battle cry, promising an impending archaic assault to follow. "Yeyeyeye!" Aurelion flapped his wings, lurching over in front of Vantor and Draven. Althira, now in front of us, looked wild and feral. Her hair whipped around her head with reckless abandon; the large black cloak she wore was now billowing in the wind behind her. The chariot lurched left and right at speed, Althira staying planted firmly with every move. "Yee woop woop!" Althira's voice rang through the night like a sword against stone. Aurelion spread his wings straight out to each side as he dashed forward, cutting through the air, his wings spanning the width of the wide dirt path we rode on. Althira let go of the reins, leaning forward to put her arms up in front of her before bringing them out to her side, mimicking the way Aurelion's wings were spread. The shadowy black smoke she controlled poured off her body like steam from spring water in the freezing air. It rushed forward, wrapping around Aurelion in totality, Aurelion took on a brilliant glow of divinity before the smoke took the form of solid white and gold armor on the colossal beast, plates of solid metal scales were now coating the wings and all vital areas. The unicorn brayed fiercely, like a mule fueled by demented torment, flapping its now armor-clad wings down once with a thunderous clap. The horn on his head let off a bright gleam as he did. The chariot barreled on behind him at ungodly speed. As we approached the group of Ravynari, there had to be twenty of them. They screamed and shouted, riding their horses straight for us, weapons at the ready, but they had no chance against what was coming. Aurelion cleaved through them, every Ravynari flying to the side, knocked from their horses. The horses falling over hit the ground with a thud. As we cleared the patrol, relief washed over me. We have accomplished our goal, and as far as I know, we have done so without causing the death of any Ravynari. While those on the ground behind us were injured, they would be fine. I turned around to look through the coach window, signaling to Ophelia that we were in the clear. My heart stopped the moment I turned and saw the image that was visible through the coach window.

www.ingramcontent.com/pod-product-compliance
Lightning Source LLC
Chambersburg PA
CBHW020035310726
48970CB00007B/2273